MW01120685

MENINGIE MAN 02

PREQUEL TO THE STEPHANIE MCBRIDE CRIME SERIES

LEE HOPKINS

°138

MENINGIE MAN

Copyright © 2019 by Lee Hopkins.

All rights reserved. No part of this book may be used or reproduced in any manner without written permission except in the case of brief quotations embodied in critical articles or reviews.

This book is a work of fiction. Names, characters, businesses, organizations, places, events and incidents either are the product of the author's imagination or are used fictitiously. Any resemblance to actual persons, living or dead, events, or locales is entirely coincidental.

For information contact:

Twitter: @leehopkins

Facebook: LeeHopkinsAuthor

Website: LeeHopkins.com

Ebook ISBN: 978-0-6486991-0-1

Print ISBN: 979-8-6205630-3-6 (Amazon)

Published by degrees138 : degrees138.com

°138

❋ Created with Vellum

ONE

MENINGIE MAN

LEE HOPKINS

With thanks to G for support, encouragement, guidance and laughter, and thanks to Grant for wisdom and friendship.

To Caz, for being the best CFO I could hope for.

Thanks go to Dr Ina Schapiro for medical insights and details about Flinders Medical Centre's Emergency Department.

Thanks, too, to Tony Buzek and Lorraine Hosking for their eagle-eyed spotting of errors.

PART ONE

Stephanie Mcbride's white SUV took the Anzac Highway towards Plympton, in pursuit of an eight-year-old red Mazda.

'Right down Marion Road!' Stephanie's passenger announced excitedly.

If Stephanie's intel was right, the Mazda only a few cars in front of her was being driven by *Diablo*, a mid-level cyber criminal who had made the fatal mistake of hacking into a business that Stephanie was keeping a close eye on.

'They've just passed the Uniting Church, coming up on the left in a few seconds. Keep going forwards.'

There were no sirens to help her part the cars in front of her, Stephanie had to rely on smooth driving and good luck. But she exceeded the speed limit by 10 kilometres an hour.

'Turn right at McEwin Avenue, coming up on the right after Nesfield House.'

'Turn left at the end of the road.' The cars had thinned out now that Stephanie was off a main road, there was only herself and a red CX-5, about 200 metres ahead.

She saw the Mazda turn right on the roundabout and almost double back on itself.

Stephanie did the same, with more gusto, and there was the Mazda, just 100 metres in front of her on Urrbrae Terrace. The Mazda was slowing down, looking to park. Stephanie continued past her prey and took the next right, Henry Street. Turning around, she nosed her car back out onto Urrbrae Terrace to see if the red Mazda was still around. It was, parked under a tree outside some houses.

Stephanie reversed back and parked on Henry Street, then she and her colleague Petra Starkey got out of the Kia Sorento and pulled their pistols out, checking that the safety was on and that the guns were ready. Stowing the guns in their shoulder holsters, Stephanie and Petra calmly walked back around to where the CX-5 was parked. The driver could have entered one of three houses, so it was a process of elimination.

Stephanie rang the doorbell on house number one, while Petra hopped the small gate into the carport. No answer. Again, no answer. A shout-out to Petra and off the pair went to house number two.

Stephanie rang the doorbell on house number two once Petra had entered the carport, blocking any escape.

An elderly woman answered and replied to Stephanie that she didn't know who owned the red car, but she'd seen it several times in the last few months and she thought it was probably a frequent visitor to the third house on Stephanie's list.

Stephanie and Petra casually walked up the driveway of house number three. Pretending to be Jehovah's Witnesses, the pair separated at the top of the driveway and Petra quietly placed herself at the back of the carport. Stephanie rang the front doorbell.

'What do you want?' came the grumpy reply.

'The Kingdom of Heaven is at hand,' called out Stephanie.

'Bugger off!' came the reply.

'This is Stephanie McBride from the Police, open up or I'll enter by force.'

'Shit!' came a new voice from within, followed by the sound of furniture being turned over.

Stephanie pulled out her pistol and aimed at the door lock. It gave way under the force of the bullet and Stephanie darted in.

Petra, hearing the gunshot, raced around to the back door and finding it unlocked pulled her gun and entered.

Inside the pair found two men in their late 20s, two laptops still open, and a guilty expression on both of them.

'No need to shoot, for fuck's sake!' cried one man.

Stephanie and Petra cable-tied the men's hands and separated them into two rooms so that two conversations could take place without interference.

Over the course of the next fifteen minutes they determined that one man, Stephanie's, was indeed *Diablo*. A check of their computers found that they were planning on breaking and entering a mattress manufacturer's computer network. They also found something disturbing: the men were being bankrolled by a Chinese syndicate, one known for its willingness to use violence to meet its ends.

It was one discovery that Stephanie hadn't seen coming, and that scared her. Why was she blind-sided? And was Chinese syndicate violence about to arrive on the quiet streets of Adelaide?

Child-sized. White, with white lilies draped over the top. Gold edging and gold handles.

The whole community of Meningie attended the service of Lily April Wilkins. Deaths happen in country towns, but it's usually the death of an elderly pensioner or the suicide of an out-of-luck, end-of-their-tether farmer. The death of a six-year-old girl stood out as uncommon, and the town wanted to come and pay their respects.

Father Rob Bower from the Catholic Church took the service, and the Reverend Janette Masterton from the Anglicans helped, ushering visitors to the seats and offering words of solace to those overcome with emotions.

Of which there were a few, because Lily was a popular girl. Like her parents, she was active and curious. She was good with ball sports and was a keen hot-shotter, the tennis coaching program for kids. Popular with her schoolmates, her teachers loved her as a caring student who had no problems standing up for others. Her parents were besotted with her.

Dave and Sarah Wilkins sat at the front of the RSL Hall, their lips tight and their hands interlocked.

Two weeks earlier, at a 'bring your child to work' day at Derringerry, a local farm, Dave had turned his back for a second to talk to a colleague and Lily slipped between some gates that shouldn't have been open and was crushed by an incoming herd of cattle. Dave was powerless and helpless to get to his daughter caught up in the legs of the herd. He couldn't reach her and nothing could be done for her.

It was only later in the funeral's day that Dave would

notice that there was no representative from the farm's Chinese owners, other than the farm manager Alan Peters, Dave's direct boss. No-one from higher in the company paid their respects. He was numb from crying, but still felt anger at the company's refusal to acknowledge any liability. For now, he focused on making sure his wife Sarah was okay.

The sun was hot at 11am, and the hall's ceiling fans pushed the air around and provided what little relief it could. The hall was packed, and there was a growing collection of townsfolk left outside. Many had driven up from Kingston and across from farms in Coomandook, Coonalpyn and the Council offices in Tailem Bend, such was the popularity of Lily and her parents. Even the local hotel put a sign on the door saying the staff were at a funeral and the hotel wouldn't re-open for business until 2pm.

Dan Robinson, Dave Wilkins' best mate and best man, had driven up to Adelaide the day before to collect the flowers, which his mum had stopped from wilting by placing them in buckets of water and directing the house air-conditioning onto them. The cafe and the Thai takeaway both contributed food, and the town sporting clubs provided urns of hot water and tea and coffee. The RSL Hall provided the crockery.

Despite the heat, the day was sombre. No one likes it when a child dies.

After the ceremony, while tea, coffee and food were being served, Dave came up to Dan.

'Thanks for your help, mate.'

'No worries. It's the least I could do,' replied Dan. 'The flowers look beaut, hey?'

'That they do. You back in Adelaide tomorrow with clients?'

'Yeah, I've got a training session to run. But I need to

check a few things off with Kelly first, to make sure I'm hitting the right marks.'

'You don't think you can wing it, anyway?'

'Before recently I would have said Yes, but Kelly's helped me see that there are sometimes better ways that blasting them like a bull in a china shop. She's knocked my confidence a bit, but it's all for the better, I hope.'

'Yeah, well, your confidence needs to be up when you're presenting, I reckon. You never know what you can achieve with a good dose of confidence in your sails. Good luck with it. Are you working with Kelly this afternoon?'

'Yeah, she's taken the whole day off and so she will kindly spend two hours with me, working on my presentation. Do you want me to pick anything up for you and Sarah from Adelaide?'

'Nah, she'll be right.'

'Let me know when you and Sarah are ready to move to the cemetery.'

'Will do. And thanks again, mate.'

'Pleasure.'

03

'Bugger them,' he thought. 'Serves them right for stuffing me around. Let them wait another couple of hours.'

Dan Robinson instructed his phone's personal digital assistant, Siri, to stop playing his voicemail and turned his attention back to the road.

He deliberately didn't answer calls while out driving, it was too dangerous—he'd often get distracted and wander over the road—so he let the calls go through to voicemail and listened to the briefer, one-way conversation later.

It annoyed him. One of his three clients had rung, wanting some password information. It didn't sound urgent.

'Siri, navigate my way home.'

Dan turned the engine over while Siri worked out the quickest way out of wherever he was in Adelaide and home to Meningie.

'It will take approximately one hour and fifty-three minutes to reach home,' Siri said. 'Turn left at the end of this road.'

Dan, comfortable with technology, had changed Siri's voice from female to male. 'Hey Siri, who's the man?'

'You are, Dan Robinson.'

Dan chuckled to himself.

Twenty-eight-year-old Dan turned out of the car park in his twelve-year-old silver Corolla and let Siri navigate him away from his new client's offices. Only when they reached the South Eastern Freeway did he say, 'Siri, read me my new emails.'

04

'**Dan, do you have a marketing plan?**' asked Kelly, standing in Dan's kitchen.

'Nope. What's one of them?' replied Dan.

'A plan to grow your business through effective marketing.'

'Sounds useful. Where do I get one?'

'Ha ha. Well, it's a bit more complex than that. You

create one yourself, by thinking through the answers to some pretty deep questions.'

'Thinking. Sounds horrific. Do I need one? I'm happy with the clients I've got at the moment, and happy with my advertising on Google Ads.'

'Well, Ads is one tactic you can use to grow your business, yes. But what happens if one of your clients pulls the pin on a contract, or goes out of business. Or the cost of advertising climbs through the roof and becomes unaffordable. Then you'd be stuck with fewer clients and less income. Marketing helps keep you in the minds of decision-makers and potential clients. It helps cement you in with existing clients and helps you find new ones.'

'Okay, I can see the potential. But what's all this "thinking" that I've got to do?'

'Well, you have to think through the answers to some deep questions, as I've said. But the beauty of a plan is that it is something you can refer back to when life gets hectic and it can help get you back on track. It helps you find the "why" of your business, which drives so much of your motivation and energy.'

'Okay, so where do I go to find these questions?'

'Ah ha! It just so happens that I have a very useful template here in my hand and, if you're willing, over the next hour we can answer the questions and get a real handle on your marketing for the next six months.'

'And what happens in six months' time?'

'You fill in the plan again. But this time you have the old plan to look back on and guide you.'

'Strewth. I don't know about this. It sounds like a lot of hard work for nothing. But you've never steered me wrong before, Kels, so I'll trust you on this one. Let me get a couple of beers from the fridge. Take a seat.'

'I won't have a beer, thanks, Dan. I'll stick with my water bottle.'

'Suit yourself. There we go. Now, let's look at this paper you have in your hand.'

'It's a ninety-day plan, but I reckon we can use it as a half-yearly plan for now. Once your business is full, you can change to ninety-day plans for flexibility.'

'Fair enough. Who designed the plan?' Dan took the orange form from Kelly and turned it over in his hands.

'A very clever marketing company in Sydney called Basic Bananas. They use it themselves in their own marketing.'

'Fair enough. Let's get started. Do I answer the first question, "What's my purpose?"'

'Yes, let's think of a reason why you're in business.'

'Well, to make me money so I can put beers in the fridge and petrol in the car.'

'Oh, that's all well and good, Dan. But is there an underlying reason why you're in business? Say, to change the world, or to best utilise the skills you have to help businesses with their IT needs?'

'Oooh, I like that one, Kels. Utilising the skills I have. Helping other businesses. Yes, I like that, that sounds like me.'

'Okay, good. That's the "why" sorted out. Very good, Dan.'

'Well, you thought of it, Kels, I just agreed with you. You did all the work.'

'Well, now that you know the sort of answers we're looking for, I'm sure you'll contribute more fully.'

'Say Kels, have you filled in this plan for your own business?'

'Oh sure. I did a marketing course with Basic Bananas.

It was extremely helpful to pinpoint how best to approach our customers and potential customers. The whole course was brilliant. I'm still using their material three years later.'

'That's good to know. It's not like you're trying to fob some nonsense on me, then.'

'Oh no, this stuff works. Now, let's consider the next question… 'Who. Who are your target markets?'

'What do you mean, target markets? Is this like the targeting in Google Ads?'

'Yes, in a way it is. What sort of businesses or people are you most happy working with?'

'Well, I'm happy to work with anyone who pays me, Kels.'

'Okay, but imagine you are full with clients. Which clients or people do you get the most satisfaction working with?'

'Well, the ones that pay on time, and pay a reasonable fee. I've had clients in the past who penny-pinched everything and argued over every invoice. They eventually left, and I was glad to be rid of them, to be honest. They were taking up so much of my time for so little reward.'

'I agree, those sort of clients are a right pain. I've had a couple like that, and I was so glad when they moved their account to a competitor. But if we had to put down in just a few words what an ideal client looks like, what would you say?'

'Well, someone who pays on time, recognises my skills, is open-minded and fair… is that the sort of thing you're looking for?'

'Brilliant. Just perfect. Now, what size company? Can micro businesses, for example, afford your skills?'

'No, they can't. But I would imagine they would know of someone in their world who could provide advice, for a fee. No, the company I'm looking for is a medium-sized company. Not a big company, because they have technicians on staff, but a medium-sized company can't justify taking someone on full-time but can justify having someone like me on their books for when situations crop up.'

'Perfect, Dan. See? You're doing all the work now. Well done. Great answers.'

'Ahh, it's all down to your guidance, Kels. Next question.'

'This will be a tricky one. What's your Unique Selling Proposition? What makes you different from other IT technicians out there?'

'Strewth, Kels, that's a curly one. What makes me different? Hmmm... Let me grab another beer and think about it.'

'Take your time. This question is always a difficult one to answer. It took me several months of thinking about it before I could come up with one for our business.'

'So what did you come up with? I thought all you agribusinesses are the same.'

'I know. We all do the same thing, we all offer the same services, we even drive the same cars. It's hard to tell us apart. But after months of thinking I reflected that where we were different was that we offered a 24/7 territory manager call out. Which means that if a client of mine has troubles at three in the morning, they can ring me and I'll come out to be with them in their hour of need. Our two competitors *say* they offer 24/7 service, but from word around the farms they are hard to get hold of and only talk on the phone. We turn up on site whenever we're needed. And we don't charge a call out fee, either. Which the other two do.'

'Well, I'm impressed. But that's still no closer to me coming up with a unique whatever you called it.'

'No, you're right. So what makes you unique, Dan? Why would a company use you rather than a competitor, assuming you have competitors?'

'Oh yes, I have competitors. From what I can tell, they fall into two camps: graduates with a computer science degree but no job, and former IT technicians who have been made redundant. The kids don't worry me, but the old hands, they know their way around the systems. They are my biggest threat.'

'So, what would stop a business from hiring one of those older IT techs?'

'Cost, maybe. These older techs are charging big bucks.'

'Okay. So maybe you provide more value for money. What else? Why would someone hire you rather than an older tech?'

'... Strewth, Kels. I dunno. Can I think on it?'

'Of course. Like I said, it took me months to find the USP for our business. Okay, next question: Marketing Goals. What are one, two or three things you want to achieve in the next twelve months in your business?'

'What, like have more clients?'

'Yes, but not just 'have more clients', you have to say how many you want.'

'Well, I reckon I could handle another three clients easily, or five at a pinch.'

'Okay, so how about we say 'grow my business by four more clients, to make a total of X clients'? How many clients in total do you want, how many do you think you can handle?'

'Well, I have three at the moment and I've got tons of spare time, so another four would give me a total of seven. Seven clients would be the limit.'

'Okay. Grow by four to make seven. And how are you going to do this?'

'I have no idea. Word of mouth, I guess.'

'How did you get the three clients you currently have?'

'Through Google Ads.'

'Okay, so online advertising is one tactic. Have you thought of other tactics you could try, like newsletters, or videos?'

'No, I hadn't. Well, that's not true; I *had* thought of them, but I dismissed them as too time consuming for no reward. To be honest, Kels, I don't know enough to create a monthly newsletter or video.'

'Oh, you're just saying that out of modesty, Dan. You've been playing with computers forever, you know lots. You're the man everyone around here asks for advice and help with their computer. I reckon there's a lot you could talk about, a lot you could share in a newsletter. And don't forget, you only do one a month. You could always do some research on the web first before writing it.'

'That's true. How long would it have to be?'

'Well, that's the beauty of online publishing; it's as long as it needs to be, and no more. I know of writers who publish short, and I mean really short, newsletters one month, and then a long one the following month. It depends entirely on what they have to say.'

'Wouldn't any newsletter I write be boring to read? I'm not skilled at writing.'

'You'd learn, and there are plenty of free newsletters on the web on how to write effective newsletters. And the newsletters wouldn't be boring to your target audience, because they are interested in what you will write about. And don't forget Grammarly and ProWritingAid—they will pick up any spelling and grammar errors.'

'Kels, you make it all sound doable. Is it really as simple as writing an essay each month and emailing it out?'

'Sure. You have a subscription form on your website that captures email addresses, and you use a mailing service to send out your newsletter to them. The mailing service handles all the back-end processing, like making sure your emails go out at a set time, and it handles all subscriptions and unsubscribes. And they are low cost or free to begin with, so there's no risk.'

'And you reckon this is a way to grow my business?'

'There's no one way to grow a business these days, Dan. Marketing is doing as many things as possible to create touch points where people—target customers—can interact with you and get a good taste in their mouth. But having a regular newsletter helps build your credibility. It shows that you know what you're talking about, that your thinking is sound. The people around here trust you and your advice; why not show that same expertise on a bigger stage?'

'Okay, Kels. You've convinced me. I'll create a newsletter.'

'Glad to hear it. Now, what else can you do?'

'What else? Strewth! I could always do a video, or blog.'

'You could do both, Dan, at the same time. A regular or semi-regular video, short, under five minutes, talking about one topic at a time. You could record them on your phone, using your earbuds' mic for better quality audio.'

'Do you do videos, Kels?'

'Oh sure. I was as nervous as anything when I first started, but I got the hang of it after a while and now think nothing of it. I have a rig in my car so I can record a video while I'm driving between clients. We have it set up at work that the videos only go out to clients, not the general public, so I don't get the harassment that I would if every male idiot out there could see them. But the clients seem to like them, and I always try to give solid information and ideas.'

'Okay. Well, I'm not so confident about doing a video, Kels, but I think a newsletter would be a good place to start, hey?'

'Absolutely. So let's fill in this form. The goal is to grow by four customers. The next step is to create a newsletter, name it and organise an online mailing service account where you can design your newsletter so it looks professional when it goes out. Like I said, you can pick mailing accounts up for free and only pay when you hit a larger number of subscribers. Now, the big question is "by when"—when are you going to have an account set up, a newsletter template designed, and your first newsletter written and ready to send? Oh, and also have the sign-up form on your website.'

'What about one month from today? Is that too soon, or too far away?'

'No, that sounds about right. There's a lot to do, Dan, in setting up a newsletter. But it's all worth it once you've done. It's like flying a plane; the take-off is all slow and grunty, but once you're up in the air, it's increasingly easy to get moving along at a cracking pace. Well, congratulations, Dan, you've written a marketing plan!'

'Ha ha! Well, I don't know about that, I reckon you wrote most of it, I just nodded.'

'Well, I might have helped a little. Only because I've written lots of these myself and know their value. But now you have this template document you can refer back to, to keep you moving forward and focusing on what you set out to do. I see too many farms try different things and give up too soon before what they are trying can take effect. They rush to the shiniest object and think it will be their salvation. Honestly, Dan, the old methods are still around because they work. Stick with what's proven to work, do one thing at a time, and grow your business in a way you can handle. That's what this plan will help you achieve.'

'Well, thanks again, Kels. You sure I can't get you a beer?'

'No, I'm sure. I'd best be off, anyway. You've got a lot to think about.'

'Ha ha, you're right. Well, if there's anything I can ever do for you...'

'I know. It's no problem, Dan. If my printer gets stuck again, I'll call you at four am.'

'Ha ha. I know you will.'

05

Three month's later, the State Manager of Anthol Logistics, Bruce Abernathy, sat down with Derringerry's farm manager, Alan Peters.

'I won't lie or beat about the bush, Alan. Your head-count's too high for the size of your farm. Lose someone.'

'We run a tight ship here, Bruce. I know you've just taken us over, but we don't have any slack to lose someone.'

'I've looked at your figures, and for the size of the farm and your throughput, you're one too many. You need to cut about $50-60,000 from your salary and wages line. That's one person. Look, I have tried juggling the numbers myself. You're not making enough money to be viable.'

'I confess I'm shocked, Bruce.'

'I know. That's why I've come down here to Meningie personally, rather than send one of my area managers. Now, walk me through your staff here and let's see if we can be as kind as we can be in the situation.'

At 65 years of age, Alan was not new to having to let staff go. But it still hurt. The staff were like family to him, and even the ones he didn't get on with were still entitled to a fair go in his eyes. He turned to his computer, called up the staff wages and salary spreadsheet, and let his gaze slowly slide down the list of names. Running a farm was always tricky; there was never enough staff to go around during the good times.

Derringerry wasn't operating at peak capacity at the moment, but it was always threatening to 'go big'. Alan always kept one or two people on for those periods when it suddenly ramped up and all hands were needed on deck. You needed hands that were experienced, not travellers passing through. He was loath to give up anyone without a fight. The farm had been sold to Anthol Logistics, a Chinese-owned conglomerate, because it could pull its weight during peak periods and was therefore worth something to its owners. But to do that, he needed to have his entire crew on board. Losing someone was not, to him, an option.

Anthol Logistics had a bad reputation in the industry. They were asset strippers, building up farms to make them look profitable, then selling them at a high price. Their reputation was such that no one counted on a long career with them, or a career with a living, respectable wage. Promotions were non-existent and salaries stagnated for years.

Alan Peters started at the top of the list. 'Jono Anderson...'

06

Time passed. 'Darl, look at this!' David 'Davo'
Wilkins called out. He held his phone up so his wife could
take it from him while he sat on the couch.

'What am I looking at?' Sarah asked once she'd come
from the kitchen where it was her turn to make dinner. Like
her husband, she was toned in body, as keen athletes often
are. Both the same age, 28, they put a positive stamp on the
local football, cricket and netball competitions. Both were
doing their best for each other to move forward with their
grief. But their loss of Lily coloured every aspect of their
lives.

'A blinding goal from DeFrancese against Liverpool.'

'Why aren't you watching it on TV?'

'Just checking my emails and Spiro sent this clip. I'll
watch the game after training tonight.'

'It's a great goal, lover,' Sarah agreed as she went back to
the kitchen and the quick pasta dish she was preparing.

All 182cm of prime alpha male got up from the couch
and came into the kitchen.

'You know what? I reckon we should invite Spiro and
Liz over for dinner.'

'Okay, what night do you propose? I have summer
netball training Monday night, you have cricket training
Tuesday night, every other Wednesday night I have yoga
with Shandra, Thursday night is admin night for the clubs
and Friday night is pub night. Leaving just Saturday and
Sunday, and I don't enjoy doing anything on a Sunday night
except rest and prepare for the next week.'

Davo looked down at the ever-present-when-there's-
food-about hounds, Caz and Sophie. Caz was a ten-year-old
yellow Labrador, Sophie was a six-year-old black and white

Jack Russell. Both had a love affair with food preparation time in the kitchen. Sophie had even been known to sit quietly in the early hours of the morning, on her own in the dark, staring at the fridge.

'What do you reckon, girls? Do you fancy a dinner party?'

He guessed that the answer would have been yes, because at dinner parties he surreptitiously fed them both from the food on his plate.

Well, not-so-surreptitiously, because Sarah had spied him doing it frequently but hadn't bothered to say anything.

'Not during the week,' Sarah demanded, 'there's no space, lover. If you can find a Saturday that's free in the next three months, then fine.'

'Challenge accepted! Now, I'd better go get changed for practice.'

07

Dan belonged to an online group of entrepreneurs on Facebook, Kate Toon's 'Misfit Entrepreneurs'. It was a ragbag collective of entrepreneurs who had read Kate's book on entrepreneurialism, enjoyed her twisted sense of humour and enjoyed sharing the weird and wonderful of the web.

A frequent commenter on Dan's sarcastic posts was a lady called Hannah, recently they had started an online friendship based around sarcasm. Hannah lived in Sydney, married with two young children, and was a mumpreneur (a stay-at-home mum who ran a business from home). She sold scented candles and personalised, embossed leather bookmarks on Etsy. Hannah and Dan were catching up on one of Hannah's Facebook status updates.

'You remind me of a software update. Whenever I see you, I usually think "Not now!"' Dan wrote.

'Lol. Hilarious, Dan. You're on fire this week.'

'Cool - thx. Seen some funny memes lately, thought I'd share.'

'I like a good sarcastic meme. Makes such a change from the boring shit I normally see on Facebook.'

'Hey, fancy continuing this on Pickant?'

'Sure, send me a link.'

Hannah's face popped up on Pickant, a popular online video platform.

'G'day, Hannah. Where were we? Oh yeah, sarcasm. That's why I stick with the misfits. I've got the space to be myself, but darker and more sarcastic. You share some funny stuff too, you know.'

'Yes, but not as many as you. Which is why I love reading your posts; they cheer me up.'

'Do you need cheering up? You strike me as having a good sense of humour.'

'Oh yes, I need cheering up. It's a long story for another time, but your posts are a highlight of my day.'

'Go on, I've got some free time before my next client meet-up. Tell me why you need cheering up.'

'Well, after the birth of my twins, I developed postnatal depression, which I haven't been able to shake off. It's been over three years now. I get the blues terrible some days, and it's only because I have to attend to the girls I get out of bed at all. My husband works long hours, and so when he gets home he's exhausted and wants to watch some sports and go to bed. I don't have many friends to socialise with, they're all at work during the day and have their own families to look after at night. Your funny Facebook updates cheer me up.'

'Wow. That's a sad story. Sorry to hear it, for your sake. I'll make sure I keep up my sarcasm ratio for you.'

'Thanks.'

'Here's one: There are only three things that tell the truth—drunks, small children, and leggings.'

'Ha ha ha. That's fabulous and so true!'

'My mum prints out motivational sayings she finds on the web. She's crazy about them. Me, I don't go for all that shit, but it keeps mum happy. Hang on and I'll go see what her latest one is.'

A minute or so later, he was back.

'Here we go. *If you don't heal what hurt you, you'll bleed on people who didn't cut you*. I do not understand what it means. Which is true about most of the sayings that mum prints out.'

'It's deep. It's about pain and personal suffering and not dumping on people who don't deserve to be dumped on, I think.'

'I see. But when is it okay to dump on someone? On the one hand, people are told to be positive all the time, not be a Negative Nigel to their friends and to smile and do the best you can, and they are also told to share their feelings more, acknowledge their frailty and ask for help. Which one is it we should be doing?'

'That's a good question, and I don't know the answer. The being a Negative Nigel is old-school thinking, whereas the second option is more modern. But I agree, no-one enjoys being around a negative person. Even I find it uncomfortable when someone is "opening up" and "sharing" around me.'

'Ha ha. Look, I've got to talk to one of my clients. Are you going to be around next Wednesday, at about the same time? We could chat again then.'

'Sure, that would be lovely. Thanks.'

'No worries. See you next Wednesday.'

After the call, Hannah opened up Evernote on her computer and wrote into her daily journal.

Talked on Pickant with Dan Robinson from the Misfits group on Facebook. Seems like a nice man. Has a gsoh. Lives in country South Australia. He may become a friend. I talked about my depression and it didn't seem to scare him off, but I won't make that mistake again. That was stupid of me. We've agreed to chat again next week. Let's see if my stupid talk about my depression puts him off, and he doesn't show up.

08

Half an hour later, Alan Peters wrapped up his 'discussion' with Bruce Abernathy by reading the last name on the wages and salary spreadsheet, Alice Yates, and spelling out why the accounts clerk was invaluable to the team. Every name on his spreadsheet had a glowing reference from him and reason or reasons they should not be fired.

'You fight for your team, I admire that, Alan,' Bruce commented. 'But there must be someone not pulling their weight, someone who would not be missed if they didn't turn up for work one day. Who would that be? I know you want to keep them all, but I'm afraid you can't. That's why I'm here today, to walk away with a name. Now, come on. Who wouldn't you miss?'

A name flickered across his eyes. But he immediately had an answer for why they couldn't be let go. They were the local cricket and footy star. They were part of the town's power elite—a husband and wife team that almost single-handedly ran and shaped the cricket, football, and netball in Meningie. To sack David Wilkins, or 'Davo' as everybody called him, would be a crime against the town. At least in the town's eyes. Sure, David wasn't the sharpest tool in the shed, and he kept making mistakes in his handling of clients, but his heart was in the right place. Alan knew that he wouldn't be missed in the day-to-day running of the farm, as his job was to look after clients and that often meant he was off-site. No, there had to be someone else. There must be.

But there wasn't. Everyone else had a watertight reason their place in the spreadsheet was permanent, even the contractors.

'What about if I cancel the company cars? Surely that would save a dollar or two?' Alan asked.

'It's a thought. But all your contracts are still going; there's no contract that's not going to involve a large sum to pay out. No, you are going to have to let someone go. Are you going to name someone, or shall I?'

'Who did you have in mind?'

'David Wilkins. Word got back to me he screwed up on

the Maginty job. I gather that wasn't the first time that he's done that—screw up a client job.'

'But David is an integral part of the Sales and Marketing team. We couldn't afford to lose him.'

'But you have a whole Sales and Marketing team up in Head Office that you can call on now, Alan. I got a call from the state sales manager of Maginty about how pissed off they were. We can't afford to lose them as a client, not in this market. Is he married?'

'Yes.'

'Kids?'

'No. His daughter Lily was he and Sarah's only child.'

'Well, that settles it. He's in less of a position that causes sleepless nights. Now, I'm sacking him, not making him redundant. He screwed up with Maginty and that's a no-no in our company. We'll pay him his wages and any owed holiday up until this Friday, but he's got to go.'

'This won't make you popular in this town. He's already threatening to go legal over Lily's death.'

'Popularity is not my worry, Alan. I'm here to make a profit, not administer a charity. The company lawyers will make sure the company is protected. Now, I'd best be going and leave you to it.'

09

'Oh, that's perfect!' she exclaimed.

Ros Robinson was someone who exclaimed a lot. It was in her nature. She got excited about things. Little things and big things. Big things like the business success of her son, Daniel. Little things like a neatly balanced accounts book for a client, or a delicious main course or a dessert at a friend's place. Or an apt saying she'd read on Facebook.

Tonight, it was a saying she'd read on Facebook.

———

'YOU NEVER KNOW HOW STRONG YOU ARE UNTIL BEING STRONG IS THE ONLY CHOICE YOU HAVE'

———

'That's me!' she yelled out to no one else at her home printer.

Ros liked motivational sayings. She followed Avocado Wolfe, an American self-titled health guru who promoted a variety of pseudoscientific ideas such as Raw foodism, alternative medicine, and vaccine denialism. He wrote self-help sayings, and Ros was an eager audience for just such things.

Ros liked to print out the sayings she found on the internet and post them on her fridge. Every two or three days she'd select her latest favourite, print it out and stick it to the fridge. Ros was the Pollyanna of Meningie.

There had been a few men over the years who had attempted to woo her, but men rarely achieved the high standards she set. It's not that she hated men, she'd say to friends, just that each one she'd met had so many obvious faults.

One way Ros kept herself busy was by entertaining her friends, showing off her cooking skills, and by going to reciprocated evenings, where something tasty was always on the menu.

The other way she kept busy was by loving her son, Daniel. She loved her son dearly, but if she listened to her heart, there were niggles. He was slightly overweight. He slouched. He spent all of his time on his computer. He didn't read books, particularly self-development books. He didn't have a girlfriend and didn't try to get one. He'd go down to the hotel on a Friday night and drink far too much with his friend Davo, then drive home. All correctable niggles, she'd reason with herself, so best to remind Dan of his obligations and direction now and then. Which she did, usually when she and Dan intersected in the kitchen. The rest of the time, Dan was in the study, busily working on his computer, or out with friends on the weekend.

One evening Dan stopped at the fridge to get a beer.

There was a new saying that his mum had found on the internet. 'More of Mum's mind and body nonsense,' he thought.

Ros came into the kitchen to make a cup of green tea and saw Dan standing next to the fridge door.

'Well, what do you think? It's good, isn't it?'

'DON'T ASK WHAT THE WORLD NEEDS. ASK WHAT MAKES YOU COME ALIVE, AND GO DO IT. BECAUSE WHAT THE WORLD NEEDS IS PEOPLE WHO HAVE COME ALIVE' — BRENÉ BROWN

'Yes, mum. Excellent.' Without a shred of enthusiasm in his voice.

'Oh, Dan. You need to be more enthusiastic about things. Especially about re-tuning your mind to emit higher vibrations. Your life would go so much smoother if you let me retrain your brain.'

'Maybe next year, mum. I'm a bit busy at the moment.'

'Well, you could help your mum out now, by taking me round to the Prescott's. I want to have a drink while I'm there and so I don't want to drive.'

'But mum, you never have more than two glasses of wine when you're out. You know that. You'll be fine to drive.'

'Tsch. You know how Peter Prescott loves to fill up my wine glass all the time. I never know how much I've had when I go there.'

'Then, why go?'

'Well, Sheryl's doing her famous orzo macaroni and cheese. It's exciting!'

'Ok, mum, if you insist. You ready to go now?'

'Yup. Do I look presentable?'

Ros was 50, of medium height, still attractive, but the Aussie sun was being less kind to her face, giving her the start of a pinched mouth. She had long wavy streaked auburn hair that reached down her back, and she kept fit by walking, when she was not visiting friends and socialising. She stretched and twisted at Shandra's yoga clinic once a fortnight. Plus, her limited intake of alcohol helped keep her figure trim, taut and terrific, as the old advert used to say.

'Sure mum, you look great.'

'Thank you, Daniel. Now, drive me to the Prescott's, please.'

Mr John Pendlebury opened up the door of his red 1973 450 SL convertible Mercedes Benz. It was another beautiful evening down in Meningie—the temperature was still in the late twenties degrees after hitting a daytime high of thirty-five. Perfect for putting the top down and cruising down the Princes Highway to Kingston and back, catching the sunset over the Coorong on the way. Nearly four hours of motoring bliss, he thought.

He'd driven there lots of times, mostly in this Mercedes. Occasionally he'd driven down in his work car, a Toyota Prado.

Mr Pendlebury—and that is how everyone referred to him and addressed him—was like an old-school English country gentleman. A modern-day Winnie the Pooh in appearance, but without a Piglet for friendship and company. He ran his legal practice in Meningie, kept a bookkeeper on staff for his small business contractor clients, and kept to himself.

He'd been married once. But his wife had run off with a used car salesman named Dean, and he'd never remarried. He never really got back into dating. He was too hurt to want to risk loving someone again. Occasionally he had thoughts about his bookkeeper, Ros Robinson, who was also single, but he always reminded himself that work and play should never mix. Besides, she was his employee, and that sort of thing was frowned upon in his circle of peers.

So, Mr Pendlebury got into his sports car and slipped a cassette into the player. A male voice asked him if he cared to do the Fandango. He was as surprised and delighted as anybody when cassettes suddenly came back into production.

'Siri, call Kelly Germein for me.'

Siri dialled the number, and Kelly answered the call on the third ring.

'Hey Dan, whatcha up to?'

'G'day Kels. I need your help with a client problem I have. Have you got a few spare minutes?'

'Sure, I'm just driving to Coomandook. I've got about 20 minutes of free time ahead of me.'

'Excellent. Well, one of my clients has changed their primary contact with me. Whereas I used to work with a smart guy, Curt Davis, now he's moved on and I have to work with a Deirdre. I reckon she works over in Accounts and has no clue about technology. Yesterday she tried teaching me how to configure their server. She was reading from a manual. Honestly. How do I deal with her? She knows nothing.'

'I sense frustration in the force, young Obi-Dan.'

'Seriously, Kels, she knows nothing. How am I even supposed to work with her?'

'Remind me again what your contract title role is.'

'Uh, it's "Support Officer", why?'

'Because that's what you are supposed to be doing, supporting her. You need to hold her hand and let her feel she's in control.'

'But she knows nothing. I will have to hold her hand and teach her from scratch!'

'Exactly. You will have to do what you're contracted to —provide support. And that includes encouragement, training AND support.'

'But that could take forever!'

'Good. It's a great reason to extend your contract with your client because you are providing additional training. You could even negotiate a price increase because of the additional responsibilities. Think of that.'

'I never thought of that. I like it.'

'Thought you might. Now, if I were you, I'd race up to Adelaide and buy Deidre a coffee, because you will become good friends. That is if you want to negotiate a better price and increased responsibilities, which further ties the client to you, making it less likely they will leave you.'

'Kels, you're a great mate. Thanks.'

'You're welcome. Why don't you offer to write a training package for Deirdre, or at least a Welcome document, that shows you are keen to work with her and train her up? She'd probably welcome the opportunity to learn new skills and be more employable, and to secure her future at the business.'

'Honestly, Kels, you're the duck's guts. Why do you always help me out? You've helped me out since that day in school, in my first few days there, when the school bully Jack Benham beat me up and you kicked him in the nuts.'

'Simple. You have a heart of gold, and you care about people. You're loyal to your friends, and you sometimes remember the small things, like what movie they cried watching. And I'll not forget that it was you who saved me from Gene Bristol, that backpacker rapist we had a few years back. He insisted that I get in his car with him when mine had broken down, but you arrived on the scene and chased him away. A girl doesn't forget things like that.'

'Blimey, I'd sort of forgotten about that.'

'Ha ha. Well, let me know how you get on with Deirdre and renegotiating the contract. If you like, we can talk through some role-plays, have a bit of a practice one evening after work. Oh and have you put Grammarly on your computer and phone yet?'

'I have. It's great and saves me from typing something stupid. Thanks again for everything, Kels. Have a good day. Siri, end the call.'

12

Alan started the discussion. 'Thanks for coming in, Davo. How're things?'

'Good, thanks. The new, better match balls for the cricket club have finally arrived so we can look forward to a better rest of the season than the start has been. And the Maginty contract is going full steam ahead. Things were slow there for a while, but they seem to have sorted things out at their end.'

'That's good, on both counts. Look, Davo, I have a bit of bad news. I will have to let you go. Things have been slow around here, and the new owners have put us all under pressure to bring costs down. I'm sorry.'

'Strewth! I'm speechless!'

'Take your time; it's a big thing to process.'

'Why me? Are there others getting the chop as well?'

'Just you at this stage, Dave. Head Office looked at our numbers and we just don't have enough money coming in to support us all. But I expect that more will follow you shortly.'

'Why me? What did I do wrong?'

'Nothing, Davo. But Head Office has a marketing and sales team bigger than ours, and they can pick up your workload and run it from Adelaide. It's a dollars decision, nothing more.'

Alan felt bad about lying to Davo, but he didn't have the heart to say the real reason why he was being let go. Alan had to live in this town and saying one of the town's elite was useless and couldn't do his job properly wasn't the way to go about peacefully existing here. Alan knew that in reality, the lie he was spinning should see Davo be made redundant with payment for his eight years of service.

'I'm afraid I have to ask you to give back your company phone, your car keys and clean out your desk. I can give you a lift back to your house.' Alan knew that a short, sharp, clean break was the best for everyone involved, including Davo. Move Davo out while he was still in shock, that was the plan.

'In this envelope I've prepared a referral letter for you, and a paper that shows you we're paying you up to today, plus accrued annual leave. Let's go and clean out your desk.'

'That's okay,' replied Davo, still in shock, 'I can do that and drop the keys back in here in a few minutes.'

'Sorry, Davo. I have to come with you to make sure you don't damage any property or send any emails. Company policy.'

'Ok. Well, let's go, then.'

Alan's Land Cruiser turned right out of the farm gate and headed towards Meningie.

'Rather than drop me at home, can you drop me at the hotel?' Davo asked, 'Only, I meet up with my best mate after work on a Friday, and we sink a few over a steak. I think I'm going to need that tonight.'

'Sure, Davo, that's no problem.'

'I'd better text Sarah and ask her to meet me early at the pub so we can talk about it all.'

'G'day tiger!' Davo called out as he saw Dan.

'G'day ya bastard,' Dan replied. 'G'day, Sarah,' he smiled.

'Get yourself a beer and come tell us your tales,' Sarah replied.

'You want a beer yourselves?'

'No,' said Davo, 'we've only just got one.'

Dan did as he was told and came back with a pint and thinking of a story to tell. Well, at least tell Davo. Sarah probably wouldn't want to hear it.

'Okay, now you're here I'll leave you two to gasbag on your own. I'm going to go have a drink with Jess,' Sarah announced. 'Are you going to be okay, lover?'

'Sure. I'll be fine,' Davo replied.

Dan sat down as Sarah got up—kind of like pub ballet.

Davo took a mouthful of beer. 'Right then, what stories can you tell me?'

'This week I have another dickhead client who wants to tell me how to configure their server,' said Dan. 'Really. They've got no bloody idea. Some forty-year-old sheila is trying to teach me what to do. She hasn't got a clue. She's probably from Accounts or something.'

'You're kidding me?'

'Nope. I have to listen to her read from the manual and pretend that she's skilled at server configuration. Bloody hopeless. What about you? What's new in your world?'

'Well, I have something for you—something happened an hour ago that I'm still recovering from.'

'Go on.'

'An hour ago, Alan Peters called me into his office and told me my services were no longer required.'

'WHAT?'

'Yep. They fired me.'

'Did he give a reason?'

'Nope. Said it was a decision from much higher up, something about staff numbers and profitability and stuff. Nothing personal.'

'That's bullshit! They can't just fire you like that! Can they?'

'I dunno. But they have.'

'Surely they'd have to make you redundant or something if it's reducing staff numbers. They can't just sack you.'

'Well, they did. Alan said I'd receive my pay as usual, plus outstanding holiday pay, and that he'd written a reference for me.'

'How did Sarah take it?'

'She's as shocked as me. It will take a little while for the shock to wear off, then anger will probably set in.'

'I bet. Have you spoken to your Uncle John about it?' Mr Pendlebury, the local solicitor, was Davo's Uncle John.

'Not yet. I'm still in shock, I guess. I'll give him a call tomorrow, once the dust has settled. In the meantime, it's business as usual, so let's go to the restaurant, get another beer and order some food. I feel like the porterhouse tonight.'

'That reminds me of a saying I read this week: Every loaf of bread is a tragic story of a group of grains that could have become a beer but didn't.'

'Deep, mate, ha ha ha. That's not one of your mum's, is it?'

They'd fired his best mate. The news was still hard to take.

It was Saturday morning, the next day after Davo told Dan that he'd been fired from Derringerry. As they usually did, there had been a few beers sunk that Friday night, and recent Saturday mornings had found Dan coming to a little reluctantly, hesitantly.

'I'm getting old,' Dan thought to himself, 'I used to take this sort of punishment with no dramas. I'm getting soft.'

His thoughts drifted back to Davo. How will Davo and Sarah make ends meet? Sure, the insurance payout from the car-crash death of his parents helped them buy their house, but there was little else to fall back on. His parents' car insurance policy coverage was minimal, and certainly they were in no position when they were alive to pay for a better policy.

And who plans to lose their life, and the life of their spouse, in a car crash anyway? Who plans and makes sure the insurance is top rate? Rob and Janice had adored Lily, as did everyone who met her. They would have been devastated to have lost her, just as Davo and Sarah were, still.

Dan pushed his thoughts back to Davo. What could he, Dan, do to make his best mate Davo's life easier? It's not as though his own IT consultancy business was booming and he had cash to spare.

His thoughts ticked over. Nothing was coming out of the ether, nothing that would help Davo survive the tricky period until he found another job. And this was rural South

Australia—it's not as if jobs were thick on the ground, waiting for someone to come along and pluck one up.

'There must be something.'

A glimmer. Something in the far distance calling out to him. Dan could sense something, but couldn't get a grip of it, couldn't pull it closer so he could recognise it.

'Time for a coffee'. He pulled the duvet back and padded to the kitchen. Reaching into the fridge to get some milk he noticed his mum's latest saying:

'DON'T CLING TO A MISTAKE JUST BECAUSE YOU SPENT A LONG TIME MAKING IT'

Not helpful to him at that moment, Dan announced to no-one there.

Back in his bedroom with a mug of hot coffee, Dan once more reached for the nebulous thought located at the periphery of his conscious. No luck.

'I know, I'll ignore it and let it come to me when it's ready. Time for a shower.'

Two minutes into his shower and the thought that wouldn't come came. It was obvious. Davo and Sarah were hurt that only Alan Peters had turned up at Lily's funeral to represent Anthol Logistics. They both harboured ill-will to Anthol, not only because no-one came to the funeral, but mostly because Anthol was trying to strong-arm Davo and Sarah into accepting a paltry compensation, using their lawyers to bully and scare Davo and Sarah into resignation and submission. It was only because of Davo's Uncle John, Mr Pendlebury, and his insistence on fighting Anthol that Davo and Sarah hadn't been crushed by Lily's death.

Now Dan saw a way to help Davo, and by association Sarah, regain a sense of self. Davo's confidence had taken a battering, and Dan saw a way to keep Davo busy and forward-focused.

They say, down around these parts, that revenge is a meal best served cold. Well, Dan was going to help Davo get revenge on Athol, in a meal that was still warm. They would steal farm equipment and cause discomfort for Anthol's management. Sure, it would probably anger Alan Peters, and he was a good egg as far as Dan could tell, but you can't make an omelette without breaking eggs.

Revenge it was and stealing farm equipment was the game. That would help his mate. He just had to pick the right time to discuss it all with Davo. Probably not this weekend, because Sarah would be around. No, best to wait until the week started again and Sarah was at work.

'The best ideas come in the shower,' he said to himself.

15

'Sẽ không tốt.'

'What does that mean?' asked a regular customer.

'No good will come of this,' Phuoc Huu replied.

It was lunchtime, and the takeaway shop he ran with his wife Han was experiencing a boom in trade because one of the local farms had recently taken on some seasonal workers to help with managing their larger-than-usual head of cattle. Phuoc and Han were delighted with the additional revenue —they could put it towards their two children's education.

Han was busy preparing more cold rolls—they were always popular—and was assuming her usual position: head down, absorbed in food preparation, seemingly not listening to her husband's interactions with the customers. But she was listening. Intently. Not much got past her, no matter how busy it got in the shop.

Listening to a customer that is interested in Phuoc's view of the hot Spring the region had been experiencing. To which Phuoc, with his customary pessimism, had replied that he didn't think it bode well. Locals loved coming in to the shop to hear Phuoc's sayings. And Phuoc was clever enough to never let them be disappointed.

16

As he had promised, Dan sent Hannah a meeting request in Pickant, and they caught up.

'G'day, Hannah, how's your week been?'

'Great, thanks. How's your week been so far?'

'Great. I got some excellent advice from a friend about a business problem I had, and she's put me on the right track.'

'That's great. Tell me more, what was the advice about?'

Dan brought Hannah up to speed on his change of heart about one of his clients and how his friend Kelly was the catalyst.

'Wow. That's a brilliant outcome.'

'Yeah, and I'm happy because I have a new buddy in Deirdre that I can train up to help me, and I'm getting paid extra for it. So it's a win-win all around.'

'Your friend Kelly sounds smart.'

'Oh, she is. She's a territory manager for a farming group down here, works with lots of farms. Knows what's what with business. She puts me straight on lots of things.'

'Where did you meet her?'

'We've been mates since school days. I was the new kid in town, the outsider. I was being bullied by another kid, and she came and kicked him in the nuts, and after that he left me alone. We've been great mates ever since.'

'Has there ever been a romance between you two?'

'Oh, no, she's a mate. There'd be none of that going on. Mind you, she's a looker all right. Long dark brown hair, slim, face to die for. My mum would love it if we ever hooked up. Kelly is whip-smart, beautiful, kind and generous. But it will never happen.'

'Why ever not?'

'Well, I'm sure she's the same as me, we just see each other as great mates. Wouldn't want to spoil what we've got going. Besides, she an aunty to her sister's kids, and that keeps her busy on weekends. Oh, and she's got a dog she treats as her baby, so she's not clucky or anything. She's told me before, she doesn't need a man in her life; it's going well enough without one.'

'Ha ha ha, sounds like she's got her head screwed on!'

'Ha, yeah. Well, that's my big news. What about you? What's been happening in your world, Hannah?'

'My world? Oh, same old. Do you have another joke for me?'

'Sure, let me think. Oh yeah, have you ever listened to someone for a while and wondered, "who ties your shoelaces for you?"'

'Ha ha ha! That's fantastic. I could think of a couple of people I know from my husband's work that would fit the bill. Speaking of the husband, or husbeast as I call him, he got a promotion yesterday. It takes effect next month, but the extra pay will help with Christmas coming up.'

'That's fantastic news, Hannah. And the extra pay will help, for sure. What's your husband's name?'

'Carlo. Carlo Fangetti. And our daughters are Jessie and Angela.'

'Beautiful names for your girls. Your surname in the Misfits group is Ramsey. What's going on there? Are you a Ramsey or a Fangetti?'

'I'm a Ramsey in my business life. It's my maiden name. But socially, I'm Mrs Fangetti. I keep the Ramsey name because I want separation between my business life and my family life with Carlo and the girls.'

'Fair enough.'

'You mentioned last week that you have depression. How's that going for you?'

'Oh, it's all good, thanks. Really. It was just a phase I was going through. I have days like that now and then. Nothing to worry about. But thanks for asking and thinking about me. I'll let you know if I'm depressed again.'

'Okay. No worries.'

'Look, I've got to get dinner ready; we have friends over for a mid-week meal, and I've got a last-minute bit of shopping to do. Do you fancy meeting up same time same day next week? We haven't got a dinner planned for then.'

'Sure, that sounds good. My mum loves cooking for dinner parties, and she loves going to them. Me, there's nothing better than a sirloin steak down at the Meningie Hotel, with roasted vegetables and a cold beer to wash it all down. I'm not one for dinner parties and fancy food. But I often get roped into them because Mum doesn't want to drive and drink, so she makes me tag along as her chauffeur. At least I get a half-decent feed that way, even if it is sitting in the kitchen while her friends and her sit in the dining room. I catch up on stuff on my laptop while I'm there.'

'Ok, at least you get fed and don't have to make it yourself. That sounds like a winner to me! Ha ha. Ok, let's catch up next week. Have a good week 'til then.'

'You, too. And have a nice night tonight. See ya.'

CHATTED WITH DAN AGAIN. GOOD CHAT. HE ASKED
ABOUT MY DEPRESSION AND I TOLD HIM IT WAS FINE,
ALL GONE. I LIED, YES. I DON'T WANT HIM TO SEE ME
AS SOME TRAGIC, SAD, MISERABLE WOMAN WHO SUCKS
THE LIFE OUT OF OTHERS. HE'S FUNNY AND KIND AND
I WANT HIM TO STICK AROUND, SO NO LETTING HIM
KNOW THAT I'M FEELING AS MISERABLE AS ALL FUCK.
I PANICKED AND TOLD HIM WE WERE HAVING A
DINNER PARTY TONIGHT. OF COURSE, WE'RE NOT.
CARLO WILL BE WORKING LATE AGAIN, AS ALWAYS.
I'LL HAVE TO REMEMBER ABOUT THE DINNER PARTY
WHEN I CHAT WITH DAN NEXT WEEK. HE STARTED
TALKING ABOUT MY DEPRESSION, SO I CLOSED DOWN
AND MADE AN EXCUSE TO CUT THE CONVERSATION
OFF. I DON'T WANT HIM ANYWHERE NEAR MY
DEPRESSION.

17

Mr Pendlebury picked up his mobile on the fifth
ring. It wasn't close to him and he had to lean across his
dining table covered with legal papers to reach it.

'G'day Uncle John. It's me, Dave.'

'Hello, Dave, how's things? Is Sarah well?'

'Oh yeah, she's good, thanks. Look, I have something I'd
like your advice on. Is now a convenient time?'

'Sure, I'm just working on some conveyancing matters,
but I can stop that for my favourite nephew.'

'I'm you're ONLY nephew, Uncle John, ha ha.'

'Well, you have me on a technicality there, Dave. How can I help you?'

'Something's come up with my work. They have fired me. The only reason I got given was they were letting me go because of financial worries with the farm, nothing about my performance. Is there something I should know about that they're not telling me? Like, should I be made redundant, rather than just sacked?'

'I'm not up with employment law, Dave, but I'm reasonably confident that in such a situation as you describe someone would have rights to a redundancy package. But it all depends on the employment contract they signed. If they signed an Enterprise Agreement that specifically allowed the company to terminate employment and not pay any redundancy package, then the person would have no right to a claim. So, it all depends on the employment contract you signed. Do you have it in front of you?'

'No, and to be honest, I have no idea where it would be. It was seven years ago that I joined the farm. Oh, but I had to sign something when Anthol took over the farm a few months back. I can dig that up if it will help.'

'If it's an employment contract it will help indeed, Dave. Give me another call when you've found it and then bring it over for me to read.'

'Will do, Uncle John, and thanks.'

18

Dan called Davo on the phone. Sarah would be at work, so Dan had a good guess that he'd have Davo's undivided attention.

'I've got an idea. Something to help pass the time 'til you find another job.'

'As Frasier Crane used to say, "I'm listening".'

'Are you still as angry as you were last Friday night when you had just been sacked?'

'Probably angrier. I've been to see my Uncle John. He's no employment law expert, but he reckons the farm's management should have made me redundant. They can't just sack someone because they want to reduce headcount.'

'That's what I've been reading on the web, too. Are you going to go legal on the farm?'

'Probably, over Lily. Why?'

'Well, I thought to pass the time it probably wouldn't hurt to teach the farm a lesson and nick some equipment and leave it in an unexpected place.'

'Why on earth would I do that?'

'We. We would do that. Because revenge is a dish best served warm and Anthol are bastards. Apart from Alan Peters, no one from the company turned up at Lily's funeral, and the company still fudges its responses on liability for her death.'

'True.'

'We just have to be smart about it and not get caught.'

'When would we do it?'

'At night, when it's dark, and the police have gone to bed.'

'If Sarah finds out, I'll be in deep shit.'

'I've thought of that. If we go in the middle of the night, no one will miss us. And to prepare for the work, tell her you're coming over to my place to pick up some training on office IT system maintenance, to add to your resume.'

'I'm starting to warm to the idea. I can see us getting

away with it and screwing with the Anthol management. I'm starting to love the idea!'

'Good. What we need is a map of the farm where the access points are, and where some machinery is stored that we can steal. Things like welders and stuff. Can you handle that?'

'Sure. Let me finish sending some resumes out and I'll get right onto it.'

'Excellent. Naturally, Sarah cannot know about this.'

'Naturally.'

'Come over tomorrow night and we'll discuss it further.'

'I LOVE this plan!'

'Good. See you tomorrow night.'

'What will we do about gear, disguises and stuff?'

'I've thought about that. We can buy special clothing for this online. I've found a few websites. I'll show you tomorrow night.'

PART TWO

It was time for their weekly Pickant chat. Both Hannah and Dan, for different reasons, looked forward to it.

For Hannah, it meant chatting with an adult and one who was interested in, and emotionally available, to her.

For Dan, it was talking with a woman, and being able to be himself, relaxed. Kind of like talking with a girlfriend, he imagined, even if this one was half a country away.

'So, I have this great joke for you,' started Dan once they had connected online.

'Go on, I'd like a joke,' Hannah laughed.

'Well, imagine if the person who named the Walkie Talkie named other stuff. For example, stamps would be Lickie Stickie, defibrillators would be Hearty Starty, bumble bees would be Fuzzy Buzzy, a pregnancy test would be Maybe Baby, a fork would be Stabby Grabby, socks would be Heatie Feetie, and a nightmare would be Screamy Dreamy. Ha ha ha, I love that last one.'

'They're excellent, Dan. Where do you find this stuff?'

'I told you, in my newsfeed on Facebook. All my friends are weird and post weird stuff. How's your week been?'

'Good. Sold some stuff on the website, had coffee with a friend who's home on holidays. Made some scones for the girls and they loved them. All in all, a good week. What about you?'

'Good. A client had a problem with passwords; they keep forgetting them. I installed a password manager on their computer and trained them up on how to use it. It will also store all of their website logins, so all they have to remember is the main password to the programme, and the programme takes care of the rest.'

'That was very helpful of you.'

'Yeah. My friend Kelly has been helping me with my people skills, helping me be more patient and understanding. When I look back, I used to have a bit of a problem. Probably still do, but I'm getting better. Oh, and I just remembered, I will be helping my best mate who got sacked, Davo, start skilling up on IT. We've decided he will come around once a week for two hours and I'll train him up on things like server configuration, networks, and so on. It'll probably be a bit of a hard slog, as I don't think it's his natural area of expertise, but he's keen to learn.'

'That's good of you, Dan. I reckon you're a decent man.'

'Oh, I don't know. You'd have to ask my mum what it's like to live with me. She'll probably have a few horror stories. But I've got no enemies, as far as I know, so that's a good thing, isn't it?'

'I reckon it is.'

'How's your depression going?'

'It's fine, thank you. Like I've said before, it was just a moment, nothing more. A momentary lapse of reason. It's nice of you to be concerned, but really, there's nothing to worry about.'

'Well, that's good. I do worry because one of our local farmers took his own life a couple of years back. The rural life can be tough, and the banks aren't always accommodating. Harry left behind a wife and three small kids. The insurance payout paid off the loans, but Laura struggles to make a go of the farm. The kids miss their dad. My mum helps out with the books, and I look after their computer for them. So I'm sort of sensitive when people say they're depressed. Sorry for nagging you about it.'

'That's terribly sad, Dan. And that's good of your mum, you and your community to rally around—Laura, is it?—and the kids. But honestly, I'm fine. If I have another attack of depression, I'll let you know. Hey, guess what? I've found the perfect job I want once the girls go to school.'

'What's that?'

'I want the job where I push scared skydivers out of the plane.'

'Ha ha. Very good; you must share that one in the misfits group.'

'I thought you'd like it. I saw it a couple of days ago and hung off posting it in there because I wanted you to hear it first.'

'Okay, well, I have another joke for you. Why can't dinosaurs clap their hands?'

'I don't know, why can't dinosaurs clap their hands?'

'Because they're dead. Ha ha ha!'

'Oh, that's a shocker! That's a dad joke! Hilarious.'

'Yeah, I laughed and laughed when I read it. "Because they're dead" ha ha ha.'

'I must tell my dad that one.'

Good chat with Dan. He told me a couple of good jokes, which lifted my mood. He's been helping a friend who was sacked from his job.

Note to self: definitely don't tell Dan about how I feel. This bloody depression is dragging on, and I probably should go see someone about it. But I don't want to see my GP; she'll just give me tablets. I don't like tablets. Tablets aren't the answer. I read somewhere that running can help lift my mood. But when do I get a chance to go running? Once the girls go to kindy next year, sure, but certainly not at the moment. And there's no chance of going for a run after dinner because Carlo doesn't get back until late most nights. And by then I'm exhausted from looking after the girls and keeping the house tidy. Maybe next year when the girls go to kindy, then I can start running again.

Angela has been whinging all day today, whiny and not her usual self. Maybe she's coming down with something.

20

Davo came over to see Dan with the ideas and plans of what they could steal from where.

'G'day mate,' said Dan as he met his mate at the front door. 'How're they hanging?'

'Perfectly,' replied Davo, as they made their way to the kitchen and the fridge for a beer.

Davo, about to open the fridge, stopped to read a new sign on the door.

'IT IS ALWAYS IMPORTANT TO KNOW WHEN SOMETHING HAS REACHED ITS END. CLOSING CIRCLES, SHUTTING DOORS, FINISHING CHAPTERS, IT DOESN'T MATTER WHAT WE CALL IT; WHAT MATTERS IS TO LEAVE IN THE PAST THOSE MOMENTS IN LIFE THAT ARE OVER — PAULO COELHO'

'Another one of your mum's sayings, then?' said Davo.

'Yup.'

'Deep.'

'Yup.'

Think it applies to me?'

'Dunno, but are you going to get a couple of beers out or not?'

'Right,' replied Davo. 'The important stuff first, eh?'

'Precisely. And we have important things to discuss.'

Dan led the way to the study and hovered at the entrance so he could close the door behind Davo.

'So,' Dan said, keeping his voice low so as not to be heard by his mum, 'what ideas and plans do you have?'

Davo pulled a folded A4 sheet of paper from the back pocket of his jeans and flattened it out on Dan's desk.

'Here's the farm. Here's the gate into the buildings, here's the first shed, what we call the ancillary equipment shed, and here's the machinery shed. I think we're better off hitting the ancillary shed because the equipment in there is smaller and lighter. In the machinery shed are the tractors, the feed spreaders and such. We'd have to drive them out, and that could be noisy. But the ancillary shed has lots of stuff that we can steal that will be just a "quick in, quick out". What do you think?'

'That's excellent, Davo. Good work. What do you think we should go for first?'

'I reckon we grab a welder or a gennie. Something easy to pick up and put in the back of the ute.'

'Are you sure there's no security anywhere?'

'Positive.'

'It could be a catastrophe if you're wrong.'

'Nope, not wrong. There's never been a break-in, or anything stolen at the farm since Alan Peters has been there, and there's been no security equipment either. We'd all know about it if there was; there are no secrets at Derringerry.'

'Okay. So that all looks good. When should we make our first theft?'

'What about tomorrow night? I have cricket practice at seven; we could make a go of it after nine-thirty when we finish. I'll just tell Sarah that I stopped in at your place to grab a quick beer and a chat.'

'No, too risky. It ties you and me together too easily, and there are still too many people about. What about 3am? If you snuck out of the house and met me at the Catholic Church, we could go in your ute and be back before anyone was awake to miss us.'

'That's a good idea.'

'What about, though, if Sarah wakes up? What will you say about why you're leaving?'

'I could say that I can't sleep and I'm going for a drive to clear my head. I'll tell her that the sacking has played with my head and I need to get some night-time road under my feet.'

'That's great. Good thinking. Okay, we'll meet up tomorrow night at 3am at the Catholic Church. Now, here, try this on.'

Dan pulled out some black camouflage clothing from a garbage bag.

'I guessed your size,' he said.

The trousers and long-sleeved t-shirt fitted like a glove. The boots were a size too big, but nothing a thick pair of explorer socks couldn't fix.

'What are *they*?' laughed Davo.

'They're Scream masks, replied Dan. 'I picked them up at a costume shop in Adelaide.'

Davo tried one on, then looked at himself in his phone. 'Cool. They go well with the black camouflage gear.'

'Precisely. And here's a box of black rubber gloves. We should be set.'

'Why the clothing and the masks?'

'Just in case there IS surveillance equipment. Our only weakness is the number plates on your ute, but we can unscrew them at the church.'

'You've thought of everything,' Davo said, suitably impressed.

'I tried. I just remembered those old spy novels we read in English class at school.'

'Okay, so see you at three tomorrow, then.'

'Let's rock.'

21

2.50am. Both men had their alarms set to silent, and the vibrations woke them up ten minutes before three, as planned.

Davo was the first to the church, his souped-up ute rumbling its way around the pitch-black streets of Meningie. He hoped he hadn't woken Sarah up, but at least he had an excuse ready for her if he had. His flecked and smoky sunburst orange XR8 ute glistened and flickered in the moonlight. It was distinctive. He'd paid an Adelaide paint shop a chunk of money to give his car a distinctive look, and they had succeeded. Everyone around town and far away knew Davo's ute, which was a liability if there *were* security cameras at Derringerry. But Davo was convinced there weren't, that there was no security at the farm at all.

At five past three, Dan pulled up in his silver Corolla and parked up against the church's garage. He got out, fully clothed in his camouflage gear, and walked over to Davo. Davo was busy changing into his camo gear, not wanting to get ready at home in case Sarah woke up and wondered what on earth he was up to. The air was crisp, the night quiet. Both men whispered.

'You ready?' asked Dan.

'Now or never,' replied Davo.

Once Davo dressed, they unscrewed the ute's number plates and slipped into the seats. Davo backed the car into the driveway and drove forwards towards Bowman Street and the highway.

Twelve kilometres north of town, they spotted the signs to Derringerry. Davo's ute knew where to go. They pulled up at the farm gate and put their Scream masks and rubber gloves on. Davo then swung the ute into the entrance and to the right, the opposite direction to the staff carpark. On the right were two large sheds—the ancillary shed, and the machine shed. Davo swung the car around and backed into the ancilliary shed as far as he dared. There were no lights to guide him, and he could run over a piece of equipment and puncture a tyre or gouge the ute's bodywork if he wasn't careful. So just inside the shed it was.

Ute parked but engine still running in case they needed to make a fast getaway, the two men turned their torches on and looked around for something to steal.

Davo was the first to spot something—a bright red welder. They briefly discussed it, then eagerly picked it up and dropped it into the back of the ute. While Davo was strapping the welder down, Dan picked up some welding rods and a couple of helmets and popped those in the back. They'd make a noise rattling about, but let's get out of the farm first, he thought, 'then we can dampen them down'.

A final check to make sure they hadn't missed something important, like security cameras, or better equipment than a welder to steal, and the dynamic duo were back in the front seats and driving briskly out of the farm and back onto the highway.

After a minute they pulled over, removed their masks and breathed deeply for the first time since they had pulled up outside the farm. Then let out huge screams of laughter and delight. Davo punched the air and Dan got out and danced a jig around the front of the ute.

'WE DID IT!' yelled Davo.

'We did, mate. Good driving!'

The euphoria lasted a little while longer, and both men were in no hurry for the high to recede. They leaned back against the bonnet of the ute and took in the night stars, so plentiful that night.

'I suppose we should secure the rods and helmets,' said Dan, eventually.

'True. I'll also check the straps on the welder; I was in a bit of a hurry before.'

Both men did their thing, then got back into the ute.

'So where are we going to store all this gear?' asked Davo.

'I know just the place. Head back to town and out the other side. I'll give you directions.'

Dan got back into the ute and felt the camouflage netting at his feet. Emotionally, he felt successful, competent, accomplished.

He also noticed that he had a slowly dying erection.

22

8.55am. Senior Constable 1st Class Andrew Campbell opened up the Meningie Police Station and went inside. His first duty was to put the kettle on and make himself a cup of coffee, then listen to any voice messages left on the phone system.

'G'day. Alan Peters here from Derringerry. We've had a break in, and some tools have gone missing. Can you pop over and see me? Thanks.'

That was the only message. Meningie was a quiet town, and it did not require a lot of policing. There'd been the rape of a backpacker a few years back, by a local farmer, but apart from that, things were boring.

At 52 years of age, there wasn't much you could do to

shock Andrew, and his years of experience in Mount Gambier, Naracoorte and Bordertown had inured him to country policing's vicissitudes. He'd only been based at Meningie for three months, but he was comfortable with how things were going.

He was single—the police life was the one that gave him the most comfort and security—with no intentions of settling down with someone after he'd hung up his hand-cuffs and pistol. A life driving the country highways and byways, interspersed with desk duty, meant that he wasn't as fit as some of his city counterparts, but it didn't worry him. Things ambled out here, he reasoned, and there was little need for STAR Group dramatics and STAR Group levels of fitness.

Andrew finished his coffee and picked up the keys to his patrol car, a nine-speed Commodore RS. Zero to 100kms in six seconds. Fast enough to chase down anything on the highway. He enjoyed the feeling of power under his right boot.

23

Ros had just got back from her nightly walk around the town. She had been listening to some songs written by women about women, and Ariana Grande's *God is a Woman* had been on repeat in her ears.

She was feeling a bit glum, her thoughts cycling back to the year she took her young eight-year-old son Daniel away from his father and brought him to a country town where no one knew him, and no one probably cared.

Why had she left his father? Because he was boring, she

answered. The man no sooner was married than he reverted to a reject from the 1950s, wanting his meals laid out before him and a pipe and slippers after dinner.

And if truth be told, she told herself, he was boring before they married, only she refused to recognise it because she was in love with being in love. In love with the fairytale of someone caring about her and wanting to give her everything. It was only in hindsight that she saw that this man she had married had never cared for her, but instead saw her as a cook, cleaner and part-time on-demand whore. Many nights she had cried herself silently to sleep. And he was a loud snorer—some nights she never slept.

But what had moving to the country done to Daniel, she asked herself? Well, she answered, if truth be told he's done all right for himself. Sure, he's not set the business world on fire, but he has a growing online business that she wasn't sure she fully understood, but she knew he had clients and he made regular trips to Adelaide on business. He had money to buy beer, and he seemed happy. He had good friends in that adorable woman Kelly, she said to herself, and of course his best mate Davo. He had some other friends that he spent time with on weekends, watching them play their sports. She wished that her Daniel expressed more of an interest in Kelly, but she knew to leave the subject alone—Dan had told her off enough on previous occasions.

'Dan is good to me,' she reasoned with herself. He was often driving her to dinner parties and generally looking after her. He listened to her rare complaints about life and men. All in all, he seemed happy with his life and not wanting for more adventure and excitement. So, although the country life she had brought him to lack some finer things that living up in Adelaide possibly would have brought him, he didn't seem lacking in friends, adventures while growing up, and opportunities to make his mark on the world. Thinking all of this, Ros felt pleased with her long-ago decision. Twenty years ago, in fact. Her son, she reasoned, was healthy (if a little overweight from no exercise, she muttered), happy and a fine man. Not an outgoing, gregarious man, not an 'Alpha Male' like Davo, but a competent, caring, considerate, loving man, nonetheless.

Ros took a small amount of pride in how she had raised such a fine son. As she acknowledged, it was a bit of nature and a bit of nurture. He was occasionally short-tempered and brusque, especially when she was trying to mould him into something he didn't want to be (like when he snapped at her for mentioning the words 'Kelly' and 'girlfriend' in the same sentence). Or when she was trying to get him to expand his consciousness more, like she had done, and read some books she had enjoyed reading. But all men get grumpy when they must deal with change, she argued, and in any case, the rest of their relationship was delightful and comforting.

Yes, she thought, he's a good son. I've done good.

And what of me, she asked? What do I think I've done with my life? Well, she answered, she had kept herself away from lazy, rough men. There were a few in this town. She still had some looks, she reasoned, so it was natural for men to try chatting her up. Two of her clients at work would probably like to be more than clients. And her boss, Mr Pendlebury, kept staring at her in unguarded moments, which she was flattered by but was certainly not going to do anything about. *That* was a messy scenario she didn't want to be part of—dating the man who pays her wages. He was nice enough, in a Pooh Bear sort of way, but not decisive enough for her. His business, she thought, had grown out of the necessity of the service he provided, not his business acumen. And he had a thing about fountain pens which she found somewhat old-fashioned. He had only just bought himself a 2-in-1 laptop at her strong suggestion that he join the twenty-first century, but he was clueless on how to work it. He kept calling her into his office to ask her to show him where the # key was and how and when to use it.

No, she reasoned, she was better off single, concentrating on paying off the mortgage on her little house on Cemetery Road, and enjoying the frequent dinner parties she was invited to by friends she had made. None of her friends shared her tastes in self-development, but that was their loss, she reasoned. She missed the touch and smell of a man, and God knows there were rare nights when her adult toys were not enough, but all in all, she felt loved in this town she called home and loved being in the town in return, even if it meant remaining single.

24

Alan met the police car in the parking area.

'Thanks for turning up. I don't know when it happened, but someone's helped themselves to a welding machine.'

'Okay. When did you first notice it was missing?' Andrew asked, getting his interview clipboard from the car.

'Yesterday morning. One of our farm hands went to get it to repair a gate, and he couldn't find it. Looked everywhere. He came and saw me, and we both looked in all the usual and unusual places for it. So I asked around, thinking someone must have used it and forgotten to put it back. But no one claimed to know anything about it.'

'So, what makes you think it was stolen?'

'A welder is not something you forget. At least not ours. It's a Lincoln Tig Inverter, expensive, and bright red.'

'I see. And no one knows anything about it, you say?'

'That's right, which is why I've asked you to come over. If someone did accidentally "borrow" it and forget to put it back, perhaps seeing your uniform and your car might jog their memory.'

'Anyone I should interview first, a likely suspect or something?'

'No, not really. This is the first time we've had anything stolen, or borrowed without me knowing about it first, in all the years I've been here.'

'And how many years have you been here?'

'Twelve. Happy years.'

'I see. When was the welding machine last seen?'

'About a week ago. Two of my team knocked up a frame.'

'And they put it back in the right spot?'

'Yep. They say they did.'

'Okay, well, do you have any serial number for the welder?'

'Sure, we keep a record of all of our machinery; let's go up to the office, and I'll give you a photocopy of the original invoice with the serial number on it.'

25

Hannah and Dan caught up on Pickant.

'I've had a good week this week. What about you?' asked Dan.

'Great, thanks. The girls have gotten over their colds, didn't pass them on to Carlo or me, and I sold some bookmarks.'

'That's fantastic, Hannah. Well, I did a Good Samaritan deed and helped a mate out.'

'What did you do?'

'His employer had unfairly sacked him, so the two of us broke into his old place of work and stole some welding equipment.'

'YOU DID WHAT?'

'Yep, we were wreaking revenge for him being sacked. He'd been feeling down after the sacking, but stealing some stuff picked him up. We will do it again.'

'You are kidding me, aren't you! You didn't really steal from his old employer, did you?'

'Sure did. They won't miss the equipment, and my mate really got a kick out of it. So did I, if truth be told.'

'But Dan, what about the surveillance equipment? You'll be caught.'

'They don't have any surveillance equipment. And insurance'd cover them. It's a victimless crime.'

'No, it's not. Theft is a crime, and you can be convicted and lose your business, plus have a huge fine to pay. I'd have to check with my dad, who's a policeman, but I think you could do jail time. Don't do another stealing job, Dan, please!'

'She'll be right. We will only do one or two more jobs, then we'll call it quits.'

'But don't you see the path you are on? Petty criminals have a high rate of being caught. I learned that from Dad.'

'Oh, it's all right. We won't get caught. And even if we do, they'll probably just give us a small fine or something. It's doubtful they'll even miss the equipment.'

'Don't you see the risk you're running?'

'There's not much risk. There's no surveillance stuff, no one will miss the equipment. But it's cheered my mate up. So that's worth it.'

'Okay, I believe you, but I'm not happy about it. Lecture over. Tell me another funny meme you read this week.'

'Santa's been reading your posts on Facebook and is bringing you a psychiatrist for Christmas.'

'Ha ha ha, very good. I could think of a few people that applies to.'

'I'd better go. I have a client catch-up I need to prep for. See you online next week?'

'Sure. And remember what I said.'

'I will.'

Dan's been stealing from a farm. He's stolen a welder. I told him off, but I didn't want to be too hard on him in case I scare him away. He's a bloody idiot.

Angela still not feeling well. Will take her to the doctor's tomorrow if she doesn't come right overnight.

26

'G'day Phuoc, G'day Han. How're things?'

'Good, thank you, Davo,' replied Phuoc. Han looked up from her preparations, nodded and smiled, 'It's always a pleasure to see you again. What can we get for you today?'

'Sarah will have the chicken with chilli and lemongrass, and I'll have the roast duck, please?'

'Certainly. That will be a wait of about five minutes. Do you want to stay and have a cold drink, or will you come back?'

'I'll stay and have a cold sparkling mineral water, Phuoc, if you've got one.'

'Sure. Here you are. Glass?'

'No, thanks, just out of the bottle is fine.'

Davo waited until his nerves had settled a bit. All of this crime stuff was new and exciting, but scary at the same time. He didn't want to give the game away. He asked what he thought would hopefully be an innocent question.

'Hey, did either of you hear anything about Derringerry farm?'

Han looked up and looked at Davo, but said nothing, just continued with her food preparations. Phuoc was the main talker in their shop.

'Someone was saying something the other day. Now, what was it? Urm... Oh yes, a welder had gone missing from the farm.' He stopped speaking, embarrassed that he was talking about Davo's old employer in his presence.

'Really?' said Davo. 'That's a bit of bad luck. Do you know if they have found it yet?'

'No, I haven't heard anything. I gather the police are asking everyone on the farm if they know anything.'

'I hope they find it soon. Those welders are expensive.'

Davo thought to himself: how to encourage Phuoc to keep an ear to the ground and keep himself informed, without giving away my interest. This crime stuff was tricky.

'What do you make of it all, Phuoc?'

'It always worries me when the police get involved. In

my country, the police are a sign of corruption and incompetence. They are always working for someone else, not you. We have an old saying in Hanoi, "hông ăn mừng cho đến khi bạn là một trăm phần trăm chắc chắn có một lý do để —don't celebrate until you are a hundred percent sure there is a reason to". I think that the police getting involved is not a good thing, Mr Davo.'

'Perhaps you're right, Phuoc. We must wait and see. What else is happening in Meningie that you know about?'

'Well, Mr Dan has a new client which makes him thrilled. He bought two extra cold rolls for lunch the other day to celebrate, ha ha ha. Mrs Davidson's daughter in Adelaide has just given birth to twins, so she's up in Adelaide now helping to look after them. Mr Davidson has been a regular customer here since she left. Mr Pendlebury just bought his first laptop but doesn't know what he's going to do with it. He bought it on impulse after Mrs Robinson pestered him to get up to date.'

'Yeah, he still works with a fountain pen and paper. That's good that Ros Robinson persuaded him to modernise a bit.'

'The Johnson's car is playing up. Trouble with the transmission, they think. Oh, and Miss Nicole Bradley has found a job in Adelaide and is moving up there next weekend.'

'That's very comprehensive, Phuoc, thanks!' Davo laughed.

'Your order is ready,' said Han. 'Chicken with chilli and lemongrass, and roast duck.'

Davo got his wallet out and paid Han. 'Thanks, guys. See you soon.'

Davo left in his usual cheery mood, whistling some out-of-tune song. Han looked up as he left and turned to her husband.

'Tôi có một cảm giác xấu về việc này,' she said to her husband.

'I have a bad feeling about this'.

27

Life faced Andrew Campbell with a dilemma. Did he wait for Adelaide Central to send down a detective to interview Dave Wilkins, which could take up to a fortnight? Or did he interview him by himself?

He'd had a few sessions of interviewing over the years, which he thought had gone well. There was always room for improvement. If he waited for a detective to come from Adelaide, he could wait forever. If he interviewed Dave by himself, he had an opportunity to prove he was good enough for promotion. At last. After all this time of being knocked back.

He interviewed Dave himself.

28

Baker Street. Cream brick, white tiled roof.

'G'day, Mr Wilkins, you got a couple of minutes?' Andrew asked through the fly screen door. He would be glad to get out of the sun.

'Sure, come on in,' Davo replied.

They made their way through to the kitchen.

Andrew started the conversation.

'Mr Wilkins, you've no doubt heard that there was a break-in at Derringerry in the last week or so.'

'I'd heard, yeah.'

'Well, I'm going around interviewing people who may know something about it. Do you know something about it?'

'No, it's something I know nothing about, other than hearing about it down at Phuoc and Han's. Why are you interviewing me?'

'Because you have a motive. You were let go by the farm, and you may want to get revenge on them. But you're not the only person being interviewed if that's what you're worried about. As I said, at this stage, we are interested in talking with lots of people, to see if the equipment has been misplaced rather than stolen.'

'I'm betting on the equipment being misplaced. I could find nothing when I went looking for it when I worked there.'

'What sort of things did you go looking for when you worked there?'

'Oh, I dunno. Hammers, screwdrivers, the odd saw. Sometimes I wanted to borrow them to fix something around the house. But I could find nothing.'

'So how did you fix the things around the house?'

'What? Oh, I ended up borrowing tools from friends.'

'I see.' Andrew had run out of questions to ask. 'Well, if you hear of Derringerry's equipment turning up, I'd appreciate if you either call me or else tell the person who found it to return it to the farm pronto.'

'Will do. Their welding equipment is pretty distinctive; I'm sure it will turn up somewhere soon.'

'Ok, thanks for your time.' Something nagged at him, but he couldn't put his finger on it. Probably something inconsequential, he thought.

Once in the security of the car, pulling away from Dave and Sarah's house, Andrew mulled on the conversation he'd just had. The nagging thought he was unsure about was becoming clearer to him. He didn't remember mentioning exactly what was stolen. So how did Dave Wilkins know it was a welder? Perhaps someone from the farm had contacted him. Alan Peters didn't specify who he'd asked when he asked around, and he could have rung Dave to ask him. Or Phuoc, the local gossip, could have known it was a welder and told him.

'Let's have a chat with Phuoc now,' he said to himself in the privacy of his mobile office.

Andrew pointed the car toward Phuoc and Han's take-away, which might be open now, he thought, as they'd be preparing lunches for the various farms to come and collect.

———

29

The shop wasn't open yet, but when Han saw that it was Constable Andrew who was knocking on the door, she opened up immediately.

'Constable Andrew, what a pleasant surprise. Your usual cold rolls for lunch?'

'Yes, please, Han. But look, I'm here on official business. Is Phuoc around? I'd like to chat with you both.'

'He's just out the back, I'll go get him. We've not done anything wrong, I hope?'

'Not at all, Han. It's just something I'd like to clear up in my mind.'

'I'll go get him,' she repeated, as she scurried off out the back, returning with her husband moments later.

'Constable Andrew, good to see you again. Han says you want to talk to us. How can we help?'

'Phuoc, Han, I gather you know there was a theft of some equipment from Derringerry.'

'Yes,' Phuoc replied, while Han nodded.

'Well, do you know what was stolen??'

'Yes, a welder,' Phuoc replied.

'Okay. Do you remember talking with Dave Wilkins about the theft?'

'Dave? No, I don't remember. But we get many people in here, Constable Andrew; I may have mentioned it to him and have forgotten that fact. Why, is Dave a suspect?'

'He's helping us with our enquiries, Phuoc. That's all I'm at liberty to say.'

'Okay. Then I won't mention anything to him about our conversation today,' he lied. Phuoc would be the first to talk about it when Davo next came in for some food.

'That's all I came to ask. Thanks for answering my questions.'

'You're welcome, Constable Andrew,' returned Phuoc.

'I'll get you some rolls,' said Han, 'Three?'

'Yes, please Han. Here's the money,' replied Andrew, handing over a note.

'Well,' he thought to himself. 'Phuoc knows what was stolen, which means that the whole town probably knows. So that line of enquiry closes down. No matter, I'll keep searching. But this is a big brown land, and that welder is a needle in a haystack out here.'

The next person on Andrew's short list of suspects was Dan Robinson. He was the best mate of Dave Wilkins, and the two of them were reportedly as thick as thieves. Dan was the local IT guru, always happy to help someone with their computer problems and challenges. That gave him lots of access to lots of properties—time to visit him and have a chat.

Andrew Campbell knocked on the door of the house in Cemetery Road. Ros was out at work at Mr Pendlebury's, but Dan's silver Corolla was parked out the front.

'G'day, Mr Robinson. You got a moment?' Andrew asked through the fly screen when the front door opened.

'Sure, come on in,' Dan replied. He led Andrew through to the kitchen.

'Tea, coffee?' Dan asked.

'No, thanks.'

'How can I help you?'

'Have you heard about the break-in over at Derringerry?'

'Yeah. What was stolen?'

'Some welding equipment. You haven't heard of anyone trying to sell welding equipment, have you?'

'No, but I'll keep an ear out.'

'Thanks. If you do hear that someone's suddenly come into some welding equipment, can you ask them to put it back quietly, and all will be forgotten?'

'Sure, I'll do that.'

'You know, Dan, your mate Dave Wilkins has been

suggested as someone of interest, and we're trying to rule him out. He hasn't said anything to you about it, has he?'

'No, not a thing. I know he's pretty cut up about being sacked, but I can't imagine him doing it.

'That's what I think, too. I gather his wife Sarah has too solid a head on her shoulders to let him get away with dreaming up schemes like that.'

'He'd be sleeping in his car if she found out.'

'That's what I figured.'

An awkward silence descended on them. Andrew had run out of things to say without wanting to accuse Dan and Davo of the thefts straight out, and Dan was quiet because that's how he naturally was.

'Well, I'd best be off,' Andrew said, having reached the end of his interviewing skills.

'Okay.' Dan's voice was flat, but he felt not a little relief.

'Have a think about what I've said, and if you want to talk about anything, I'm always at the station first and last thing.'

'Okay, thanks.'

Andrew left, and Dan closed the front door.

His first brush with the law. He felt nervous and exhilarated at the same time. He would have to tell Davo. He had Siri send Davo a quick text to say he was coming over, then grabbed his car keys.

3.23am.

Davo's ute pulled up in front of Derringerry's gates. He

and Dan pulled on their Scream masks and looked at each other.

'You ready for another go?' asked Dan.

'Ready and willing,' came the muffled reply. 'Let's go.'

Davo parked the ute in front of the same shed, and feeling confident, turned off the ignition.

Torches on, the pair surveyed the shed and looked for something easy to move, load and unload.

There were some feeders, alley panels, a few chainsaws, a Wik Classic 2 insecticide applicator.

And a portable generator, just sitting next to some fencing wire. They loaded it up and tied it down. All up, it took four and a half minutes.

After their first success, Davo and Dan were stoked to think they would get away with it again.

Both men hopped into their seats and Davo turned the engine over. But Davo's ute wouldn't start. It turned over, sure, but it wouldn't fire up.

Again and again, Davo tried until it flooded. It meant an agonising wait for the fuel to clear the carburettor, increasing the chances that someone might turn up.

All they could do was wait for a good fifteen minutes while the fuel did its thing and the vapours performed their disappearing trick.

'So, did Sarah wake up when you left last time?' asked Dan.

'No. I slipped back into bed and she was still gently snoring.'

'I hope she stays asleep this time, even after our wait.'

'Me too. But my idea of saying I was taking a drive to reduce my anxiety is great. That'll keep me in the good books.'

'Our drive tonight is giving me anxiety at the moment.'

'She'll be right, Dan. The carbi will clear in a minute and we'll be on our way.'

'Any idea why she won't start, other than the eventual flooding? Has the ute done this before?'

'No, never done it before. Don't know why she's done it now. Mustn't enjoy working at night on a full moon.'

Dan walked to the door of the shed and looked up at the night sky. 'It's not a full moon.'

'Well, at least we know not to take it out on a full moon.'

'Ha ha ha. Can you try to start it now? Has enough time passed?'

'I'll give it a go, young Daniel.'

Davo turned the ignition key, and on the third attempt the ute roared to life. Davo steered his car out of the shed, out of the farm and back onto the Princes Highway.

All told it had taken them a lot longer than they had planned. But they still had got away cleanly, eventually, and Davo headed for the hiding spot to store their second haul of equipment. Barring the hiccup with the ute's ignition, which Davo said he'd have a mechanic have a look at, things had gone smoothly.

They were getting the hang of this stealing business.

32

The two-storey Meningie Hotel is a grand old pub, in the old country pub tradition: solid, dependable. The single-storey restaurant attached to it is old but still functional. There are white cloths on the tables. At Christmas and throughout January baubles, lights and stars hang from windows, and silver and red tinsel hang across doorways and across the bar. An old wood fire sits unloved in the summer heat, flanked by two benches. The gray carpet soaks up the wine spills from the various groups that hole up at the nearby caravan park at this time of year.

It was a typical Friday night in January, a three-quarter full restaurant of locals and summer tourists taking advantage of the promise of a decent meal that they didn't have to cook themselves. Sarah was cooking at home in a bid to reduce her and Davo's outgoings, so Dan agreed to having dinner at the hotel with his mum. Ros and Dan filled the time between Dan's demolishing of the garlic bread and the arrival of their main courses with talk of Dan's business and the latest news of his clients.

Dan was particularly pleased with how a recent run of events with one client had gone. The client was under pressure to reduce costs, and Dan's contract was an obvious target. Normally, Dan would have gone in all guns a-blaze to win the client over and keep the contract. But a fruitful role-playing session with Kelly on client management and diplomacy had given Dan some much-needed interpersonal skills and insights into client motivations. His more adept handling of his client was rewarded with an increased commitment to use his services, and an extra employee to skill-up. That would tie the client to Dan for at least another twelve to eighteen months, he estimated.

The Coorong mullet was the house specialty and Dan, in deference to his mother's insistence that he eat something other than steak, had ordered a battered Coorong mullet, with garlic bread starters. Ros ordered a Caesar Salad. Dan's dish came in three fillets, with a portion of chips and a small container of steamed vegetables. The mullet was like all fish that Dan tasted — bland. Dan's tastebuds weren't overly developed, and he could only taste strong fish such as tuna and kippers. The young Asian hotel cook tried her best, and she even added a zesty tartare sauce, but Dan's stunted tastebuds were more than a match for her. Ros, on the other hand, crunched her way through her Caesar Salad with gusto.

'Dan, there's been rumours doing the rounds that one of the local farms has been broken into. Do you know anything about it?'

'No, mum.'

'According to Mr Pendlebury, they stole an expensive welder from Derringerry. Who would do such a thing, steal from a farm down here?'

'Beats me. Did Mr Pendlebury say anything more about it?'

'Only that the farm is not sure whether it was a break-in and theft, or just an employee who has forgotten to put it back.'

'It's probably just someone borrowing some tools and forgetting to bring it back. I'm sure the welder will turn up sooner or later.'

'I hope you're right. Why steal from a farm down here? Everybody is doing it tough at the moment, Derringerry included.'

'You're right, mum; I hope they catch the mongrels if it is a genuine theft.'

'So do I, Daniel, so do I.'

It was time once again for their weekly chat, and this time Hannah was the first into the meeting.

Dan's face eventually appeared, but it was not a happy face.

'Oh no, Dan, why the sad face?'

'I have an attack of the glums, as my mum says.'

'Why's that?'

'You know how Davo and I have been stealing stuff from the farm? Well, that's all ended. They've installed security cameras.'

'Really? How do you know?'

'Because we saw them early yesterday morning when we arrived at the farm. The cameras were sitting up on the gates, pointing into the farm courtyard.'

'Goodness. How do you know they haven't already got sight of your number plates?'

'Oh, we took them off before we went near the farm. It was only eagle-eyed spotting by Davo that noticed the cameras. He yelled at me and stood on the brakes. If it hadn't been for him, we would have sailed into the courtyard and been seen.'

'But if you had no number plates, how would they have recognised you?'

'Davo's ute is distinctive; it has mag wheels and a speccy paint job. He got it done up in Adelaide for his 25th birthday. Everybody down here knows Davo's ute.'

'How do you know that there wasn't also a camera pointing out towards the road?'

'Davo put his mask on and got out of the ute and had a walk around. There were only two cameras, one facing into the courtyard and one facing the entrance to the admin building.'

'Well, that's a relief. I hope this means you will stop your revenge attacks.'

'I reckon we will. Can't see how we can continue if

they've put security cameras in place. The bastards have probably put them up in the work sheds, too. We'd probably be right there—we'd only be seen if we backed the ute into the sheds and loaded up with gear. But having one on the courtyard stops us dead.'

'Well, I'm sad for you, because I know the stealing meant a lot to you. But I'm also glad you have to stop because it means you reduce the chances of being caught. And being caught is not something you want to have happen, is it?'

'No, I guess not.'

'No. Now, what else has been happening in your world? What's your mum's fridge saying this week?'

'Hang on, I'll go and get it. It's a ripper this week.'

Hannah typed something into Evernote.

DAN HAS HAD TO STOP STEALING FROM THE FARM. FANTASTIC! NOW I DON'T HAVE A FRIEND WHO'S ALSO A CRIMINAL.

Dan returned. 'Here we go. "YOU DIDN'T COME THIS FAR TO ONLY COME THIS FAR". How's that one?'

'That's great, as in terrible. Where does she find this stuff?'

'God knows. Sometimes I reckon she's off in fairyland when she finds these sayings. There are whole bloody websites full of stuff like this. She keeps trying to get me to heal my inner child and stuff. Bloody loopy.'

'Well, don't you go all hippy-trippy on me, young man! I want you to keep your wits about you.'

'Yes, Boss, ha ha. Now, if you don't mind, I'm driving up

to Adelaide tomorrow to take Deirdre out for a coffee and some training, and I have to write her training notes for this week.'

'Totally understand. But before you go, tell me another funny saying you've come across this week. I noticed you posted a couple to the Misfits group.'

'Okay. Let me see... oh, here's one: 'Always check the height of nearby ceiling fans before giving a toddler a ride on your shoulders. How I learned this rule is not important."

'Ha ha ha! That's brilliant. And another?'

'Okay. Ahh... "A bloke just tried to sell me a coffin. I said mate, that's the last thing I need."'

'Oh, too funny. Good choices, young Dan, thank you.'

'You're welcome. Now, I'd best bugger off and get some work done.'

'Well, I'm glad to see you happier, even if you can no longer be a criminal. Catch you next week.

Oh, I forgot to ask you, how are you? How's the family?'

'Good, thanks, on all counts. Carlo is enjoying his promotion, the girls are happy, and I'm looking forward to them going to kindy next year. Business is good for me, although I'd always say "yes" to more sales. But there are enough sales to keep me busy and save up to buy an espresso machine for Christmas, which will be a surprise for Carlo. He loves his coffee too. So, all good.'

'That's excellent. Well, I'd best be off.'

'See you next week.'

'Catch ya.'

LIED TO DAN AGAIN TODAY. HE ASKED HOW THINGS

WERE, AND I SAID ALL GOOD AND THAT THE WEBSITE SALES WERE KEEPING ME BUSY AND SAVING UP FOR AN ESPRESSO MACHINE. OF COURSE, THAT'S NOT GOING TO HAPPEN. HAVEN'T HAD A SALE IN OVER THREE MONTHS.

WHY DO I KEEP LYING TO DAN? I DON'T LIE TO CARLO OR THE GIRLS, OR MY PARENTS. BUT SOMETHING COMPELS ME TO KEEP A SUCCESSFUL, WINNING FACE UP FOR DAN. LIKE HE'D WANT NOTHING TO DO WITH ME IF I WASN'T SUCCESSFUL. BUT I'M MISERABLE. I'M AS MISERABLE AS ANYTHING.

IT'S LIKE HE'S MY LIFELINE OUT OF THE MISERY I'M IN. HE IS A SHINING LIGHT UP AHEAD, OUT AND AWAY FROM THE BLACK OILY MESS.

SOME DAYS I WISH I WEREN'T HERE ANYMORE. IT'S ONLY THE GIRLS THAT KEEPS ME HERE.

WHICH REMINDS ME, ANGELA STILL ISN'T HER USUAL SELF, EVEN AFTER SEEING THE GP. I'LL HAVE TO TAKE HER TO A SPECIALIST.

PART THREE

Dan and Davo were enjoying their usual quiet Friday night pint in the dining room of the Meningie Hotel. Dan had shouted Davo a steak, and both men were contemplating their futures over a friendly pint.

'It's a bugger that the farm got surveillance cameras in,' said Davo.

'Yeah, it's a bugger all right. How are we going to teach them a lesson now?'

'Dunno. I've been racking my brains and haven't come up with anything that wouldn't point directly back to us.'

'I've had a thought,' said Dan after a minute's pause. 'What if I do what I do with Dierdre?'

'What? Install a server? Take her out for coffee?'

'No, skill myself up, only this time in hacking. There's got to be some websites where I can learn a few tricks and figure out how to hack into Derringerry's computers.'

'What would you do once you had hacked into them?'

'I don't know, steal something, maybe, or plant a virus that kills their computers. Something like that.'

'But what about getting caught?'

'I reckon there's probably little chance of that. After all, if they've only just installed security cameras after getting gear stolen, I doubt there would be any security on the computers yet. Anyway, I'll learn how to avoid detection first.'

'It's an interesting idea, mate. You sure you want to do this thing? I won't be able to help you, other than mop the sweat off your brow while you're hacking.'

'Yeah, I reckon it'll be a good thing to do. I'll do some investigating about hacking and training and surveillance and stuff. I won't just dive in and flail madly about.'

'Well, it sounds like an interesting plan. Let me buy you a beer to celebrate your thinking.'

35

Dan's investigations led him to the dark web, a part of the internet hidden from most internet explorers. Google had no links into it. It was kind of like you had to know someone to get access to it, you'd never find it on your own.

Dan found a link in a forum post on Reddit, and his initial exploration was a time suck: he found the Reddit post at 7.20pm; he next looked up from his computer at 1.15am.

This new dark web held a fascination for Dan. There was so much to explore, so much to sample and learn. He felt his head exploding just thinking about the possibilities.

But his searching was taking shape. He had compartmentalised various sections and aspects of his journey, and today he was searching for one person. D@@Mladen. An Australian hacker who, by all accounts, was legendary, rich and powerful.

He'd heard of D@@Mladen in whispers, brief half-mentions in articles he had found in his trawling of the dark web. Australian. Skilled. A teacher of some of those skills.

In the dark web you don't just look up someone's name and find their profile. It's not like Facebook or Twitter or Instagram. In the dark web you must remember that the police and other law enforcement agencies are also lurking, so there's no direct linking to someone's email account, for example. No, you leave a virtual chalk mark on a dead letter box somewhere and wait for your intended recipient to contact you. You leave enough information about yourself to hope they trust you, but not enough that the law can track you down, and thus track your contact down too.

An old-school foreign spy scenario. With stakes just as high.

Dan had found a possible link to a chat service that un-boasted several high-profile clients. The service deliberately played down who and how many used their service, which is why their reputation was good. Unlike the daylight world, silence was a powerful form of marketing on the dark web.

He left a note for D@@Mladen, giving his hacking name as 'Vextant', crossed his fingers, and left. He exited the dark web, wiped his browser history clean, and got up from his desk, stretched, felt exhilarated, and grabbed his car keys. It was time for a drive and a blast of the bands 'Stuck Out', 'Tame Impala' and some classic 'Gang of Youths'.

36

Dan logged into the dark web chat. There was one message, left there just one minute before.

'hi i'm D@@Mladen you were looking for me.'

'G'day. Yes I need your help.'

'with what'

'A mate of mine was sacked. I want to hack into his old employer's system'

'revenge ok so what do you want from me'

'I'd like you to teach me how to hack'

'have you ever done anything like this before'

'No, I'm completely new to this, but I'm eager to learn.'

'whereabouts are you based'

'In a country town about two hours from Adelaide'

'handy'

'I haven't got much money, but I could pay you something'

'no ones ever got much money'

'I could be your student'

'my own little padawan - I have plenty of those but i've never had a country student before. that could be novel. we should probably meet country padawan.'

'I can get to Adelaide fairly easily. Can you? When do you want to meet?'

'ill send you instructions'

'Cool and thanks.'

'DONT THANK ME TOO QUICKLY I HAVENT DONE ANYTHING YET'

'WELL, YOU'VE GIVEN ME HOPE.'

37

FOLLOW GREENHILL ROAD FOR 6.5KMS PAST HALLETT ROAD. THERE YOU WILL FIND A RIGHT HAND CORNER ONTO MOUNT LOFTY SUMMIT ROAD. THERE IS A CLEARING THERE. PARK IN THE CLEARING AT 3PM TOMORROW. D@@MLADEN

2.55pm. He parked in the clearing and waited. He was a few minutes early, eager to meet, so he took the time to survey his surroundings. A winding road with no spot where the police could easily stop and wait, plenty of trees to hide in and survey the road up and down, those trees could stop any drones from locking on to someone and following them. He thought it was a spot well chosen. He didn't see the person dressed in army camouflage gear walking out of the trees towards him. The first he knew was when they tapped on his window and pointed a pistol at his head.

'Get out of the car slowly.'

He did as he was told, his guts in a knot. He raised his hands above his head as he'd seen on tv and the movies. The person with the pistol motioned for Dan to walk into the centre of the clearing. A second person emerged from the trees, also dressed in camouflage gear, and came up to Dan. Both of the camouflaged people had ski masks on.

The second person ran a phone-like device over Dan; his iPhone died instantly. After that, the first person checked for weapons.

Once they had finished their inspection of him and were satisfied, they walked Dan into the trees. Still mostly in shock, Dan slowly saw the potential for death loom in front of him, but he was powerless to do anything about it. Every footstep saw him release some flatulence. Maybe it was a mistake to get into this hacking game, he thought.

'He's clean,' said the person who'd just swept him. 'What's your name?'

'Dan. Dan Robinson.'

'Do you have any other name?'

Dan suddenly realised they meant his hacking name.

'Vextant,' he blurted out.

'Okay, Vextant, why are you here?'

'I'm here to meet with D@@Mladen.'

The person facing him side on paused, then pulled off their ski mask. It was a woman. It was a woman. Dan hadn't expected that.

'Hi, Vextant, I'm D@@Mladen. Nice to meet you.'

Dan stared at her, smiled with relief and let out a long, flatulent sigh.

'I'm sorry for staring. I didn't expect you to be a woman.'

'It usually comes as a shock. But the shock is mutual. I didn't expect to meet a thirty-year-old man. I only ever meet teenage boys. What makes a thirty-year-old man want to get into the revenge game?'

'Twenty-eight. I'm twenty-eight. But never mind. A large farming conglomerate sacked my best mate, and we both reckon they did him out of his full entitlements. He should have been made redundant and given a pay out. But he wasn't, so we started stealing equipment from the farm in revenge. But the farm beefed up their security, so I reckoned I might try hacking as a way of getting back at them.'

'It's okay, Franco, you can relax.'

Franco took off his ski mask and put the pistol back in his waistband.

'Tell me, Dan, what do you know about hacking?' D@@Mladen asked.

'Nothing. That's why I want someone to teach me. I have my laptop in my car.'

'This was a meet-and-greet event,' D@@Mladen said. 'But I guess while we're here, I can show you a few things that might keep you out of harm's way. Go get it. Go with him, Franco.'

Dan returned with his Dell laptop, flipped the lid and powered it up. D@@Mladen sat down on the ground, and Franco and Dan joined her. In the next five minutes, she taught Dan how to avoid being tracked by cellphone towers and internet providers.

She also gave him an invaluable gift—the name of a secret app on Apple's AppStore that puts Siri into permanent listening mode, and also the details of a dark web search engine, a google for the dark web, that the new, all-powerful Siri could access and search through. All hidden from any surveillance technology.

The new, improved Siri received updates regularly; as enforcement agencies found a new way of tracking cyber-criminals, so the keepers of the AdvancedSiri updated the software to block them. It was an endless cat-and-mouse game, much like the commercial anti-virus software companies played with malevolent Russian teenagers.

'So, tell me, why the name "Doomladen" with the "At" sign?' Dan asked.

'It was fairly simple,' she replied. 'I wanted a short name, and English. And I used the "At" symbols to remind people that I'm female.'

'Huh? I don't get it.'

'Most men don't. Back in the eighties, there was a pop singer called Madonna. She was a gay and feminist icon. She used to wear huge pointy bras. I stole the idea. To show that I'm a woman.'

'Oh, okay, I guess. But how do I get to learn more from you?'

'From now on we meet only online. Do as you did before, leave a message in the chat room. I'll be in touch. What's the name of the farm you want to learn to hack into?'

'Derringerry.'

'Okay, I'll be in touch. Time for you to leave, Vextant.'

D@@Mladen had been true to her word. Dan had left a message in the chat room and she contacted him almost immediately. The first stop for Dan was to download the tools of the trade—hacking tools that everybody used and stood by. So Dan downloaded a dozen tools with such strange names as *ophcrack*, N*map*, and *Cain & Abel*. And at D@@Mladen's suggestion, their next online meeting took three hours while she trained him up in their use.

Once exposed to these tools and how to use them, he attempted hacks of dummy companies that D@@Mladen had set up on a secure server. This whole training period lasted two weeks, and he was a lot more confident about his chosen path for having undertaken instruction from her.

Dan picked a date for when his first attempt at hacking a business for real was going to take place. He was going to hack into Derringerry's computers on December 22nd. The office would be closed, with only a skeleton crew working on the farm, so his hacking would likely go unnoticed for quite a while.

The 22nd of December came along soon enough, and Dan readied himself. He charged up his second mobile phone, an Android, purchased online through a secure intermediary for the sole purpose of being his internet hotspot. He made sure his laptop was fully charged, and just before 7pm he headed out to his car, after telling his mum he was just popping out for a bit. Ros would wait for the ABC news on tv and would be wrapped up in it.

He turned the Corolla into Cemetery Road, drove past the Trees of Tribute and headed up East Terrace. Turning right at McCallum St, he swooped left at the end of the road and parked in the driveway of the Catholic church.

He turned the engine off and moved across to the passenger seat to give him the space to open his laptop and start his hacking. His training days with D@@Mladen had served him well—he quickly breached the server and entered the business world of Derringerry.

From there, it was only a matter of using tools such as

Metasploit and *SQLPing* to find the weaknesses and locate a place from which to cause havoc.

Dan remembered what D@@Mladen had told him: 'Get in, do what you came to do, get out, quickly'. He'd rehearsed in his mind what he would do and how long it would take him. He'd even set the timer on his iPhone to ten minutes, so he didn't hang around and increase the risk of getting caught.

He was pleased. The files he thought would be there were, and the files he was hoping wouldn't be there weren't. That enabled him to plant his virus in a seldom-opened spreadsheet. Once opened by the unwitting user, it would slowly, carefully, seed bad code into the user's computer and out across the network. Sure, there were tools available that could detect such a virus, but Dan was pleased to see that such tools had left no telltale traces of their presence on the farm's server. All was clear to leave his virus, wipe clean his entry into the system and his path once in it, and clear as best as possible his exit route. Which is what he did, and he'd been in and out in under ten minutes. D@@Mladen would be proud of him, he thought.

So, he packed up his equipment, got back into the driver's seat and reversed the Corolla back down the driveway and headed off to the hotel for a celebratory beer.

One other thing he noticed as he was driving off: Again, he was slightly aroused.

40

Davo came around for his IT instruction as usual. Stopping to grab two beers from the fridge, he noted another of Ros' printouts:

'AVOIDING DANGER IS NO SAFER IN THE LONG RUN THAN OUTRIGHT EXPOSURE. THE FEARFUL ARE CAUGHT AS OFTEN AS THE BOLD'

'You saw this?' asked Davo of Dan.

'Yeah. I reckon for once mum's got it right. Best give it a go because you are still at risk if you stand still and do nothing. At least, that's what Kelly told me last week.'

The pair left the kitchen and once inside the study closed the door and continued their conversation in whispers.

'How did the hack go?' asked Davo.

'Mate, you should have seen me. It was like I was on speed. I was working so fast, checking files, wiping traces of my visit. It all happened in less than ten minutes. It was like a dream!'

'That's brilliant, mate. I wish I could have been there to witness it. So, did you drop that virus in the system like you said you would?'

'Yep. Dropped it in a spreadsheet that Alice Yates uses and that no one will think to virus check. Made sure the code signature of the virus was installed in the 'approved' signatures list for the virus software Derringerry uses and made sure that all traces of my movements around the server were wiped clean. It was amazing.'

'That's bloody excellent, mate. Did you steal any files?'

'Oh sure, I copied all the payroll and salary spreadsheets, and the client database. Plus, I left what's called a "backdoor" on the server, so I can enter and exit whenever I like and no one can trace me.'

'You have the salary spreadsheets? Wow, can I take a look? I want to know what everyone else is on.'

'Sure; here, I've opened them up on my laptop for you. Take as long as you like.'

'This is amazing. It's eye-opening seeing what people are paid. Poor Alice deserves more than she's getting, that's for sure! And Alan Peters is pulling in some coin, isn't he?'

'Well, he deserves to—he has to put up with clowns like you every day!'

'You bastard,' Davo laughed.

'I'll go get us another beer while you're still looking,' whispered Dan.

When he returned, Davo had finished looking at the spreadsheet.

'So, now that you've done what you said you'd do, are you going to quit?' whispered Davo.

'I've thought about it. I got such a buzz from doing it that I will go back in again.'

'What?!'

'Yep. I'm bound to find some correspondence I'm sure they don't want me or the rest of the world to see. Now that I've built a backdoor, my job will be that much easier and quicker.'

'Strewth, Dan, don't go get caught or anything.'

'No chance. Now that I've got systems in place, I'm right to go. 'ANSMN: Ain't No Stopping Me Now'.'

41

Wang Wei was the recently appointed IT guru at Anthol Logistics in Adelaide. Twenty five years of age, a degree in computer science of the Uni of Adelaide, smart and presentable. And strongly recommended by Anthol's parent company. Which is why he was hired by Bruce Abernathy to look after the computer systems and website of Anthol.

One of the first things Wei did was conduct a review of the security of the various IT systems, to plug the inevitable holes. There were always holes.

Wei saw that the main system in the Adelaide headquarters was porous, and so plugged it. But of concern to him was the security, or lack of it, on satellite systems out on the farms the company owned. It would be easy, he saw, for someone to hack into any of the farms on the network and then springboard from there into the main IT system in Adelaide.

So, Wei put in place several programs to patch over the holes, intending to go to the farms himself one day and configure things at a local level to tighten up the security.

One step to the security that he instigated was to install an artificially intelligent monitoring system, named *Evie*, over the entire network that scanned for anomalies and differences in files, and notified him when something was awry and in need of further investigation.

Evie was smart enough to know with reasonable confidence when a file had been altered for business by an employee with proper access to the file. It was also smart enough to know with a reasonable confidence when the file had been altered by a rogue operator. And *Evie* was learning and improving all the time.

So, it was with some excitement that Wang Wei received an email and a text message on his phone from *Evie* saying that some files had been accessed, and one altered, by a potential rogue operator at a farm of the company's.

Wei went into Bruce's office with the news.

'Hi, Bruce, thanks for making time to see me. I got an email this morning from one of my IT monitoring systems. Files at the Derringerry farm have been altered suspiciously.'

'I see. Do you know what files, and by whom?'

'Yes, a payroll spreadsheet was altered, and several general data correspondence and farm maintenance folders have been looked at. I don't know by whom at this stage.'

'Okay. What will you do?'

'I'll contact the police to see if they have a cyber-crime branch—they probably do—and work with them to track and trace the hacker. I've already called the farm and told them to not open the payroll spreadsheet, in case they have infected it.'

'Well done. It sounds like you have it under control. Can they hack into our main system here?'

'No. I've stopped that from happening. But all it takes is one software update by someone somewhere and the whole system could be exposed. It's a constant battle to stay on top.'

'Well, keep up the good fight and let me know how you get on with the police. I'll ring Alan Peters, the farm manager, and let him know what's going on. Can you liaise with him, please, as well?'

'Will do.'

Wei made his way back to his office and put in a call to SAPOL, asking if there was anyone who could help with a potential cyber-crime attack. The switchboard operator said there was and put him through to a number that rang through to a voice mailbox. He left his number and rang Alan Peters with the bad news that his system had been hacked, but good news that they potentially had identified the file that had been hacked and that the rest of his files were probably uncorrupted.

Within half an hour, SAPOL rang Wei back.

'Hello, Wang Wei, my name's Stephanie McBride. I'm a computer crime expert at SAPOL; I understand one of your systems has been breached, am I right?'

'Hi, Stephanie. Yes, one of our farms was breached last night. From my initial investigation, nothing bad seems to have been stolen, judging by the log files, but there is the possibility that a payroll spreadsheet was opened and infected.'

'Okay. First things first; quarantine that spreadsheet and make sure no one opens it. Secondly, remotely install *PenalTee* on the farm's network, that way we can make sure that any future fishing expeditions by your hacker are monitored and recorded.'

'I've heard of that app, but I don't have a copy of it myself.'

'It's a handy little program that buries itself on your server and makes itself invisible. I'll email you over a link to the download page. Thirdly, give me your office location. I'll drop by you and get some login details and any records you have of what's on the farm's computers. I'll pay a visit to the farm this afternoon. Whereabouts is the farm?'

'Thanks. The farm is in Meningie, an hour and a half away. We're on Greenhill Road, in Keswick. Number 26. I look forward to working with you.'

42

Three in the afternoon. Back in his office after a half-day out on the road, Senior Constable 1st Class Andrew Campbell listened to the message on his answer machine while drinking his coffee. A honeyed voice, posh. Asking him to call her back.

'Hello, Constable Campbell, my name is Stephanie McBride. I'm a cyber-crime expert working for SAPOL in Adelaide. I am calling to inform you you have a potential case of computer crime down there. Can you call me back, please, when you have a moment? Thanks.' She left a mobile number.

There were no other messages to listen to but damned if he would ring her back straight away as if he was her slave. She could wait for me to finish my coffee, he thought.

43

'*Fanculo questo!*'

The swearing Rocco Santofanti had earlier that day attempted hacking into Santos, a large oil and gas exploration company headquartered in Adelaide. Now he was being offered a 'deal'—help the police with their other cyber-crime enquiries in exchange for a quiet word with the magistrate, explaining how Rocco was doing 'good works'.

Rocco reluctantly agreed to help to make his mother's life easier. The less time he would spend behind bars, he reasoned, the more time he would have to be back under his mother's control. And she firmly believed that her son was a 'good boy' who was led astray by 'bad boys'. The less time he spent locked up, the happier and less stressed his mother would be. And all good Italian boys knew it was important to keep their mother happy.

But he had a condition—no one must know of his co-operation with the police. His life would be a living hell if anyone found out. So, Stephanie McBride, the civilian working as a subject matter expert in 'C' branch of the South Australian Police promised Rocco that his work would remain confidential. Rocco had lost all of his computer equipment in the arrest, so Stephanie provided Rocco with an ancient and beaten-up laptop and a cheap mobile phone. And had tracing software installed on both so she could see what Rocco was up to at all times. If Rocco tried to disable the software, it would notify her, she told him matter-of-factly.

At eighteen years of age, Rocco was an Italian boy who had grown into a man's body but still hadn't achieved maturity. He liked to think he was cool, smart and manly, whereas to forty-something Stephanie McBride, with two teenage boys of her own, he was just a pimply, gangly boy with ideas way above his station.

This was how it went down.

'So, Rocco, why does a smart young man like you get mixed up with hacking?' Stephanie asked.

'I dunno. It was just something to do.'

'Surely, you knew of the risk you were taking, of getting caught?'

'Sure, I know lots of things. I know how to get into Santos. Someone else must have tipped off youse police.'

'You need not say anything, Mr Santofanti,' said his lawyer. Stephanie ignored the interruption.

'I can assure you, Rocco, that no one tipped us off. I caught you through your own errors.'

'I doubt it.'

'You know you are in for a hard time, don't you? First, the remand centre where we will keep you is not a happy place for pretty boys. Second, no magistrate will look favourably on someone hacking into businesses to relieve their boredom.'

'I can look after myself.'

'I'm sure you can, Rocco. I'll leave you to think things through. But just know this, the last two hackers we caught ended up serving seven years each. Seven years is a long time to get to know your cellmates, and you'll get some pretty screwed up cellmates to call your friends. Drug dealers, paedophiles, murderers, rapists. All the good folk. All looking to make you their pretty pet.'

'I can look after myself,' Rocco repeated, but this time with not so much bravado.

'I'm sure you can, Rocco. I'll just leave you while I attend to some paperwork. Enjoy your stay.'

A uniformed officer led Rocco back to the holding cells.

After leaving Rocco to slow-cook in his own thoughts for a few hours, Stephanie had him brought back to an interview room, where his lawyer was waiting.

'So, Rocco, how have you enjoyed your time in our cells? I hope everything met with your satisfaction?'

'Hilarious.'

'Good, now that we understand each other, I will propose something. Of course, you have every right to turn it down, but I hope you at least consider it.'

'I'm listening,' confirmed Rocco.

'So am I,' said his lawyer.

'There's a hacker in Australia who goes by the name of Doomladen. I'll assume you have heard of him. He is a person of interest to us in several cases, and we'd like to meet with him. Your help in arranging that meeting will be of value to us, and we would put in a good word with the Magistrate who hears your case, that you have been co-operating with us and that they should take this into account in sentencing.'

'Be careful what you say next, Mr Santofanti, you don't have to do anything for the police. You will appear before a magistrate anyway; there is no guarantee that the police will do anything to help you.'

'So what if I know this Doomladen? What makes you think they'll listen to me and meet up with you?'

'I think someone smart like you can convince someone like Doomladen to at least consider a meeting. Or an exchange of contact details. You could do that, couldn't you, Rocco?'

'Sure. Easy.'

'Careful, Mr Santofanti, the police aren't offering to put anything in writing,' said the lawyer.

'Here's the problem, Rocco. If we put things down on paper, make you a formal, written offer... well, a document like that is easily leaked. Now, I'm guessing that you wouldn't want anyone else to know that you're helping us, would you? That could get messy, couldn't it?'

'What if I helped you, with no paperwork? How do I know you would tell the magistrate I've been helpful?'

'You have my word, Rocco. But other than that, you're right, there is no guarantee. But life is nothing if not a risk, an adventure, is it? Hacking is an adventure, a risk. So is working with me. And I don't know what the magistrate will think of your co-operation, but you can imagine that what I tell them will help you in some regard. Imagine getting less time in prison and more time home with your family—more home cooking and less of the pigs' swill that is served up in prison. I will leave you here with your lawyer to discuss my offer. When you're ready, we can talk again.'

45

Dan fired up Pickant on his desktop and made sure his Røde USB microphone was plugged in and working. Moments later, Hannah joined the meeting, and she saw a beaming Dan in her monitor.

'G'day,' she said, 'What have you done that you're smiling like that for?'

'Ah ha! Wouldn't you like to know?' Dan replied.

'Yes, I would, actually.'

'Well, you know how I was helping my best mate Davo get revenge on his old employer for sacking him?'

'Yes, I seem to remember telling you off for stealing, and being glad when they installed security cameras and stopped you.'

'Well, I figured out a way to continue avenging Davo's sacking. I now hack into their computers and wreak havoc that way.'

'You do WHAT?!'

'Yep, I hack into their computers. I've been in once already, left a virus, and got away cleanly without a trace. Whaddya think? Cool, huh?'

'Idiotic is what I think it is. Dan, you can't be serious. You could do jail time if you're found out.'

'But I won't get found out. I followed a hacking mentor's instructions, wiped any trace of my presence there clean away and covered my tracks on my way out. It was textbook stuff, except that there are no textbooks for hacking. And I feel fantastic about what I've done.'

'Feel fantastic? How can you feel fantastic when you could go to jail? Stupid is what you should be feeling!'

'But I don't. I feel clever. Smart. More powerful than I was before. I was clever enough to break into a company's computer system and drop a virus in there. And get out again with no one knowing. That's clever, as far as I'm concerned. And Derringerry had it coming to them. They shouldn't have sacked Davo to avoid a redundancy payout.'

'Dan, I admire your motives for your actions, really I do. I like a bit of Ned Kelly anti-hero but hacking into companies is big-time stuff. I'm sure it's not just a small fine and a smack on the wrist. There are real consequences here.'

'It's fine, and I have it all covered. Like I said, I left no trace, and I actually left a backdoor in place so I can enter their system whenever I want, no dramas. And I dropped a virus in place that will slowly eat their data, but so slowly that they won't at first notice it, so it will infect their backup copies as well. There'll be nothing they can do to protect themselves. I'm doing all this for Davo.'

'I'm sure Davo appreciates your motives, Dan, but your methods are just not cutting it with me.'

'Look, I appreciate your concern, but nothing will

happen. No-one knows I hacked into Derringerry's computers, no one knows about the virus, no one suspects there's anything wrong.'

'I hope so, Dan, for your sake. I really hope so. Oh, listen, that's Angela crying in the background. Poor love, she's still not well. I've taken her to the GP, but no-one can figure out what's wrong with her. I'd better look after her. See you here next week?'

'Yep, of course.'

'And promise me you'll think about our conversation today?'

'Yep, I will. Take care. See you next week.'

DAN TOLD ME HE'D HACKED INTO THE FARM'S COMPUTER. IDIOT! I TOLD HIM THE RISK OF GETTING CAUGHT WAS TOO HIGH, AND THE PENALTY FOR CYBER-CRIME WAS STIFF. BUT I DON'T KNOW WHAT THE PENALTIES FOR CYBER-CRIME ARE. I MUST ASK DAD ABOUT IT SUBTLY.

I FACE A MORAL DILEMMA: DOES THIS DAUGHTER OF A POLICEMAN REPORT A CRIME, OR DOES SHE STAY SILENT AND PROTECT A FRIEND WHO IS ALSO A CRIMINAL?

ANGELA STILL UNWELL. I'LL TAKE HER TO THE CHILDREN'S HOSPITAL TOMORROW TO SEE IF THEY CAN SHED SOME LIGHT ON WHY SHE'S SO FLAT. HER SISTER IS AS BOUNCY AS EVER.

46

'Country towns. Country bloody towns. Never a decent restaurant or well-stocked bar,' Stephanie McBride thought. 'Except in rare places like The Zone on Kangaroo Island. Or Sarin's in Port Lincoln.'

But not in Meningie late on a weekday afternoon.

She decided on the Laphroaig scotch whisky but would have preferred a thirst-quenching Auchentoshan scotch. Only the Cheese Factory Restaurant didn't stock it. So, Laphroaig it was, to accompany her order of grilled chicken. Not a typical combination, but there was nothing typical about Stephanie McBride. Tall, willowy, well-spoken, honey voice to go with the long wavy honey hair. You'd never guess that she had born two healthy identical twin boys, now late-teenagers. And that she could out-swear them both.

When she went out for a quiet drink with her husband or her colleagues in 'C' Branch—Commercial and Electronic Crime branch—she ordered a scotch, not chardonnay. She didn't mind a good Sauvignon Blanc and had been known to enjoy a quiet chat over an expensive Merlot, but neat scotch was her drink.

And here, in a jaunty little restaurant on the southeastern edge of Lake Albert, next to the cheese museum and opposite the caravan park, she would nurse her Laphroaig while she waited for her meal.

'What a simple case,' she mused to herself. 'A forced entry into a farm's computer system, one known viruses deposited, no files stolen that we can see, no clues as to the attacker's identity, no ransom note, no obvious insight into motive. Hopefully, this won't take too long to wrap up; I've got enough cases on my plate as it is.'

Stephanie had a Masters Degree in Cyber Security from Deakin University that she'd paid for out of her own pocket. She undertook the degree while living in Geelong and working in the Victorian Police as an IT analyst. She then leveraged that qualification into a civilian officer's role with the South Australian Police as a senior investigator in their cyber-crime branch.

Moving to Adelaide wasn't a big deal—her sons Matthew and Joshua would head off to uni back in Melbourne. They had already been accepted into Deakin for Bachelors degrees, one in 'Communication' and the other in 'Creative Arts', and would be living with their paternal grandparents in Melbourne while they studied. Her husband James was an author and so could work anywhere there was power for his laptop or iPad. He even had one of those fancy new laptops that could be charged off a power bank brick. Truly portable. He wrote historical romance novels, bodice tearers, under a female pen name. He was quite successful.

'So, let's consider motive. Who would want to hack into the farm? Who's got a grudge? Any outstanding creditors? What about ex-employees or former IT contractors? A former lover of a farm worker who's out for revenge?' she mused. One, she thought, a David Wilkins, ex-employee. Might have a grudge against the farm, she thought. Currently in litigation with the company over the death of his daughter.

'And let's look at the farm's computer equipment. Cisco server, with Dell desktops and laptops. Pretty solid stuff, no one ever got sacked for buying Dell or Cisco.'

Her grilled chicken arrived, generously portioned, and she stopped musing for long enough to pick up her cutlery and slice a piece of chicken. It tasted good, but not as good as she could cook in her own kitchen, surrounded by her cherished spices and herbs.

'I'll send Rocco down here,' she decided. 'He'll like to get away from South Road and see a bit of the country.'

Rocco was her 'project', a teenage boy who'd mixed it with the wrong crowd and got caught trying to hack into a large oil and gas company. He was waiting for his turn with the magistrate and had promised to help Stephanie in the meantime. In exchange for a 'good word' with the magistrate, Rocco kept a watchful eye on D@@Mladen, an Australian hacker who had pulled off some successful heists, and probably more besides that no one knew about. Stephanie was trying to track D@@Mladen down and bring him to justice, and she had Rocco keep a watch on his activities as best he could. The dark web was not a friendly place for law enforcement agencies.

Another sip of her scotch and she devoted her attention to the chicken and her surroundings. It was comfortable at the Cheese Factory, and sitting outside as she was there was a view of Lake Albert. There were worse places to have a chicken meal and a scotch, she accepted.

47

'G'day, Dad. How are you? Enjoying your day off?'

'I'm always happiest on a day off. I'm good, Hannah. How are you, and how're my beautiful granddaughters?'

'Ha ha. All of us are good, although Angela hasn't been herself recently. I took her to the Children's Hospital, they ran some tests and stuff, but there was nothing that they could find that was wrong with her.'

'Poor love. What are her symptoms?'

'Lethargy, and she's off her food. She's always tired and occasionally whingy and tearful. The spark's not in her eyes, either.'

'Poor thing. Well, I'm no doctor, but I know a grandpa's love is a powerful thing. She can rest here on the couch and watch some tele if she wants. Is Jessie okay?'

'Yes, Jess is fine. It's only Angela I'm worried about. It may just be a phase she's going through, but I've tried all sorts of foods, and so far, nothing is making a difference. Dad, I'm really worried that she might have inherited my bipolar disorder.'

'Is that possible? Do infants and kids get bipolar?'

'Apparently so. The Mayo Clinic reckon kids of any age can display symptoms of bipolar. I really hope she's not got a depression going on.'

'I can understand. I'm worried too, now, and I know your mother will be when she gets home from work and I tell her.'

'Ask mum to ring me so I can talk to her about it. I want to know what I was like as an infant.'

'Well, I spent much of that time out on patrols, but I do know you were a bright and bubbly child, never happier than when playing with friends or else playing with your dolls.'

'I have a feeling of my childhood being a happy one. I guess everything fell apart after the birth of the girls. That's when my depression came and took the ground from under me. I feel really sad for Carlo—he married a happy young woman. Now he's married to a miserable old hag.'

'Oh, darling. You're not a miserable old hag. Look how well you look after the girls! And you're always cheerful when you see your mother and me.'

'I wish you were right, Dad. But Carlo spends long hours at work, and I sometimes wonder if that's because he doesn't want to come home.'

'You should see the number of stressed-out executives we see in a working day. All of them working long hours because the job demands it. All of them wishing they could be at home and instead drowning their pain in alcohol and drugs. We have a real problem in our society at the moment, and no one's willing to address it or do anything about it. So, we and the paramedics have to pick up the pieces and mop up the remains—cars driven into trees at high speed, drownings in the bath, hangings in the shed. Suicide is the biggest killer of the under 40s. I'm sure Carlo would much rather be at home than at work, hon.'

'I'm sad to hear about your work, Dad, and I hope that Carlo looks forward to being at home. I always try to ensure we do something fun on weekends as a family.'

'Good to hear. Now, what was it you wanted to see me about?'

'A friend of mine is writing a novel. It involves some cyber-crime, and she wanted to know about sentencing and penalties, punishments and stuff. Do you have any thoughts on that?'

'Well, cyber-crime is not something I see in my work. That's the remit of the Organised Crime branch. But I do hear of cases now and then.'

'Can you tell me what you know, what you've heard?'

'Sure. Well, one case I heard of involved someone attempting to hack into a bank branch. It turns out they found out somebody's password by ringing up and pretending to be from the bank's head office. They tricked this junior bank clerk into giving away their login and password details, then used those details to log into the bank's secure system. It was only when they repeatedly tried to access some customer accounts that the bank's IT people were alerted, and a trace put on all network traffic. By some technical wizardry I don't know about nor understand, they tracked down the bloke trying to break into the accounts and liaised with the Organised Crime boys and girls, who sent a patrol car out to pick the bugger up. Apparently, it came as a surprise to him that he could be caught.'

'And how much time did he get? What was his punishment?'

'I forget how long he got. Something near five years rings a bell in my brain. Plus, no unsupervised access to a computer for five years after.'

'Any other cases?'

'Let me see. Oh yes, there was this one case, a pimply young girl it was. Was angry with her parents so tried getting their cars repossessed and the house taken back by their bank.'

'And the punishment?'

'Well, she was a juvenile, so a good behaviour bond, plus no unsupervised access to a computer for several years.'

'What is the average time that someone can go to jail for hacking?'

'Well, that depends on the seriousness of the crime. A teenager being angry with their parents or a teacher differs vastly from an organised attack on a business. The levels of security that they have had to go through figures into the final mix, as does what their goal was. But you can expect the average hacker to spend between two and twelve years behind bars. Plus, an equivalent time after their sentence has been served where they have no unsupervised access to a computer, whether that's a traditional computer or a smartphone. Now, how you monitor that is a moot point.

But if they get caught again, they can expect some serious jail time; we're talking in the decades.'

'Has anyone been jailed a second time here in Australia?'

'Oh, sure. Hacking is big business. Lots of it is going on. It's just that you don't read about it in the papers or see it on tv. Because the businesses that have been hacked don't want you to know someone has hacked them. It would be bad for business. So, they wear the loss and pay security consultants large sums of money to make sure it never happens again. And they take big steps to make sure it stays out of the media's eye.'

'Have the banks been hacked?'

'Oh, sure they have. Their systems are more robust than most, but they'll never let on that their systems get hacked all the time. Most of the time nothing substantial gets stolen, but every once in a while some enterprising hacker gets away with a large payday.'

'That's amazing, Dad. All of this going on and no one knows anything about it.'

'You'd be surprised at what goes on out of view of the media's cameras. We see many things during a typical day. Ninety-nine percent of the time there's no one there to witness it and no one interested enough to care. It's a tough world out there.'

'How do you not suffer from stress and burnout?'

'We do, all the time. There's no support network for us, no structures in place to provide help when you're doing it tough. You just have to tough it out or go under, and most cops go under eventually. They retire from the force and make a living in the security services. Or as prison guards. But even prison guards suffer high rates of PTSD, too.

Having a good family really helps buffer you from what you have to deal with daily.'

'Oh, Dad! I never knew policing was so hard. If I'd have known, I probably wouldn't have been such a nightmare as a teenager.'

'Oh, you were never a nightmare. A handful, yes, but you were never hell on toast. Certainly nothing that your mother and I couldn't handle with patience and a lump of four-be-two, ha ha. But next time you see a police officer think kindly of them—they may well have had to scrape somebody off the road that day or taken a frightened and abused child away from its parents.'

'And you say there are no support structures. Do you mean that there're no resources for the police officers to tap into to help relieve the stress?'

'That's right. Oh, there're links on websites, but there are no actual support services, counsellors and stuff. You just have to deal with the mess you see every day in the best way you know, which with some officers means alcohol or drugs.'

'So how have you survived for so long?'

'Your mother is a rock for me. She stopped me going off the rails quite a few times. I have my fishing, my Sudoku. And these days I also have my granddaughters to keep my mind focused on the positives, not the negatives. I want to be a good grandpa to them, giving them a positive role model. I can't do that if I'm stuck in a bottle. That's why I don't drink these days.'

'Don't you have a wine after work, or a beer on your days off, anymore?'

'I haven't touched a drop since the girls were born. Mind you, I have days where that record is sorely tested.

But I take tablets to control the urges, and with your mother's support, I get past the urges and back into the positive.'

'Do you miss the drink?'

'Sometimes, but I just think of the girls and my brain sorts itself out. I remember reading a quote once, that with a big enough "why", the "how" sorts itself out. Anyway, that's enough about me. Was I helpful for your novel-writing friend, do you think?'

'I'm sure they will be delighted with what you've told me. Thanks very much for that, Dad.'

'Well, it's no problem. Now, help me prepare dinner for your mother. I'm cooking a Thai stir-fry; you can cut the beef into strips for me.'

SPENT A COUPLE OF HOURS WITH DAD TODAY, ON ONE OF HIS DAYS OFF. I NEVER KNEW COPS HAD IT SO HARD. I REALLY FEEL FOR HIM AND HAVE A NEW APPRECIATION FOR ALL HE DID FOR ME AS A YOUNG GIRL. HOW HE DIDN'T KILL ME WHEN I WAS A TEENAGER IS BEYOND ME.

FOUND OUT ABOUT HACKING AND PUNISHMENT. CRIME AND PUNISHMENT. THERE'S A BOOK IN THAT, HA HA. DAN COULD GO TO JAIL FOR UP TO TWELVE YEARS. I HAVE TO WARN HIM. BUT HE'S JUST NOT LISTENING AT THE MOMENT. HE'S ON HIS QUEST TO BE A HERO FOR HIS MATE, AND HE'S NOT LISTENING TO REASON.

BLOODY MEN.

48

Buoyed by the success of his first foray into the semi-serious end of the hacking world, Dan thought he'd have another go, this time attacking a shoe store in the city who once sold him a pair of shoes the soles of which came apart after two months. He didn't bother taking the shoes back to the store to complain; in fact, they were still sitting in their box at the back of his wardrobe.

Dan drove out to the Catholic Church with his laptop and his burner cellphone.

He located the shoe shop's online presence and negotiated his way around the various virtual doorways that led to the administration back-end of the 'real' company.

From there it was easy to navigate the various directory paths until he finally found what he was looking for: the accounts books. The shop used Xero as their bookkeeping package; cool, because D@@Mladen had given him print-friendly instructions on how to get around a Xero package. With the instruction sheet next to him, he followed the directions and with delight ended up at a locked virtual 'safe'.

It took more time than he was happy with to find a username and password combination that opened the safe, but he eventually got there. He had been inside the shop's computers for over ten minutes, and D@@Mladen had been forceful about getting in and getting out quickly. But at last he was at the safe's now open door.

Inside the safe was a text file, nothing else.

He double-clicked on the file.

To whoever thinks of attacking this store, you're too late. This site is being monitored by SAPOL's Commercial and Electronic Crime Branch and your movements are being tracked. Smile, you're on camera. Regards, Stephanie McBride

---

Dan slammed the lid of his laptop down and vowed to put tissue paper over his webcam before he went out on another adventure. He turned his burner phone off and headed home.

Over a beer in the kitchen he went through what he'd done, trying to find clues where he had stuffed up, wondering if he really *was* being tracked. Arguing with himself that he probably wasn't, he reached out to D@@Mladen to get her views on the situation. There was no point telling anyone else about tonight's failed hack, he told himself, meaning that he wouldn't be telling Davo or Hannah. Just D@@Mladen.

49

Of course the site wasn't monitored. The cyber-crime branch had far too many live cases for monitoring to take place. At least, active monitoring, the sort that provided intel within a short space of time. Like days.

No, it was sometimes weeks before someone read the monitoring file and tried to match up existing cases with those incursions monitored weeks before. The monitoring file was useful for providing extra detail to prosecutors, but that was about all.

Stephanie looked at the digital file on her desktop — the name of the file was in bold, signifying that they had monitored an incursion since the file was last open. Every detective in the cyber branch had an instance of the file on their desktop, hoping someone in the branch would open it. Supposedly, if you had some spare time, you were supposed to open the file and check its contents, looking for patterns that signified other known players in the cyberworld's eternal game of chess.

'Not today' Stephanie thought, and got up from her chair, strolled over to the cheap pod coffee maker, decided against one of the branch's coffees and announced to her colleague Petra that she was off to 'Grounds for Coffee', a nearby cafe that made a tasty brew, with the owner roasting imported Columbian beans.

It would have annoyed Stephanie to know that the owner also imported fine Columbian marching powder as well, in boxes where the smell of the coffee overpowered the smell of the cocaine, and the sniffer dogs were powerless to detect it.

Stephanie took a seat at the cafe's feature window and contemplated her lot. She was in the throes of another depressive episode. Being Bipolar was a roller coaster of an emotional ride, with some days being hypomanic and feeling like she could crack every case she had wide open, and other days where even the simplest case was overpowering. In between she enjoyed 'normal' days where she resembled the majority of her colleagues and had a balanced, jaundiced view of the uphill task she was facing.

No-one knew of her Bipolar condition except her private GP and a treating psychiatrist. She even kept it from her husband James, the one secret she kept from him. It scared her that he would think less of her, walk out on her. So she held on to her secret like a talisman, clenching her teeth through her bad days and forcing herself to put one foot in front of the other.

The medications she took evened her moods out mostly, although they put weight on her. She was constantly battling her weight, running up the kilometres on a walking machine at home in a frenzied attempt to out-metabolise the psychopharmaceuticals.

Weakness was frowned upon in the force, and admitting to Bipolar would ruin any chances of promotion, or leadership of task forces and groups. So the secret stayed with her, and she nursed her skim-milk latte and grappled with her current problem: was James having an affair?

She didn't think so, but she'd become so caught up in her workload she had been neglecting him. They hadn't gone out for their usual mid-week movie dates. Or any dates, really. Not for at least a couple of months. Had he sought company elsewhere? He was always heading out to cafes during the day to write; what if he was secretly rendezvousing with other writers? What if he had his own private life that he kept hidden from her? He seemed attentive enough when she got home from work, asking her about her day, cooking dinner for her when she was too tired for her favourite stress-relieving pastime.

She decided to work past her exhaustion and pay attention to James. She and he were in a new city, with temptations all around. It would be best if she and James stuck together, she reasoned. 'I'll cook him dinner tonight, despite feeling like crap, and tomorrow night we'll go out to the movies. There's bound to be something on we'd both like to watch.'

It was time for their weekly meet. Hannah was first into the meeting room, Dan a few minutes late. That delay was enough to spook Hannah—she worried that she'd pushed Dan too hard about being a criminal and he would not show.

'Oh, you're here, I'm glad,' said Hannah when Dan eventually showed up.

'G'day, sorry I'm late. I was up in Adelaide and only just got back. There were some roadworks on the freeway that slowed things up. Did I miss anything, ha ha?'

'Yes, you missed me pacing the floorboards, worrying that the police had caught you.'

'No chance of that. I know what I'm doing, trust me.'

'Well, to prove it to me, make a million dollars fly into my bank account.'

'Ha ha. Sure, give me your bank details and I'll hack in and deposit a million bucks in there. Easy. I'm already a millionaire several times over, just from hacking the farm, ha ha. Hey, I have a new saying for you: "Your baby might be adorable, but so is my cat, and she cleans her own bum".'

'Ha ha ha, that's very good. Ok, you have successfully gotten rid of my grumpy mood. Question: virus protection, which do you prefer: Norton or AVG?'

'Neither. They stuff your system up. I use the built-in virus protection of Windows Defender, which comes free from Microsoft with Windows. It updates all the time, so I never have to worry. And I make sure I don't do anything stupid like click on dodgy links in emails. No virus protection system will protect you if you deliberately click on a dodgy link.'

'Interesting, ta. It's always useful to talk with a techie about technical issues.'

'Just ask away, anytime.'

'My turn to share something interesting. And it concerns you. I spoke with my dad the other day about hacking and punishment. It turns out the courts take it very seriously, giving between two- and twelve-years' jail time to offenders. That's in NSW, I don't know about South Australia.'

'Wow, twelve years is a long time. But you don't have to worry, I will not get caught. I've had training from a real-world big-time hacker, and she's making sure I don't get caught. I have all the tools, I know how to use them, I've planted the viruses and backdoors to make sure I can enter and exit with ease. I know what I'm doing, Hannah.'

'Famous last words. I worry that you will get caught.'

'Look, I'll stop hacking into the farm after my next go. Promise. All I want to do is read their HR files and I'll leave a happy man. No more hacking.'

'Promise?'

'Promise.'

Rocco sat back and considered his options. He could either work with this Stephanie McBride chick, and get a reduced sentence, but risk having his co-operation becoming known to his tribe of friends, or he could continue to plead 'guilty', not co-operate and face the full wrath of the court. He knew from others that the courts take a dim view of teenage boys hacking into businesses.

He swayed back and forth, tossing the arguments and the 'what ifs' around in his head.

Eventually, he reached a decision: work with the police to track down D@@Mladen. Decision made, he focused his attention on the problem of the country farm and the potential cyber-crime. A country farm with a sophisticated artificial intelligence-based anti-intrusion system? Whoever heard of such a thing? Still, there it was, and the reports showed the evidence that someone had snuck into the computer system at a farm called Derringerry and opened and downloaded a spreadsheet, and had a general look around various folders in the system.

Rocco looked around at the open area he was in at C branch. A simple white plastic trestle table, probably bought from Officeworks, was his desk. A cheap office chair to sit on. Both housed in an old nineteen-eighties office building on South Road, Keswick, just up from Vili's bakery. Two storeys, grey concrete exterior, cream interior walls and aluminium window fittings. No posters on the walls. Nothing inside to inspire a young man to aspire to better things. In fact, just the opposite. Rocco found himself feeling slightly depressed. It was a functional building only, not one to inspire and encourage. He could understand why cops spent so much time out of the office in coffee shops. The conditions there were better. So was the coffee.

'Back to the AI program,' said Stephanie.

Rocco streamed his consciousness as he opened the report in a browser tab.

'A single attack. Entry timed at 7.02pm. Exit at 7.14pm. Only one file opened, a payroll spreadsheet. A database file and the payroll spreadsheet downloaded. Many folders accessed, a list of them provided, with times of entry and exit.'

Rocco compared the list with the folders he could see on his laptop now that he had access to Derringerry's computers.

'It looks like the intruder opened up the folders to see what lay inside, then according to the timing logs they exited out of the folder and went on to the next one in rapid succession. Just like I would do if I were looking for something. It looked like the intruder stopped searching when they found the payroll spreadsheet. I can understand why they hunted around for a bit,' he said. 'The folder that housed the spreadsheet wasn't named something logical like "payroll" or "salaries". No, it was named, "stipendi". It would take an Italian or Italian speaker to understand that. Perhaps the person who set the spreadsheet up in the first place was Italian.'

'So, the intruder probably wasn't Italian or an Italian speaker. That narrows it down to about, oh, one million South Australians. And that's assuming the intruder was from South Australia. If they were a foreign hacker out for a bit of fun on a Tuesday night, or morning where they were, they could be anyone,' said Stephanie.

Rocco continued. 'There were no clues where the intruder came from. No IP address worth believing, not when even script kiddies know how to mask their IP address and bounce themselves around the globe. The Derringerry hacker cleaned up at the end of their session. It was the last thing they did before exiting out of the computers.'

The only useful information Stephanie McBride and Rocco had to go on was that the intruder arrived just after 7pm on a Tuesday night, they had accessed the payroll spreadsheet and the client database, and that they didn't speak Italian.

'Okay, Rocco. Let's keep a watch on the farm and see if someone tries to break in again. Have you quarantined the spreadsheet and the client database? Kept a copy of all the files and folders? Got the AI program specifically looking for an intruder?'

'Yep. All of our programs say that the spreadsheet was opened but not infected. But they downloaded it. Maybe the hacker will try to insert a corrupted spreadsheet into Derringerry's files next time. They might try during business hours so that their entry is masked by the general busyness of the system.'

'Okay. I want you to monitor the farm for me, watch the files to see what else gets moved about and opened, closed and saved. Set up an immediate notification for yourself and me when something out of the ordinary happens.'

'Righty-ho.'

'And I want you to monitor the dark web. Keep an eye out for D@@Mladen and let me know if you find anything. I'll open up your laptop permissions so you can search in there. I'll go back to my other forty-seven cases.'

There was another case that Stephanie had found added to her caseload. A shoe shop in the city had been attacked, and the hacker had got in all the way to 'the note', the note Stephanie left in all cases of hacking, figuring that if someone had hacked into it once, chances were good that someone else would try to hack into it. The note acted as a deterrent, she argued. If nothing else, it would scare a newbie hacker and make them think twice about hacking again. But it was aimed at deterring junior hackers from hacking; those who had been around a while knew that the police weren't looking, they just reacted to break-ins, that they weren't proactive at all. They had too many cases to look into to spare resources on monitoring every potential hack.

52

'Damn, that didn't work. Let's try the Reynolds trick,' Dan suggested to himself.

'Nope, that didn't work either.'

Dan's iPhone lit up and a suggestion from Siri filled the screen.

'Dan, have you read this article? It suggests an alternative to the Reynolds program. It may be of value to you at this time.'

Dan picked up his phone and read the article. It gave examples of where the Reynolds trick didn't work and possible reasons why, and suggestions on how to succeed.

'Thanks, Siri, good find.'

Siri was getting better at listening to context and subsequently searching out the murky corners of the dark web and finding useful information.

The Reynolds trick was a way of having an Excel spreadsheet slowly corrupt itself. You could 'set and forget'; it would look after itself and corrupt both the source spreadsheet and any copies. And it was near invisible; it would take a practised eye to spot it. And if someone opened the spreadsheet, made adjustments and saved it, it would go to work.

But it hadn't worked on Derringerry's payroll spreadsheet, he was convinced, because he'd heard nothing from Alice Yates, and she would have been the first on the phone to him if something was wrong, because he was the town's IT guru. So, Siri's suggestion of an alternative program was timely, and it worked. That pleased Dan no end because he'd already spent six precious minutes trying to get the Reynolds program to work, and D@@Mladen was always warning him to 'get in, do what you came to do, get out as quickly as possible'. The last thing he wanted to do was hang around and get caught. Hannah's pleas were not falling on deaf ears, even though he was supremely confident in his abilities.

Even though he'd done what he set out to do—insert a virus into the payroll spreadsheet—the confidential files of the HR lady, Annie Riverside, were calling to him like flickering Christmas tree lights to a cat. Maybe if he downloaded the files, he could find out more information about the staff at the farm, more information that maybe he could blackmail them about. Completely 'out of scope' of his current mission, it was true, but a delicious thought. He was enjoying this hacking game more and more.

So, he downloaded the HR filing cabinet for future investigation and finally thought about closing the backdoor and wiping digital traces of his entry into the farm's computers clean away. Finally, completely out of Derringerry's server and computers, he punched the air above him.

'This deserves a beer,' he said out loud, to no one there.

53

The artificial intelligence-driven security software that Anthol Logistics installed on all its servers was again triggered by Dan's incursion, only this time instead of notifying just Wei, it also notified Rocco and Stephanie McBride.

'Are you seeing this?' Wei asked Stephanie in WhatsApp.

'Yes, I'll dig into it.'

'Rocco, can you run a trace on the intruder into Derringerry's server, please?'

'On it.'

A few minutes passed, then Rocco contacted both Stephanie and Wei. 'A reverse DNS lookup was crap. The closest I can get is a geographic location of the South East of South Australia. It could be Meningie, but it could equally be Kingston or Mount Gambier or any place in between and around.'

'Thanks. They're not trying to break in from Russia or Latvia or China or something?' Stephanie asked.

'No. Well, yeah. They tried bouncing me around the globe, but the one place all the bounces originate from is the South East of the state. But that's as close as me and the software could get.'

'There's a chance that it originated in Meningie, Rocco?' Wei asked.

'A chance, but not a strong one. It's just as likely they were hacking from Mt. Gambier or Kingston. Or Naracoorte.'

'Goodness, Rocco, you've been studying up on your country towns. I'm impressed! Lol' said Stephanie.

'Nothing that Google Maps can't teach me, boss.'

'Very good, Rocco. Now, can you tell what was stolen or copied?'

'As far as I can tell all they have done is have another look at the payroll spreadsheet and copy the HR documents folder. Would anything important be in there?'

'Yes, there would be,' replied Wei. 'The personnel files of all staff, past and present, are in there, there could be some secrets in there that would not like to see the light of day. Both the company and the employees themselves might prefer things to be kept hidden.'

'Okay. Rocco, you and I are going down to Meningie tomorrow to see if we can pick up further clues from the staff there as to who would be interested in HR files.'

'I'll let Alan Peters know to expect you both,' said Wei. 'Do you have a rough time you'll be there?'

'I estimate mid-morning,' replied Stephanie. 'Rocco, I'll pick you up at eight-thirty.'

54

Safely back at home and in his bedroom, Dan moved his pillow out of the way and put the back-rest pillow on his double bed. He fired up the laptop and took a swig of his cold Coopers Pale Ale.

HR folder, password protected. Easily broken; there we go. One hundred and eighteen files in the HR folder, he noted. This could take a while.

'Let's narrow this down for the moment,' he breathed to himself.

He opened the folder named 'Wilkins-David'. There should be something more interesting here, at least.

More folders: *Complaints, Dismissal, Engagement, Pay-increases, Superannuation, Training.*

'Okay, two folders of immediate interest there,' he thought.

Dan clicked on the *Complaints* folder icon and saw five

pdfs and five Word docs. The Word docs were the replies back to the complainant, it turned out. The pdfs were the letters of complaint.

Five different companies had complained about Davo, one—Maginty—in the last month. The complaints all read the same:

Dear Alan,

I sadly have to write to you about the conduct of one of your employees. Dave Wilkins has been servicing our company for over three years now, but he has yet to get an order right.

Each order is short when it's delivered, usually of something essential. I've watched when Davo enters the order into his laptop, and all looks good at this end. But somewhere along the way our order is changed and what we get is not what we asked for. Most often the missing item is essential, but sometimes it's swapped for a cheaper replacement.

Davo is always nice and pleasant, and good to work with, but in the latest order we were waiting on many kilos of sirloin for our restaurant customers, but received the same amount in short loin. Either Davo is incompetent or your abattoir supplier needs a serious talking to. Either way, with this order our customers went ape shit.

Davo is in all the instances of incomplete or plain wrong orders nothing but apologetic and keen to make amends. He has given us discounts

AND BONUS ITEMS BEFORE, BUT I KNOW FROM MY OWN EXPERIENCE OF RUNNING A BUSINESS THAT THIS BEHAVIOUR IS NOT SUSTAINABLE.

DON'T TAKE THIS THE WRONG WAY, BUT KINDLY REMOVE DAVO FROM OUR ACCOUNT AND INSTEAD GIVE US SOMEONE TO WORK WITH WHO CAN DO THE JOB.

YOURS IN FRUSTRATION,

TOM KNEEBONE

STATE SALES MANAGER

MAGINTY FOOD WHOLESALERS

Dan's best mate was not the accomplished hero alpha male Dan thought he was.

Dan felt crushed, like the complaints against Davo were complaints against him. He finished off the beer, put his laptop aside and slinked out to the fridge, hoping not to meet his mum out there.

She'd only want to talk about her latest saying.

He stood at the fridge and without meaning to, contemplated his mother's latest printout.

'IT'S OKAY TO NOT BE OKAY ALL THE TIME.

BUT ALWAYS KEEP MOVING FORWARD'

'My best mate's not okay. I'm not okay with that. But I'll keep moving forward with my plans, because I want to enact his revenge for him, and because I said I would. I'm doing it for him,' he reasoned.

He grabbed another Pale Ale from the fridge and headed back to his bedroom and the laptop that held such disheartening secrets.

Next, Dan looked in the *Termination* folder.

A copy of the letter from Anthol head office confirming

the termination date and amount owing in leave. Cold, matter-of-fact. As if casting Davo aside was an easy, casual thing to do. No sweat, no emotion.

Another letter in the folder, this time from Derringerry, confirming the date of Davo's last day with the farm, what benefits such as leave will be paid, and a request for the company car keys and any farm property to be handed over to Alan Peters, Farm Manager.

Yet another document, this time a memo from Bruce Abernathy, State Manager of Athol Logistics, to his HR team, c.c. Alan Peters, that the recent mix-up of the Maginty order was one mix-up too many and that he was stepping in and sacking Davo for incompetence and for putting a major client account at risk.

One last document, a letter of reference from Alan Peters, thanking Davo for eight years of service and that he should be proud of what he had achieved there.

'What had he achieved?' thought Dan. 'Davo has never told me of any achievements that bear remembering.'

Another gulp of beer.

'Blimey O'Reilly,' thought Dan. 'How am I going to break this to Davo? What will it do to him? He's already beaten up, how do I tell him the real reason he was sacked? And why didn't Alan Peters tell him? Too scared? Oh, strewth. I need to think about this before I go telling anybody anything. I know, I'll talk to Hannah tomorrow, she always knows what to do. I can't tell Kelly because she and Sarah go to yoga class together, and I'm not sure how Sarah would take it to know the real reason they sacked her husband.'

55

She met her colleagues at The Historian in Coromandel Place in the city. It was a boutique pub with a good menu and—most importantly for Stephanie, which is why she suggested it—a bar well stocked with whiskies.

Wednesday night was always a quiet night in town, parking was easy and the Histo was as comfortable a place as any to while away a few hours in chat.

'How's your farm case going, Stephanie?' asked Harry Myers. Harry was a long-serving member of the police force, moving from foot patrol, to cars, promotion to detective, domestic violence and now commercial and computer crime. He wasn't trained in IT like Stephanie, but he knew his way around the law and how to treat those who were assisting the police with their enquiries. He was also a team player, which helped in busy branches like his current one. It was too easy for people in the cyber team to chase rabbits down holes and never quite surface again. Cops like Harry made surfacing again all the more palatable.

Stephanie took a sip of her deep, dark brooding Lagavulin scotch.

'Good thanks, Harry. We've just had a second incursion, so the perpetrator is starting to leave clues. I'm assuming it's the same perp in each case, as a farm is not exactly gold bullion for the usual hackers to attack.'

'Any ideas on what they're looking for?'

'Well, so far they've stolen a payroll spreadsheet, a client database and a folder full of HR files, so I'm thinking a disgruntled former employee. But it's early days.'

'You've got safeguards in place?' Harry was referring to the standard C branch practice of putting software on the servers so that intruders can be tracked and traced.

'Well, that's one of the surprises in this case. It turns out the farm in question is owned by the Chinese and it's their standard practice to have an AI bot sitting on all of their servers, watching everything that is going on and reporting when something looks amiss. For example, when the second incursion happened an hour ago, within minutes I had a report on my phone telling me an attack was in progress. The report told me what files had been opened, what files were downloaded, and what files had been deleted. All in a neat little easy-to-read document. Not just lines and lines and lines of server logs.'

'Well, that's cool. Why does a farming business have such a sophisticated monitoring and reporting tool?'

'I don't know. I haven't asked yet, but I will when the time is right. I know the Chinese have a strong interest in our farming practices and land, but I haven't heard of them hacking into farms. Perhaps this is a first. Except that the tracing we have been able to do on the farm's server keeps coming up with an origin of somewhere in the south-east of the state. Sure, the pings bounce all over the globe, including China, but the origin of those bounces is the south-east. I can't get any closer than that at this stage, but maybe a third incursion will reap something.'

'And you have one of your project boys helping you?'

'Rocco, yes. He's a boy who got caught trying to be tougher than he is. He's easily led. So far, he hasn't come up with anything on D@@Mladen, but it's early days. Meanwhile, he's helping me with software installs and reading server logs. Like you, I've got a full desk of cases to get through. It's helpful having someone else who does the dull computer work.'

'But that's where the secrets are buried, Stephanie, you know that.'

'That's true in some circumstances, but AI programs like the one I saw in action tonight are the future, Harry. They highlight the anomalous behaviour and report it in near-real time. And the report isn't just lines and lines of logs, but actionable content that gets down to the key facts quickly. Making it easier for us to apply our professional knowledge and training to the real issues, not the ghosts and whispers we might find hours and days after the fact.'

'I'm not convinced.'

'Okay. What's the one failing we have? When we're looking for something, we only use our own levels of ingenuity. We only search for bodies where *we* would have buried them. We are limited by our imagination. But AI isn't. Good artificial intelligence learns from its past—and this is the most important bit—learns from the experience of other AI bots as well. It co-learns. We humans can't do that. I can't take all your experience and knowledge and apply it to my cases. All I can do is hope to learn from your case reports what you have done and what you have found out. But an AI bot can learn from other AI bots and apply that knowledge in real time. And that's exciting, Harry.'

'When you put it like that, it is. But I can't help but think what it would be like living with that on a day-to-day basis. And I'm picturing a desk full of cases, just like we have now, and mounds of server logs, and software like this adding a bright glossy report that is useful but missing essential details because the software thought them unnecessary to report.'

Stephanie took a mouthful of her Atlantic salmon. Paused. Took a sip of her Lagavulin.

'But the software learns what is important over time, an incredibly short amount of time. Because if we used the software, we could have the software engineers change what's reported and what's not incredibly quickly. In hours or days, not months and years like now. And the software could learn from what other police forces are doing with it and shape itself to that standard too, if we chose to.'

'I'd be interested to know how much this AI bot costs, not that I can see the powers-that-be coughing up for one.'

'I have no idea, but when I get a clear moment, I will find out. I find the whole thing fascinating.'

'I can tell.'

'Well, it is, because soon only governments and large corporations will be able to afford to play *mano e mano* in an AI world. Small players will be pretty quickly wiped out by AI-equipped police forces.'

'Won't it be like *Close Encounters of the Third Kind* all over again, machines playing tunes to each other while we sit back and watch them slug it out?'

'Maybe. Or maybe it will be like an arms race, where détente is quickly reached, and no one risks starting a global cyber war.'

'War or not, good luck with that software.'

56

Hannah and Dan met up again on the video conferencing service Pickant.

'G'day, how art thou this fine day?' asked Dan in his best Shakespearean voice.

'Good,' Hannah replied. 'All is good here, thank you for asking, kind sir. And how art thou?'

'Yea, verily, I say unto thee, my cup runneth over with delight.'

'Ha ha ha. I can't keep this Shakespearian stuff up.'

'Don't worry, neither can I. I've reached the limit of my Shakespeare. Although I do remember a famous saying, 'Two beer or not two beer, that is the question.' Written by Shakesbeer.'

'Ha ha ha, that's hilarious, Dan. I studied Macbeth at school, and the funniest thing for me was that the soldiers all cut off a branch of a tree to hold in front of them while they marched towards Macbeth's castle in hopes that he will somehow think they are all trees and not an army. The second funniest thing is that it worked!'

'That's insane! How drunk was Shakespeare when he wrote that?'

'Ha ha ha. I know, right?'

'Anyway, I need your help today, for I am troubled,' said Dan.

'Oh, goodness, what's wrong?'

'You know my best mate, Davo?'

'Your partner in crime? Yes, I vaguely remember you mentioning him.'

'Well, you know how I told you they sacked him, but he should have been made redundant?'

'I remember.'

'It turns out Davo was sacked because of incompetence going back years. The state manager of the farm's owners personally asked for his head after he received a complaint letter and a phone call from the farm's biggest client.'

'Oh, no! Have you told him of your discovery?'

'No, I don't know what to say. How do you tell your best mate that he's not fit for the job and hasn't been for quite a while? What would you do in my situation?'

'Wow, Dan. Thankfully, I've never been put in that position, but I feel for you. Your best mate is kind of like a role model for you, I am guessing, and now he's no longer that role model in your eyes. It seems to me that there's some good counselling material right there, for both of you.'

'I know. But we don't have any counsellors down here, and I'm not sure I'd go to one even if there were. That touchy-feely stuff is not for me. But I ask you about all this because I trust you, Hannah. What would you do if you were me?'

'Well, I wouldn't tell Davo what you know. He's probably feeling miserable anyway, so having his best mate tell him that he knows he's incompetent is not going to cheer him up. And I'm guessing that his wife probably wouldn't welcome the news either.'

'Right.'

I would let sleeping dogs lie. If Davo involves lawyers over his dismissal, the facts will all come out, anyway. I see no benefit for you to break the news to him. Does he know you have read his personnel files?'

'No, I haven't told him yet.'

'Well, that's a good thing. Does he know that you've even downloaded them?'

'No, he doesn't know I've downloaded anything apart from the salary and wages spreadsheet I pulled last week. He's seen that, I showed it to him.'

'Okay. Then, for now, play it cool. Don't tell him you hacked into the farm again. Let him think you are biding your time, being cool about things. Or that you are WORRIED ABOUT BEING CAUGHT.'

'Righty-ho. I'll play it cool. Thanks.'

'You're welcome. Now, tell me a joke, funny man.'

'Life is like a game of chess. I don't know how to play chess.'

'Ha ha ha. Very good.'

'Thanks, and thanks again for your advice. I feel calmer. Now, how are the girls and the family?'

'Oh, Jessie is fine, but Angela is flatter than a sheet of photocopy paper. She's been like this for a little while now. I've taken her to the GP and the Children's Hospital, but no one can find anything wrong with her. I'm at a loss to explain it. She's off her food, she doesn't enjoy play times like she used to, she's just mopey and cuddle-obsessed. I ask her if anything is wrong, but she just shakes her head. My big fear is that I have passed my depression onto her in my genes. But that wouldn't explain why her identical twin sister hasn't come down with anything like this. I'm at a loss.'

'Maybe Jessie needs something to trigger her, and it hasn't happened yet. What could have triggered Angela?'

'Triggered? Where did you learn such words, Kemosabe?'

'Ha ha. Hang around my mum for long enough and you soak them up like kitchen towel.'

'Well, you might be right. I don't know what triggered Angela, if that's what happened. She just went from bright and bubbly, like her sister, to sad and clingy. She hasn't been told off or anything recently. At least, not that I can remember. She just went to bed one night and woke up the next morning all depressed. At least that's what it looks like.'

'That's sad. I hope you figure out a solution. Maybe take her back to the Children's Hospital for a second opinion?'

'I think you're right. That's what I will have to do.'

'Look, I've got a client ringing me on my phone—you can probably hear it—and I'd better answer their call and solve their problem. Catch you next week?'

'Sure. Take care, Dan.'

Had a good catch-up with Dan today. He was asking after the girls and I talked about Angela and how I think I might have passed on my depression to her. I secretly worry that my own depressed behaviour might trigger Angela. Dan seemed genuinely concerned. Bless him.

The same as I'm genuinely concerned that he has hacked into the farm again, this time stealing HR documents that talk about his mate Davo. It turns out Davo's not the competent adult Dan thought he was. That's got to be a blow to Dan. I advised him not to tell Davo what he's found. If Davo needs to know, it will come out when the lawyers get involved.

I'm feeling better at talking about my depression with Dan. It doesn't look like I'm scaring him off being sad like this.

57

Dan was scheduled to meet online with D@@Mladen. However, a car-meets-truck incident on the Princes Highway meant Dan was late from an urgent meeting in Adelaide with a client. With no mobile phone signal, Dan had no way of contacting D@@Mladen to let her know of his delay.

Meanwhile, Ros was home on a day off to attend to some things, and she was looking for some scissors. Not finding any in the usual places, she wondered if Dan had them in the study, so she entered the room and searched around amongst the piles of papers to find a pair.

Her activities didn't go quite according to plan, because she accidentally moved the computer mouse and the blank screen suddenly lit up.

There, on the screen, was D@@Mladen, waiting in the dark web chat room that Dan had foolishly but inadvertently left unattended for several hours.

'Hello, Dan?' asked D@@Mladen.

Ros was unsure of what to do, so she sat down in Dan's chair to think about her options. This brought her into view of the webcam on top of Dan's monitor, and both parties finally got to see each other.

'Oh, hello,' Ros said.

'Hello. Is Dan there?' asked D@@Mladen.

'No, he's not. Are you one of his clients? Can I help? I'm Ros Robinson, Dan's mother.'

'No, I'm just a friend. I was due to meet up with him online right about now. You don't know when he's going to be home, do you?'

'Sorry, I don't. He rushed out this morning saying he had an urgent meeting with a client in Adelaide that he needed to be at, then he was out of the door and gone.'

'Oh, okay. Well, I won't take up any more of your time; I'll go.'

'Can I leave him your name so he knows you called him?'

'It's okay. I'll send him a text. It will be fine.'

'Oh, okay. Well, if you are going to text him, can you also remind him he promised to take me to the Docherty's tonight for dinner? They're cooking boned and rolled turkey breast!'

'Ha ha. I'll certainly let him know. You know, Mrs

Robinson, your fridge sayings are famous. What's the latest?'

'Oooh, it's a goody. Hang on, I'll just nip to the kitchen and get it.'

'Okay.'

Twenty seconds later, Ros was back.

'PLEASE BE PATIENT WITH ME. SOMETIMES WHEN I'M QUIET, IT IS BECAUSE I NEED TO FIGURE MYSELF OUT. IT'S NOT BECAUSE I DON'T WANT TO TALK. SOMETIMES THERE ARE NO WORDS FOR MY THOUGHTS.'

What do you think of that?'

'That's great, Mrs Robinson. 'Sometimes there are no words for my thoughts'—I sometimes feel like that.'

'Do you, dear? I do, too. Sometimes a client will do something, and I don't have the words to say to them right there on the spot. It's only later, when I've had time to stew about it, that the right words come. But by then, of course, it's too late. The moment has passed.'

'That's very true. Well, I must be off. I'll let Dan know about your dinner tonight. Who was it with again?'

'The Docherty's. It will be a lovely night. If you're ever down this way, I'll cook you a meal and show you my latest saying.'

'Well, I'd like that, thanks. Bye, bye.'

'Bye.'

And with that, the screen went blank and Ros Robinson got up and went back to the kitchen, not knowing that she had just spent quality time with one of Australia's most respected and wanted cyber criminals. If only she knew, the stories she could tell around the dinner tables of Meningie.

58

Stephanie and Rocco met with Alan Peters and discussed the HR files, their contents, and the implications of them having been stolen. Like all HR departments everywhere, the contents in those files showed the best and worst of humanity's capacity to lead and be led. There were scandals, criminal behaviour, unethical behaviour, affairs, romances and more. All intermingled with the vast majority of behaviour, which was orderly and civilised.

But some elements of the files would not lend themselves well to being aired in public. It would either be embarrassing for the farm or embarrassing for the individual concerned.

But none of the files in and of themselves would bring the farm down, which was Alan Peters' main concern,

'So Alan, is there a likely hacker who knew what they wanted and got it? An ex-employee, perhaps, or a supplier or current employee chancing their arm?' asked Stephanie.

'Oh, there are always possibilities, it's true. But I honestly can't think of anyone in our recent past who would have a vendetta against us, or have the skills to carry it out.'

'What about David Wilkins? He recently got sacked— could he be a suspect?'

'I doubt it. Davo has a heart of gold. He's a big boofhead, not all that skilled in the finer points of computer use. I understand he repeatedly asked young Alice Yates for help when he got lost in his computer and couldn't find his way out of a screen. I can't see him suddenly turning into a hacker.'

'While I'm down here, Alan, I would like to read the HR files to see if there're any clues I can pick up as to the hacker's identity or motive. Is it all right with you if Rocco and I look through your files?'

'That's fine. You can use the meeting room if you like.'

'Thanks. And where does everyone go to get lunch?'

'There's a Vietnamese takeaway that's opened up on the main drag. Their food is great and reasonably priced.'

'Thanks. Rocco, let's leave Alan to get on with his work and you and I retire to the meeting room to do some reading.'

Stephanie's method of using hackers who had been caught and were awaiting a court date was not without controversy. Her boss thought it was a brave thing to do, which in a bureaucracy was another way of saying 'professional suicide'. But Stephanie took the risk of working with youths like Rocco because they had more up-to-date information about her primary quest, D@@Mladen. They could, she argued, get closer to D@@Mladen than she had so far been able to. All she wanted, she told her 'projects' as she called them privately, was to get D@@Mladen to agree to a meeting. Not turn himself in, because he would never do that, she argued. But he might at least meet with her, and Stephanie might get his help with the overwhelming numbers of foreign attacks on South Australian businesses. Maybe he would have some ideas on how to better protect the state's businesses and citizens. It was worth a shot. Direct requests from her to him had so far met with stony silence.

So it was that Rocco, the latest in a line of 'projects', was reading for clues on a farm in country South Australia.

After two hours of reading, Stephanie asked Rocco for his thoughts.

'Well, I can see why the folder was password-protected. There's some juicy shit in here.'

'I agree. But do you see anything that screams out 'revenge'?'

'Not so far.'

'Me neither. I'm hungry—want some lunch from the Vietnamese place? I'll shout you.'

'No, thanks, Mum made me a pasta salad, just in case.'

'And you've had it in your bag all this time, not in a fridge?'

'Oh, it's all right. It won't kill me.'

'As a mother myself, I know your mother would want to clip you around the ear for that. But suit yourself. I'm heading down to the takeaway. Won't be long.'

59

'Hey Dan, have you heard about the hacker over at Derringerry?' Phuoc called out without looking up from his cooking duties. His wife Han kept her head down and focused on her rice paper roll and mam nem preparations, pretending not to listen.

'No,' replied Dan, calmly. 'Tell me about them.'

He looked at the tall blonde woman next to him, guessed she was probably five years younger than his mother and discounted her as a mere tourist. He was sure she wouldn't be interested in eavesdropping on this conversation.

'Apparently someone's broken into the systems at Derringerry and stolen some secret files.'

'Really? And how did you hear of this?' Dan asked with a genuine concern that he took pains not to show.

'Ahh, you know, word gets around. A small town like

this is just like the small town where I grew up in Vietnam. Full of intrigue and gossip.'

'It sure is, Phuoc,' agreed Dan. 'When did they break in? And do they know who it is?'

'Last week. No one knows who the hacker is, but the police are going to post a reward of $10,000 for information. And they will send a whole load of police officers down here to question everyone.'

Stephanie's eyes widened. The 'whole load' was just her and Rocco, hardly a sight to invoke fear in wayward computer jockeys. So too was the reward. There would be no reward in this case, it wasn't high profile enough. A mention on the CrimeStoppers Facebook page was about the best she could hope for.

'You're a wise man, Phuoc,' said Dan. 'What's your view of the whole thing? Is it going to bring the whole town into the news for the wrong reasons again, like Gene Bristow, the backpacker rapist from a few years ago?'

'I have a bad feeling about this, Dan. No good will come of the police coming down here. If the police come, the media will come too, and nobody will be safe from their prying eyes. There's an old Vietnamese saying, 'Hoạ vô đon chí'—'Misfortunes never come singly'. But here are your rolls. And yours too, Miss.'

He left the digital chalk mark on the digital wall and waited. A response didn't take long.

'Hello, Vextant, how's things?'

'Good. Here are my numbers,' and Dan typed in his Authenticator numbers.

Authenticity of his end confirmed, he waited for D@@Mladen to type in hers. A match, both ends confirmed. It was safe to talk in the video meeting software.

'How's the hacking been going?' D@@Mladen asked.

'Well. I've made two successful attempts at the farm and got clean away on both of them.' Dan replied.

'How do you know this, country padawan?'

'I followed the instructions and training you gave me, about getting in and getting out again, and I adjusted the logs so that my entry and my "business" was deleted. I checked to see if there were any monitoring programs on the server and computers, but there weren't any. And I left a backdoor so I can get in again whenever I want.'

'Good, well done.'

'Don't forget, this is just a country farm. There's been no security here for decades. It was only when they installed a couple of security cameras that they stopped my best mate and me from stealing equipment.'

'Even so, Vextant, you can't take security too seriously. Things change, programs change. What worked last week might not work today. Programs that were the gold standard last week are possibly old hat and worthless tomorrow morning.'

'Yes, Obi-Wan.'

'Correct response. Anyway, did you achieve what you set out to do?'

'Yes, and no. Yes, because I got into the system, twice, and got out again before they could spot me. No, because I had to go back in a second time to fix what I couldn't achieve the first time, which was the planting of a virus in a payroll spreadsheet.'

'But you got it done on the second attempt, yes?'

'Yes, but even then there were complications. The virus wouldn't work, so I had to go off searching for a work-around. But that only took a few minutes, and I was out again pretty quickly.'

'How quickly?'

'In and out in under ten minutes.'

'That's a bit long for a routine, low-level job, Vextant.'

'I know. I was trying the Reynolds trick for spreadsheets and it wasn't working. But Siri found a workaround for me, and all was as good as gold. I downloaded some HR files for curiosity, cleaned up and got out. Easy as.'

'And what are you going to do with the HR files?'

'I'm not sure. I first thought I'd see if I could find anything to blackmail the company over, but there are over a hundred files in the folder. So I cut to the chase and read the files in my mate Davo's folder.'

'And did you find anything interesting that you didn't already know?'

'Yeah, and that's what has stumped me. I've been carrying on my business ever since I read his folder. I've been pretending nothing's changed, but everything's changed.'

'I don't follow, explain.'

'Well, I've been carrying out my normal day job business, seeing clients, handling telecalls and videocalls. Working on an Operations Manual for a client. All my normal stuff, all the while hoping that inspiration would strike and I'd know the way to handle what I've learned by reading the files.'

'And what have you learned?'

'That my best mate, the bloke I was best man for at his wedding, my soul brother, is incompetent at work. It seems he has stuffed things up for years, but no one wanted to tell him because of local town politics. I can understand someone being crap at something, one or two things maybe, but it seems like my mate is lucky to hold down a job. Several of the farm's clients have asked that he be moved to another account, away from theirs. This goes back years.'

'And you want to know what to do with that information, is that right?'

'Yeah. Because I'm buggered if I know what to do with it, and how I've been dealing with it up 'til now hasn't given me some blinding flash of insight.'

'One thing you must be thinking of is whether to let your friend know you know something that perhaps he doesn't. I have to say, that's not a wise thing to do. I don't recommend you share your knowledge with anyone. What I do suggest is that you search the files for dirt on the company and leverage that to your friend's benefit. When you have some dirt like that, check in with me first before you attempt to go using it because information like that can backfire VERY quickly! I've seen other hackers get caught trying to collect ransom demands; their greed impedes a safe transaction.'

'Okay, I'll run everything past you first. I wouldn't have the first clue about blackmailing anyone, a person or company.'

'It's an enormous path to go down, Vextant. I'd hate to see you lose your footing.'

'Okay, thanks for looking out for me.'

'You're welcome. Now, is there any more I should know about the farm hacks?'

'No, I've filled you in on all the details.'

'Okay. So now, what are you going to do next?'

'Well, I thought of pulling off another hack, but a

different company this time. Just as a way of cheering me up, I think.'

'Well, that's possibly a useful strategy. Did you have a particular company in mind?'

'Yeah, I thought I'd hack into Anthol Logistics, the new owners of the farm.'

'Okay. What is your optimum outcome from the hack, should you go ahead with it?'

'I don't know.'

'That's not a good enough reason to hack a business, Vextant. You need clear goals, otherwise you are just fishing about, chewing up valuable time and massively increasing your chances of being caught.'

'Well, it would be a fishing expedition, because I don't have any goals. I thought I'd just look around and see what I can find.'

'Not a good enough reason to go in. Why don't you compile a list of Directors and download the HR files for them to see if any of them have been up to naughties?'

'That's a good idea, thanks.'

'No dramas. I'm full of good ideas, ha ha ha.'

'Okay, that's what I'll do for my next hack, which is good because it will take my mind off things. I don't know how I will look Davo in the face and pretend all is good.'

'Listen, you and Davo will be fine. It's not like you found out he's cheated on his wife or shagged a sheep or something. '

'Ha ha. True. I guess a couple of beers and it will all fade into the past.'

'More than likely. A good laughing session between the two of you and things will be as they were.'

'Thanks for being here, D@@Mladen. I appreciate all you are doing for me.'

'You're welcome, young padawan. Now, go off and be awesome. Do me proud.'

'Will do. Thanks.'

'But before you go, how's your mother?'

'WHAT? I don't follow.'

'I met your mother online the other day, remember? I'm just asking how she is. She offered to cook a meal for me if I was ever down that way. I might have to take her up on that offer, ha ha.'

'Strewth, well, she's fine. She's stressing over a dish that she promised she'd cook for some of her friends. She's been trying it on me, some sort of seafood pasta dish, and it doesn't taste that good. But I'm no cordon bleu cook or anything, so what would I know, ha ha?'

'Ha ha, well, I'll insist she not cook that dish for me, then.'

'Are you really thinking of coming down here? It's nearly a two-hour drive from Adelaide, you know.'

'Well, I wasn't planning it, but you never know your luck in a big city, Vextant. Now, I've got to chat with some others. Don't forget about having a goal for your hacks and remember to run everything past me before you go off and try blackmailing someone.'

'Will do, and thanks again for looking out for me..'

'You're very welcome, Vextant. Bye.'

'Rocco, go get me a coffee, please. Here's some money.'

For Rocco, it meant a break from sitting at a cheap

plastic table on a second-hand office chair, staring at a too-small monitor. It was a nice stroll up to Vili's café in the morning sun, and it was better to run an errand than to spend all of his time staring at log files, hoping to catch sight of D@@Mladen.

For Stephanie, it was a chance to check up on what Rocco's been up to and see if he was playing along nicely.

As it turned out, Rocco *had* been playing nicely with his new friends. He hadn't tried contacting his mates, nor had he tried to infiltrate any websites. This pleased Stephanie no end; her last project had decided the pep talk she had given him wasn't a strong enough disincentive to return to a life of crime. He had undone several months of investigative work on a case and had used his SAPOL-provided laptop to break into a small hardware chain and siphon off some funds. Stephanie had sorted it all out, and the fiasco did neither the boy nor Stephanie any favours, but the magistrate threw the book at the lad, so there was some justice, at least. Even an appeal over the harsh sentence was turned down.

All of which would ordinarily invoke a rebuke from a senior officer and the end of Stephanie's 'project' experiment. But 'C' branch was 'all hands to the pumps', overflowing with cases to be solved, and criminals and kiddies to be investigated and prosecuted.

There was no rest for the wicked, and no rest for the good, either. Extra pairs of trained hands, wherever they could be found, were welcome to pull up a chair and get down and dirty.

It didn't help Stephanie or her colleagues that hackers could come from anywhere in the world, for any or no motive, and could be bored teenagers or cashed-up organised criminals. At first, you could never tell what or why or who was in play; only with repeated hacks, with telltale hints from files ignored or files accessed, could you piece together a composite profile of the hacker. And those profiles, like the police-instigated psychological profiles of the 1970s, could be wildly inaccurate, causing the officer to doubt themselves, their methods and their career choice.

As an example of this inaccuracy, Stephanie and her colleagues believed that D@@Mladen was male. The attacks that D@@Mladen had carried out, the near-misses of cyber chases, the quasi-religious loyalty of her acolytes, led the 'C' Branch and their counterparts in the other States to assume that she was a he. And that he was in his thirties. And that he lived in Sydney or the Gold Coast.

One particularly fervent police officer in Queensland even claimed to have nearly caught D@@Mladen in a car chase around Brisbane.

Nearly.

Except that D@@Mladen wasn't in Brisbane on that day, she was home in Adelaide, sleeping off a post-hack buzz after a particularly successful foray into a private Swiss bank, wherein she netted a considerable sum of money and the ownership rights to a Monet.

But back to Stephanie and her colleagues. Stephanie, Harry and the crew were flat out like a lizard drinking, and grateful for any assistance they could get. Rocco was unpaid help, but skilled in the work, so he was very welcome—if one put aside the fact that he had recently been caught committing the very crimes he was now helping to solve and would shortly be up in front of a magistrate himself.

As for Rocco himself, he was working on getting his sentence reduced, and he was looking after number one—himself. If he helped take down another hacker, well, so be it; 'it serves them right for not being smart enough to evade capture.' In the meantime, he was learning about how the police go about catching hackers like him, he was learning who the key players were (and Stephanie was certainly a player, in his book), and he was learning where the future of hacking was going. All valuable information on the inside of the prison walls.

So, everybody was working.

Stephanie, for her part, had spent a few hours researching Rocco—his movements, his cyber trail, his friends, his family. Even his extended family.

Stephanie could afford to do this, even with her busy caseload, because she was special. So special she was like no other in the whole world, at least that science knew of.

Stephanie didn't sleep. Along with Bipolar Disorder II she suffered from FFI—Fatal Familial Insomnia—and spent her nights reading, watching movies or researching the lives and loves of friends and acquaintances in the various corporate, State and Federal databases. She could do this easily, even though it was strictly forbidden, because she was a skilled hacker herself, and knew how to get around and through the various systems without being caught.

Stephanie kept her secret illness under control through the wonder drug Quinicrine. With it she stayed fully functional; miss a dose and she was attacked by blurred vision, migraines, dry mouth and a tongue that resembled sandpaper. She'd contracted the illness after suffering a fever just after the birth of her twin boys; she took great pains to stay on top of her condition and stay fully functional.

The upside of her condition was that she had twice the productivity of her colleagues.

The downside was that she was a ticking time bomb. FFI sufferers rarely lived for more than eighteen months after contracting it; Stephanie had 'enjoyed' its benefits for nearly two decades. She had a regular Skype call with a specialist at John Hopkins who was probably the world's foremost expert on the condition.

But even the specialist had no idea when her luck would run out.

D@@Mladen left a chalk mark on Dan's digital fence post. 'Meet me soon. No urgency.'

Dan returned the mark that evening when he'd finished his trip up to Adelaide to work with Deirdre. Siri had pointed out the mark while he was driving back home, listening to his emails.

'Hello, young padawan,' D@@Mladen smiled when they had exchanged their authentication.

'Hello, Obi-Wan' replied Dan.

'The thing is, I shouldn't be calling you my young padawan. You're older than me. But saying 'old padawan' is somehow weird. What should I call you, Vextant?'

'I dunno. 'Padawan' is fine with me. I agree with the 'old' bit—I don't feel old. But I guess I am, compared to the others you've dealt with.'

'Indeed. I usually deal with angry or bored teenagers, not men. Or women, for that matter. Syrus is probably the only high-ranking, high-achieving female hacker still around, still pulling off fine-art heists and emptying bank accounts.

'I've never heard of her. Where's she based?'

'New York. Runs the S-Collectif there. High-end stuff, multi-million dollar heists and bank trawls. Is for hire, so she doesn't just line her own pockets and those of her crew, but you have to be very cashed-up to get her attention. She's also skilled at finding planted agents, and quite a few cops in the early days met untimely ends trying to infiltrate her organisation, or catch her in a sting.'

'She sounds heavy duty.'

'Oh, she is. I've met her. I've even provided intel to her team when she was working an Australian angle. I was well compensated.'

'That's interesting. Now, what did you want me for? You said you wanted to catch up, but it wasn't urgent.'

'Oh, yes, I'd like to meet up with you again.'

'Really? That's great. But why?'

'To see how you're getting on. See how you're using the tools I gave you. To offer encouragement and support, that sort of thing.'

'Wow. Okay. Well, I'm flattered that you want to do that. When is a good time to meet with you? I'm pretty flexible.'

'What about Thursday night? I'll send you the location.'

'Sure, Thursday night is good. No, wait. Mum wants me to take her to a friend's place for dinner. Oh, screw it— you're more important than that. I'll tell her I have a work drinks to go to for one of my clients. What time Thursday night?'

'Nine-thirty too late for you?'

'Well, it'll be after midnight that I get back here. But okay, nine-thirty it is.'

'Good. I like to wake up, have dinner somewhere, then meet with my padawans. You sure your mum's going to be okay with her driver not being available?'

'Ha ha. I'm sure she'll get over it. I try to look after her because she's been very good to me and helped me out with lots of stuff, but she can drive herself for one night, it won't kill her.'

'Okay, it's settled then. Thursday night, nine-thirty, at a location I'll send you the address of later. I'm looking forward to seeing you, Vextant.'

'That's mutual. See you then.'

'That's funny,' Dan said to himself after he'd hung up from the call. 'I feel, oh, I don't know... flirty'.

63

Wednesday night. Just after seven pm, the time of the evening when he most liked to hack. He'd had dinner, he'd had a beer, he was relaxed.

He crossed himself to appeal to a god he didn't believe in; he'd seen countless European footballers do it so he figured it was worth a shot.

Anthol Logistics. The parent company of Derringerry. A Chinese-owned international conglomerate of farms, feed producers, livestock exporters, animal welfare inspectors and equipment manufacturers. Big in Australia and New Zealand. Big exporters to China, Russia and northern Europe.

They no doubt had teams of IT specialists, Dan thought to himself. But they probably all went home at six o'clock, leaving the place empty until the next working day. He really should have left this particular hack until the week-end, he thought, but this one quick trip in to leave a back-door won't hurt anyone.

He was nervous about breaking into Anthol. A farm is relatively easy—no one's interested in a farm, he thought, and the security would be low. But a nationwide exporting business—that is the hack that will get the attention of someone in the organisation, someone who may well have the resources to play the game in reverse and hack the hacker.

But conversely, a hacker who breaks into such an organisation and gets away cleanly gets a certain number of 'points' with which to keep score and boast about in TheHackerNews, HackForums and Reddit. Fifty points, in this case, for leaving a backdoor in place and exiting cleanly.

Dan cracked his knuckles and put fingers on keyboard. Time to get down, get in and get out.

64

Wang Wei's phone beeped at him. He was out at dinner with his partner Barry and was enjoying a 'Trucker' burger and a ginger beer at *Burgastronomy* in North Adelaide. The particular beep meant it could only be one thing—a computer intruder alert at work. The AI system he'd had installed was working silently in the background to make sure that it monitored any penetration attempts, then recorded, traced and thwarted.

Wei looked at the report of the in-progress intrusion. So far, nothing had been accessed other than the top level of the system. A deft program planted, which would be deleted once the intruder exited.

Wei shot back a request to the AI program to save the planted program for further analysis; he thought his new friends at SAPOL would no doubt like to find out more about this hack, seeing as they are already investigating one of his company's properties.

He went back to his burger. The AI program would take care of things, he thought. He'd get a full report once the intruder had left empty-handed.

65

Dan accessed Anthol's computers easily enough. A few extra hoops he had to jump through, but nothing he wasn't prepared for by D@@Mladen's training. And he'd planted the backdoor securely in place where no one would think to look. That was his total mission for this trip. Get in, place a backdoor, get out. No looking at files and spending precious time when there was more important work to be done. Quick and easy. Time to go back on the weekend when no one would be around. On Saturday he'd have a wander around, find some HR files to download, some possible mischief to create. But not tonight. Tonight was all about staying in control, of being tight, lean, focused.

Dan logged out of his systems and leaned back in his chair. Tonight was good. Sharp. Cut.

Of Power and Patience. Strategic. All was good.

66

Stephanie McBride's phone buzzed at the same time as Rocco's—it was the AI algorithm from Anthol Logistics calling with a report.

She checked it; intrusion in progress, intruder recognised from their movements as probably the same intruder that broke into Derringerry, no location could be traced closer than 'within South Australia'. One program deposited, now quarantined. All systems and files mirrored and protected so that further intrusions would just find dummy empty files with the original file names.

This artificial intelligence program is very clever, she thought. As an aside, Rocco thought the same thing. It was certainly going to revolutionise the game, they both thought.

Stephanie made a mental note to arrange a time to meet with Wei again, soon, to find out what more could be uncovered or predicted from the algorithm. In fact, she told herself, there was no time like the present.

WEI, CAN WE GET TOGETHER AND DISCUSS THE IMPLICATIONS OF THIS, PLEASE? IS TOMORROW TOO SOON FOR YOU? STEPHANIE MCBRIDE.

HI STEPHANIE. WHAT ABOUT TOMORROW AT 10?

THANKS, WEI. UNFORTUNATELY, I'M IN COURT TOMORROW MORNING. DO YOU HAVE TIME LATE AFTERNOON?

4.30?

I'LL BRING COFFEE AND ROCCO. THANKS.

SEE YOU THEN.

Possibly the same hacker that hacked into Derringerry, she thought. Who did she have as suspects for that case? Oh yes, a computer geek living in Meningie by the name of Dan Robinson. No evidence other than he's the local computer geek and is best mates with someone sacked from the farm. So there's a motive, sure, but is there enough to pull him in and have a chat? And read the riot act to him? Why not?

If only her workload permitted a meeting with Mr

Robinson soon, but she was bogged down with cases and court appearances. Even with her ability to double the productivity of her colleagues, she was still under the pump. A four-hour round trip to Meningie, for a ten-minute chat, was not the most efficacious use of her time at the moment. Sure, she could video-chat her interview with Mr Robinson via the police station in Meningie and her office on South Road, but in her experience face-to-face was far superior an interviewing technique.

It looked like she was going to have to devote some extra time at home to solving some of her outstanding cases. 'No chilling with Gene Hackman, Will Smith and *Enemy of the State* for me tonight'.

67

It was their weekly catch-up video meeting.

'There's been a lot happened since we last spoke,' Dan said.

'Really? What's gone on?' Hanna asked.

'Well, I took your advice and didn't tell Davo about the HR files. I didn't tell him about hacking in again at all.'

'Good, that's a wise decision.'

'I also met up with my hacking mentor, which was good. But weird. Confusing.'

'How so?'

'Well, she said she wanted to meet up to talk about hacking and my progress and stuff. Regular stuff. Which is good of her and I appreciate it. But at the end of the call I felt like I'd been flirting.'

'Flirting? What did you say?'

'Something regular, like she said, 'I look forward to seeing you,' and I replied, 'me too', or something. But I ended the call feeling definitely flirty.'

'Well, it doesn't sound particularly flirty. Did she flirt back?'

'No, she ended the call after I'd spoken. I don't know women at all well, was she flirting?'

'Well, women flirt in mysterious ways, Dan. Sometimes not saying anything is flirting. Just a look can be an act of flirting. Did she smile coyly when she ended the call?'

'I dunno. What's 'coyly'?'

'With a sort of half-smile, maybe with her head turning away but her eyes looking at you.'

'No, not that I remember.'

'Well, I guess you'll find out when you meet up with her. I know, as soon as you meet up with her demand to know if she was flirting with you. Insist that she gives you an answer. That will win her over and make the meeting go smoothly.'

'Ha ha. You know, I will try that out, see how more smoothly the meeting goes. "So, D@@Mladen, do you want a piece of me, huh?"'

'She'll melt right into your arms and sigh.'

'Ha ha ha. Hey, I found a new saying this week and thought of you: "He said there was no spark between us anymore. So I tasered him. I'll ask him again when he wakes up".'

'That's a classic. I'm grateful that there's still a spark between Carlo and me. It helps me get through the long days of just me and the girls.'

'Is it draining being on your own?'

'Yes, very much so. Plus, it's hard on the girls, they don't see Carlo until the weekend. But I'm also grateful he plays with them a lot on the weekend. He's a great dad.'

'I've never really had a girlfriend, so can't imagine what it's like to be married. It must be comforting, I guess.'

'Oh, yes, comforting. And warm. And funny. And infuriating. And bad-tempered. And sometimes shouty. But the nicest bit, I guess, is the commitment to be with your best friend for the rest of your life. To raise children and together experience all the highs and lows that life dishes out. It is special. But you've never had a girlfriend? What, ever?'

'Well, there were a couple of pashes and fumbles with Rebecca Stoneham in Year 11, but nothing apart from that, no. There's not a lot of single girls down here. Everyone pairs off early and all that's left are the rejects like me.'

'Oh, Dan, that's so sad! You're not a reject. I think you're lovely. I enjoy being your friend.'

'Thanks, and that's mutual. But the only women I see these days are my mum, my friend Kelly, and the employees I work with for my clients. Oh, I had a couple of one-night stands when I was in the Air Force.'

'You were in the Air Force? Did you fly planes?'

'Ha ha. That is the most asked question whenever I mention I was in the RAAF. No, I didn't fly planes. I was a clerk, pushing paper and emails around.'

'Where were you based?'

'Melbourne for two years, then Perth for two years, then back to Melbourne.'

'How long were you in the Air Force for?'

'Six years. That was my initial contract. I could have served longer, but I didn't like what the service life did to people. You become hard right-wing, ultra-conservative, narrow-minded. And you end up relying on drugs and drink to cope with days that aren't anything special. So I left after six years and ended back in Meningie, living at my mum's and trying to build a life as an IT guru.'

'Did you do drugs while in the RAAF?'

'Oh yeah, all the party drugs. One of my mates knew someone in Customs who seized all the drugs that came in on flights. She used to siphon off stuff and sell it to my mate at knock-down prices. I think they had a thing going on and that's why he got them so cheap.'

'That's amazing. What a life you've led, young Dan!'

'Do you want to know the second most asked question I got asked when I was serving? "You're in the Air Force? I know someone in the Air Force. Joe Bloggs, has something to do with planes. Works in Queensland. Do you know him?"'

'Seriously, people asked you that?'

'Questions like it, yeah. "There's only 22,000 people in the Air Force and I know most of them, but Joe Bloggs escapes me, sorry."'

'Ha ha. But what of these one-night stands in the Air Force? What happened there?'

'Well, after too much drink and drugs, you're all loved up and thinking that everyone is beautiful. Twice I ended up going back to the same girl's place. But it was all very difficult the next morning, coming down and all. She was a clerk too; I'd seen her around and to be honest not thought anything of her. She certainly didn't attract me. But add drink and drugs to the mix and anyone is a movie star. You ever done drugs, Hannah?'

'Me? No. My dad is a cop, and I was given big lectures on drugs all the time. It scared me hearing about what they did to people, aged them, ruined their health, their teeth, their looks, and so on. I guess it was the looks that scared me the most. I wasn't the most attractive girl in my class and I needed to stay as good looking as I could if I was to hope for a date with one of the 'A' league boys, ha ha.'

'I don't do drugs now. Can't afford them and not interested in the party life anymore. But I'm partial to a beer. Never went in for fancy wines and stuff. I had mates in the RAAF who joined wine clubs and such; they were always boasting about their cellars. Me, I'm happy with a Coopers Pale Ale. Or a Stella.'

'I haven't drunk since I fell pregnant, and I was never a big drinker, anyway. One of dad's friends worked in the sexual crimes unit; she told me stories of rape and torture that made me never want to lose control of my body and my words. All in all, I had a boring teenage life, ha ha.'

'Truly, you didn't miss much. Getting off on drugs and drink is great while you're in it, but it's as boring as all fuck for anyone watching. And there's the hangover the next day to deal with, of course. I tried Tequila one night at a party. Loved it. Drained nearly half a bottle. Everybody was so pretty. Hugged my toilet hard that night, and it took me a week to get over it. Probably should have gone and had my stomach pumped at hospital, the recovery would have been quicker.'

'Yes, I remember teenage parties where certain girls and boys would get all drunk and silly. The girls would get all flirty, think that they were fashion models, and end up sliding off chairs and down walls onto the floor. The boys would all think they were hard men, start swearing a lot, and stagger all over the house we were in, holding on to furniture. I don't think I missed anything.'

'Now that we're older we know better, hey?'

'Ha ha. Too right. I'm glad Carlo's not a big drinker. Just a quiet beer when he comes home from work, a couple of glasses of wine with dinner on the weekend. He's not a big drinker. Wouldn't be with him if he was. Hey, I was wondering, have you been committing any criminal offences lately?'

'As a matter of fact, I have. I had a few visits to local companies to test out their systems, which was fun. And I hacked into the company that owns the farm where Davo used to work. I've not done any damage yet, but on the weekend I'll go in and have a nosy around.'

'Oh, Dan. You do worry me that you'll get caught, you know.'

'I know. But I've been checking everywhere for capture programs and so far, touch wood, there's been nothing to cause anybody any concern. You'd be surprised how easy it is to break into some companies' computer systems and do damage. Really. I'm astonished myself at how insecure and ripe for exploitation most Australian businesses are.'

'Aren't we always being told to be careful with our data, not to give our passwords out, and so on? There's always some IT guru in the press going on about it.'

'Yeah, it seems that way, doesn't it? But I think individuals are more clued up on this than businesses. Businesses just connect their computers to the internet and expect things to be secure. And they're not. It truly has been easy for me to go wandering in various businesses systems. If I wanted to, I could do all sorts of damage—wipe hard drives, corrupt databases, sell passwords and personal data. It's just too easy.'

'Well, don't go doing those things. That's not the Dan I know. Oh, listen... the girls are waking up early after their nap. I've got to go. Catch you in a week?'

'Love to. No doubt I'll have more tales to tell of Australian computer systems.'

'I hope not. But I'll catch you anyway. Bye.'

'Bye.'

Dan is still hacking into companies.

He told me he was in the Air Force, and that he's never had a girlfriend. Wow, that's amazing. I know some of my school friends have gone on to have careers without getting caught up in relationships. Some of them seem happy. That's not the life I'd want to lead, but good on them if they're happy. I don't think Dan is particularly upset by not having a girlfriend.

68

'Thanks for seeing us again, Wang Wei. Here's your coffee.'

'Thanks. Let's go up to the boardroom, it's free this afternoon.'

Wang Wei had hooked up his laptop to the big display array in the boardroom, and it was currently showing the *Evie* data that the latest report was derived from.

'Here's the entry time, the server the intruder hacked into and the path they took.'

'I see,' said Stephanie. 'They weren't in for very long, were they?'

'Just two minutes,' added Rocco.

'That's right. Long enough to have a quick look around and to deposit this.' Wei opened up a window showing program code. 'A backdoor payload. All the intruder would have to do next time was execute the code and they would, in the old days, be free to wander the corridors of power.'

'And these days?' asked Rocco.

'Free to wander a spoof server with empty dummy files. As soon as *Evie* recognises them as an intruder, she funnels them off to the virtual server. They see lots of filenames, but all the documents and folders are empty of real data.'

Rocco let out a low whistle. 'Impressive.'

'We think so, that's one of the reasons we invested in *Evie*.

'So, your intruder of yesterday got in, left a backdoor, and got out again. Did they leave any trace of who they were?' asked Stephanie.

'I installed *PenalTee*, as you suggested,' replied Wei. 'It could only narrow the pings down to south-east South Australia, I'm afraid. I'm confident enough in its assessment to believe that we're not dealing with a foreign invasion but a home-grown opportunist. Other than that, they were careful enough to wipe their feet and hands as they entered and left. There was nothing left for us to find.'

'Damn,' said Stephanie.

'That's what I thought. So I've asked *Evie*'s developers to run their track and trace code earlier in the process, as soon as the intruder enters. This means that *any* access of the servers is tracked and traced, tying up further resources in the clouds, but the payoff is we get to see who is knocking on our front door before they enter and potentially start causing damage. As *Evie* learns over time who is who—who the legal regulars are, who the illegals are—the pull on resources will be less and less.'

'*Evie*'s report said that the intruder was possibly the same one that accessed the Derringerry farm,' Stephanie said.

'That's right. If you look at this window, here..., you'll see that the timing was the same, three minutes past seven pm, and there were similar patterns in how long files were interrogated. At that stage, *Evie* was less sophisticated than she is now, and she couldn't funnel the intruder off to a dummy server. So our intruder then got access to files that would be impossible now.'

'From memory, a payroll file,' commented Rocco.

'That's right. And in a subsequent hack, a folder of HR files,' Wei answered.

'There is a finger of suspicion, Wei, that a gentleman from Meningie is involved. There's no evidence, yet, but we will have a chat with him shortly, to see if he can help us with our enquiries,' said Stephanie.

'That would be good,' Wei said, 'we had to do a fair bit of work to protect the servers and files at the farm from any further intrusion. I gather the HR files are sensitive because of some personnel issues from a few years back. The payroll file was re-inserted into the farm's filing system, but it was unchanged. Still, it's confidential information and employees have a right to feel their pay and banking information is secure.'

'Absolutely. Okay, I think that is all we need at the moment, Wei. Thanks very much for seeing Rocco and I at such short notice.'

'My pleasure. I hope your chat with Meningie Man works out for the good of all. I'll walk you down to Reception.'

69

The next day, lunchtime.

'Fancy a pizza for lunch, Rocco?'

'Sure, if you're buying.'

'Ha, ha. Of course I'm buying, Rocco. What do you fancy?'

'A "meat lovers". Where are you getting the pizza from?'

'Oasis in Torrensville. They do great pizzas, and they deliver.'

'I'll have a look at their menu, boss.'

'Good idea.'

Two minutes later, Rocco placed his order with her. 'A small "mix meat" and a can of Coke, please. It's the "Small Classic Pizza" offer.'

'Certainly.'

'What are you having, boss?'

'I'm buying a medium sized mix meat pizza, and we're sharing. You'll still get your Coke, and I'll have one of their Coke Coffee cans.'

'Do you like Coke with coffee, boss?'

'I'm partial to it now and then. I've been exercising a bit more at home recently, so I reckon I've earned some syrup, don't you?'

'Whatever you says, boss.'

'You run another check for D@@Mladen for me, please, and I'll order the pizza and Cokes.'

'Sure. Running a check now. Nothing's coming up; he's been quiet recently.'

Stephanie McBride already knew. She'd run some checks last night while she wasn't sleeping, as much to satisfy her own curiosity as to check up on Rocco. 'Well, that's annoying, isn't it?'

Other than continuing her investigation into D@@Mladen, and delving deep into the internet habits of Rocco's extended family, Stephanie McBride had spent last night finishing off her reading of Lawrence Block's various series. She'd read all of his Tanner books and found them very 1960s, which was fair because that's when they were written. She'd read all the much darker Matthew Scudder, the ex-detective who grappled with alcoholism (Stephanie McBride had grappled with alcoholism as well, and won. Now it was she who was in control, not the alcohol). She'd thoroughly enjoyed the professional hitman Keller series, and laughed at gentleman burglar Bernie Rhodenbarr's antics. It was a Bernie book that had occupied her last night, *The Burglar Who Counted the Spoons*.

'Here's something that's just come in, boss. D@@Mladen is talking to someone called Vextant. Ever heard of them?'

'Can't say I have. Can you see what they're talking about?'

'No, it's encrypted. The logger just shows who is talking to who.'

'To whom, Rocco, to whom.'

'Whatever.'

'Can you try to crack the encryption for me? It would be handy to see what they're talking about.'

'Trying now, boss... Nope, nothing is working. I'll keep trying.'

'I'll run some checks on the latest suspect in our list, *Crackerjack*, and see if we can't get a fix on them, at least.'

'I've tried everything, boss. I can't crack their encryption.'

'Save a log file of the conversation, Rocco, and let the decryption software run overnight. In the meantime, can you run a background check on Vextant and let's see what that brings us.'

'Roger that, boss.'

'Thanks. Our pizza won't be long, and I've got another case from ACORN to interview. After lunch, we might go for another drive. Are you up for it?'

'Always, boss, always. Get me away from these awful chairs and tiny monitors.'

'I know what you mean.'

70

CHANCES LANE, UNLEY. YOU TURN OFF UNLEY ROAD RIGHT BY GREENHILL ROAD AND MAKE YOUR WAY DOWN CHANCES LANE UNTIL IRWIN LANE POPS OUT ON YOUR LEFT. HEAD DOWN IRWIN LANE AND PARK IN THE CARPARK NEXT TO NUMBER 34, ON YOUR LEFT. I'LL BE WITH YOU AT 9.30PM.

At 9.25pm Dan parked in the carpark, the only car there, and waited.

Bang on the dot of 9.30pm, a BMW R 1250 R Spezial motorbike pulled up, and the leather-clad rider pulled off their helmet to reveal D@@Mladen. She reached behind her and conjured forth a spare helmet. And so it was that Dan found himself riding on the back of a fast motorcycle for the first time in his life. He was holding onto D@@Mladen's waist while trying not to grip too tightly, but his nerves on being on the back of a bike that was going fast and weaving in and out of traffic were such that he probably gripped a little tighter than a gentleman should.

The ride was a quick one; ten minutes later D@@Mladen pulled to a stop at the Kensington Baseball Club, pulling the bike up the curb and onto the grass. They sat down facing each other. It was summer, there was no hint of moisture in the ground to stain their clothes—one less thing for Dan to have to explain to his mum when she next did the washing.

It pleased Dan that the journey was over, at least for now. He knew there'd be the return to his car in Unley to negotiate.

'Well, what do you think? The bike handles well, doesn't it?' beamed D@@Mladen.

'Yeah, I guess. I've never been on the back of a bike before.'

'Really? You've never ridden?'

'I had a 50cc mini bike when I was a kid, but I kept crashing into things and falling off. Bikes and I never really hit it off. Even push bikes seemed to conspire against me.'

'Ha ha ha. Well, that probably explains why you held on so tight and didn't lean into the curves and bends. I had to fight you for a while going around some of those corners.'

'I'm not surprised; I was a bit scared.'

'Well, that's very honest of you to admit it. Normally when I take my padawans for a spin, they are all shaky when they get off the bike but try to be oh-so-casual about it. They fail miserably. But enough of this small talk.'

She reached around to the satchel hanging off her back and pulled out a mirror, a razor blade, two ten-dollar notes and some white powder.

'Want some?' she asked.

His natural caution told him to say 'No, not anymore'.

But Dan was sometimes a pragmatist, especially when it was a mentor and an attractive younger woman doing the offering, so he calmly said 'Yes, but you first'.

D@@Mladen snorted a line of coke and passed the mirror over to Dan, who mimicked his mentor and then had a sneezing fit afterwards.

'Sorry about that,' he said, as he pulled a clean tissue from the pack in his trouser pocket.

'No problems,' said D@@Mladen, not wishing to smile at his discomfort. 'Plenty more where that came from'.

'You know, I always feel like a bumbling country idiot when I'm with you,' he said.

'Do you? I don't mean to intimidate. Sorry.'

'Oh, it's probably not anything you're doing. It's just me. I'm a country lad, raised around cattle and open spaces. You're a city girl, used to navigating through the twists and turns of city life. You can do things with computers that I can only dream of, if I even know what to dream. I mean, there's probably stuff you do with computers that it would never occur to me could be done. It's not in my world. You move in a totally different world from me. That world is intimidating for a country man, that's all. You're personally not intimidating. Well, except when you go too fast in traffic or take bends and corners at frightening speeds.'

'That's very honest of you, Vextant. Very insightful. I guess you're right—we do come from different worlds, and now you're trying to move into mine. But I have an unfair advantage. I've been here for a long time and have learned many tricks. You are just starting on your journey. Given enough time, you will one day appear magical to bored teenagers and wannabe hackers, I promise.'

She leaned forward and patted him on his knee.

'Now, tell me of your latest hack; how did it go?'

'Well, it was a really quick visit. I had the goal of going in just to leave a backdoor for a later, bigger look around. So I was in and out in five minutes. *Metasploit* and *Cane & Abel* showed me a path into the system, and since the server was Windows, it was all pretty straightforward to navigate. I downloaded nothing this time, just left a backdoor.'

'That's very good, Vextant. You weren't tempted to have a wander around and maybe find something juicy?'

'No, I remember your words about having a goal and keeping things tight, so I just got in, planted my backdoor, and got back out again. All the while, keeping an eye out for any telltale software that might be tracking my presence. I saw nothing.'

'That's impressive learning. I'm very pleased to hear that you didn't go off on a fishing expedition to find hidden treasure, but instead stuck to the script and played it safe. Well done.'

'Thanks. I'll make a hacker out of myself yet.'

'Oh, you're already one of those, Vextant, I'm pleased to say. I just want to make sure you stay a free one, not a caught one. That's my goal. Now, time for more training for you. Let me show you something.'

She again reached into her satchel and pulled out an 11-inch notepad, fired it up and scooted her bum next to Dan so she could show him her screen while she worked her magic.

'See here, Vextant, what you are about to be trained on is a chess move. Servers on the big players come with various stages of access. It's not just one simple hack in and Bob's your uncle, there are levels that you have to pass through to get to the juicy stuff. The juicier the material, the deeper the level and the harder to break in. With me so far?'

'Yep. Are you sure I'm ready for this advanced stuff?'

'Oh, yes, I'm sure. I wouldn't be sitting next to you in the middle of a baseball diamond if I wasn't, would I?'

'I dunno, you could have strange tastes.'

'Ha ha ha. Well, there is nothing wrong with my tastes, country padawan. Now, listen up and pay attention. You use your normal tools to break into the first few layers, that's easy enough, but when you get deeper, you have to watch closely what you're doing because there are landmines and tripwires deliberately planted in the deeper levels, set to go off if you make a false move. Now, I've planted some landmines on my server for you to try to avoid. Take the notepad and try to get as deep into my company as you can.'

'Blimey, these keys are so small! How do you type on them?'

'Ha, that's because I have delicate lady fingers, Vextant, not the hulking great mallets for fingers that you have. No wonder you have a 17-inch laptop.'

'Well, I use the number keypad a lot, and they usually only come on 17-inch laptops. But I'll try typing with my fingers on tippy-toes.'

'Good, that's good ergonomics. Your typing teacher would be pleased to hear that, I bet. Now, shut up and concentrate, this is serious business.'

'Yes, *mein General*.'

For several minutes Dan worked hard to log in to D@@Mladen's server. Eventually, he found a username and password combination that gave him access. To level one.

'In, at last,' he said.

'Good, now look around and try to find something which leads you to believe there are hidden gems awaiting your deft touch.'

'Here's something,' he eventually declared. 'Now, I'll just use some password crackers to get behind that firewall.'

That wasn't so easy, but, eventually, he found a combination that let him in.

'Ha! The next level.'

'Well done, Vextant, that only took... six minutes. That's an encouraging time, but also a little slow. You need to speed up your tools.'

'How do I do that? I was working as hard as I could.'

'You need to take your safety brakes off. Take off your training wheels. Go into your password crackers and turn off the monitoring settings. They're only there for newbie hackers to read back over the log files and see how long it took them to crack a password. If you turn them off, your password crackers will go faster, trust me.'

'I do, so I shall.'

'Now, find the next portal and try your password crackers again.'

'On it.'

This time he felt the software go faster, he could feel it in his bones. Maybe, he mused to himself as the software did its thing, maybe he could be cut out for this hacking business. Especially with a mentor like D@@Mladen teaching him the ropes. He felt a surge of power again, like when he was hacking the farm and Anthol Logistics for real.

He also felt a tingling in his groin.

'Into level three,' he triumphantly announced, 'and the password software was going faster this time, I could feel it.'

'Good. Now, hunt around for some stuff that might be worth a look. Tell me what you see.'

'Well, there are some log files, a folder with some images in, let's see, a folder saying 'HR'; let's go in there and have a look.'

No sooner did he click on the folder to open it than his screen started flashing red at him.

'What the...! What's happened now?'

'Ahhh, Vextant. You've tripped a tripwire and set off an alarm. You'd best make your way back to level one and exit as quickly as possible.'

'Bloody hell!' he exclaimed, as he feverishly back-tracked and attempted to get out before he could be trapped inside, and his whole cyber presence captured, analysed and traced. Thankfully there were no audio signs of his dilemma, no sirens or alarms ringing out through the laptop's speakers. That would have woken up the neighbours.

'Out!' he finally shouted, sweat on his forehead and the palms of his hands.

'Good. Well done for getting out so quickly. But not well done for triggering the alarm in the first place. Do you know what you did wrong?'

'No. What did I do, or didn't do?'

'The folder you clicked on was not a folder at all. It was a .exe file masquerading as a folder.'

'That's a mongrel trick, how did you do that?'

'How doesn't matter now. What matters now is the learning you gained from this. What did you learn?'

'I guess that I shouldn't trust everything I see to be what it says it is.'

'Very good, that's exactly the lesson. That, and always make sure you can get out as quickly as possible, cleaning up as you go along. The last thing you want to do is leave trails of your existence in the system. Better to get out and try again later when you have gotten over the adrenalin rush of alarms going off. And also note this: servers don't always hide alarm programs like this one. They can hide tracers, ping bots, programs that trigger your webcam, all sorts of nasties. Which is why you should always tape a piece of paper over your webcam when you're out playing around in someone else's garden.'

'Strewth! I never even thought that you could disguise a program to look like something else. How do you know I haven't been recorded hacking into the farm, or Anthol?'

'Because I went in with you when you went into the farm, hiding, if you like, in your footsteps. I didn't see anything to cause any worry. But I can't be piggy-backing into your territory every time, Vextant. That's why tonight I wanted to warn you of the dangers out there and prepare you to face them.'

'Thanks. But it's scared me a bit.'

'That's good, it was supposed to. You need to keep your wits about you when you go off hacking. Tonight you got a good reminder that you can never be too careful. And from what you've told me tonight, I know you'll keep that lesson close to your heart.'

'Indeed, I will. And thanks again. Strewth, I feel that I've just jumped into a bigger league, but that I'm unprepared for it.'

'You have jumped into a bigger league. Your successful expedition into Anthol was proof that you are ready to play a bigger game. But with the increased thrill and excitement comes an increased necessity for caution and vigilance. I trust that you are ready, otherwise I wouldn't have suggested we meet tonight.'

'Well, thanks for the vote of confidence. I'm still a little shell-shocked.'

'Understandable. Let's finish up here tonight and I'll take you back to your car. You have a lot to process on the drive back home.'

Five minutes later, after another snort of cocaine, Dan cautiously got onto the back of D@@Mladen's BMW and pulled his helmet on.

Ten minutes later he was back at his car. D@@Mladen cut the engine, put the bike up on its stand and pulled her helmet off. He got in his Corolla, started the engine and buttoned the driver's window down.

'Thanks for tonight,' he said.

'You're welcome,' D@@Mladen replied. Then she did something Dan didn't expect. She leaned into his car and kissed him on the mouth. Once, but firm. Like she meant it. No sooner had she done that than she pulled her helmet back on, swung her right leg over the bike, the engine roared to life and D@@Mladen raced off, leaving a bewildered Dan attempting to hold that kiss in his memory. What a night it had been for him. Eye-opening in so many ways. It was going to be a distracted and long journey home. And Dan knew from experience what cocaine did to the male sexual organs. It's why prostitutes hated clients who visited them all coked up.

71

'Are you ready, Rocco?'

'As I'll ever be, boss.'

Stephanie turned the car onto South Road and headed south, Rocco in the passenger seat, his laptop open and tracking the beeps and position of a hacker. The hacker went by the name of *Crackerjack* and he or she was easy to track. Stephanie guessed that they were new to the hacking game, from the beginner's mistakes they made.

Rocco had tracked *Crackerjack* in the dark web and noted where they hung out. Their conversations were often 'in the open', meaning they were unencrypted, which was a typical newbie mistake. So too were the tools they used—tools that were designed by the world's security services but 'sold' to the dark community's newest and most gullible members as the latest 'cool' toys, must-haves to 'beat companies at their own game'. The tools came with their own tracking devices built in, and it was child's play for security services like SAPOL to hitch a ride and capture a criminal, even if that criminal is a wet-behind-the-ears teenager.

So now Stephanie McBride and Rocco were tracking the physical location of *Crackerjack*'s computer as it moved from one suburb to another. All Stephanie had to do was find the car with the computer in, probably a laptop—although the rich kiddies were using pimped tablets these days—and make an arrest.

The average human being would have no chance of finding anyone with such pinpoint accuracy. GPS systems for the world user were accurate to around 50 metres, 20 metres on a good day. But the GPS that security services had access to could pick out a car in a carpark. Or, and as was pertinent to Stephanie McBride and Rocco, pick out one car driving on a road with many other cars around it.

So Stephanie McBride drove, Rocco navigated, and the two of them worked as a team to find out just how old *Crackerjack* was.

Crackerjack had used the gee-whizz tools to break into four companies so far. A construction company, where the access was used to search for accounts details that would enable *Crackerjack* to transfer monies to their bank account (they were unsuccessful). A retail shop where similarly no financial accounts could be found (they were hidden under a series of innocuous folder names). A plumbing supplies business where the accounts information was clearly labelled, but hidden under a password that *Crackerjack* couldn't break (using a password cracker that was also made by the same 'hackers' that made the access tools). And finally, a car rental company that allowed *Crackerjack* to rent out a Lexus sedan for nothing for a fortnight.

The rental company had the foresight to place Bluetooth trackers surreptitiously into the rear seat pockets of their cars, and it was this information, combined with the placement tracking information provided by the hacking tools, that enabled Stephanie McBride and Rocco to be so confident about the direction they were heading and the arrest they were going to make.

Except that as they were heading down south to the suburb of St Marys, Rocco's screen suddenly went blank and all connections with the SAPOL server and the tracking software were severed.

'*Fanculo questo!*'

'What is it, Rocco?'

'The laptop's died on me. I have power, but no screen.'

'Can you fix it?'

'I'll try.'

'I'll keep driving.'

But despite him powering the laptop down and back up again, repeatedly, the screen refused to work.

'It's no use, boss. The laptop's dead.'

'Damn. Okay, we'll head back to the office and get another one. We may still be quick enough to catch *Crackerjack* out driving.'

Meanwhile, across town, D@@Mladen smiled and again gave thanks to the hacking gods that allowed her to gain access to the very laptop that Rocco had been using. A simple bit of code and Rocco's laptop was completely disabled. Sure, it could be fixed, but only by re-installing Windows over a wiped hard drive. 'That should slow them down for a little while,' D@@Mladen said to no one there. 'And they'll think it was just a hardware failure.'

72

'G'day, Hannah.'

'G'day handsome. How're things? Do you have a joke for me?'

'Sure. Interviewer: "How would you describe yourself?" Me: "Verbally, but I have also prepared a dance".'

'That's funny. How's your week been?'

'Good. Well, good and certainly interesting. Want to know more?'

'Ooh, do tell!'

'Well, remember we were talking about my mentor last week, and how I felt that flirting had gone down in our last web video, but that I was unsure of who was flirting, D@@Mladen or me?'

'Yes, I remember. So what happened at your meet up?'

'*Well!* All went okay. She picked me up on the back of her motorbike and then proceeded to try to kill me by racing through the suburbs of Adelaide, weaving in and out of traffic, and taking corners at insane speeds. We ended up at a baseball diamond somewhere, where we had a line of coke, and she got me to try out my skills on her server. I failed and set off some alarms, but she reckoned I still passed.'

'This doesn't sound flirtatious to me, Dan. But I'm nervous about the line of coke and where that might lead.'

'No need to panic, and it isn't flirtatious. So, we finished her schooling me, and we do another line of coke, and she dashes back through the suburbs of Adelaide to my car, with me on the back holding on for my life.'

'With you so far, but still not seeing the flirty bit.'

'Well, we turn up at the carpark, and I get in my car and wind my window down to say goodbye. Suddenly, she's whipped her helmet off and she's giving me a long, hard kiss. Then she whips her helmet back on and roars off on her bike.'

'Wow. Now THAT's flirty. What did you do?'

'Nothing I could do. By the time I'd recovered she had disappeared into the night, and I was left on my own, in my car, in an empty carpark late at night, with two lines of high-grade coke in me. It was a confusing drive home, that's for sure. I tried holding on to the muscle memory of the kiss, but it disappeared with the need to concentrate on driving out of Adelaide and onto the freeway.'

'Well, I certainly think your question about who was doing the flirting has been answered. Have you heard from her since?'

'No, not a word. Maybe she's off on some adventure somewhere. Or this is how she breaks in her pupils. Flirts with them to keep them interested in her, then plays with their emotions. I don't know. But I do know one thing: she's a good kisser. I'd be up for a second go if it were offered.'

'You won't know for sure. I'd keep an eye on her and keep something of myself in reserve if I were you, at least until she discloses more about herself. Don't go falling in love or anything. You'd just be falling in love with the idea of falling in love. Some silly romantic notion. I've seen it happen to friends of mine from school—they fell in love with a boy from school, or uni, and thought it was for real.

Three years into a loveless marriage, after a big expensive wedding her parents have crippled themselves paying for, they wonder what on earth ever happened. Don't go doing that, Dan, please.'

'Okay, I'll keep a watchful eye out. And it was only a kiss; we haven't been on a date or anything.'

'That's true. Well, young Dan, it has been an adventurous week for you. Anything else happening?'

'I've been helping Davo with IT training. I'm using the same manual I wrote for Deirdre, and after a slow start, he's making progress. Now that I know he's not the sharpest tool in the tool shed, my expectations are lower, but he's coming along fine. And speaking of Deirdre, she keeps surprising me with how quickly she's picking things up. She's turning into a nice little asset in her company. I got an email from my client the other day to thank me for what I've done, which was nice. I will have to write Deirdre another training manual, for the next level up.'

'That's fantastic, Dan. All that hard work with Deirdre has paid off. Can you do the same for any of your other clients?'

'Yeah, possibly one other. But they're only a new client, so I don't want to lay the hard word on them just yet. But I feel that my contact there is looking for another job. Nothing they've said, it's just a hunch. I've been known to have hunches turn out wrong. I'm not Mr One Hundred Percent with them, ha ha.'

'Well, you were right about the flirting, Dan, so I wouldn't be so quick to dismiss your intuition.'

'True. Hey, I just received a message from her. Let me read it... She wants to meet up tomorrow night, at some random carpark in some fast-asleep suburb. Should I go? What should I say?'

'I'd absolutely go. If she was only playing with you, she might not even mention the kiss. She might just want to train you up more. But you won't know if you don't go, as the saying goes. But I wouldn't reply straight away. That will make you look too keen. Leave it an hour or two before replying, Dan.'

'Okay. I'll wait awhile. But this is an interesting development, isn't it? And what if she wants to kiss me again? That would be exciting. Wouldn't it?'

'Easy, tiger. All you know is that she wants a meeting. It could be to apologise for the kiss, for leading you on, you don't know. And if it is because she wants to kiss you again, please remember what I told you about falling in love with falling in love. Don't rush headlong like an excited puppy. Be cool and calm and keep your shit together. Promise me?'

'I promise. Tell you what, do you sleep with your phone on silent?'

'No, why?'

'Because if you did, I'd text you after our meeting, to let you know what's going on. But I don't want to wake you in the middle of the night when you're fast asleep.'

'No, I'd appreciate not being woken up. Just text me the next day. But that's a lovely thought, Dan, thank you.'

The rest of the conversation was uneventful. Hannah repeated her concern about Angela and the passing of bipolar genes from mother to twin daughters. Dan, for his part, was distracted by the thought of meeting up with D@@Mladen once again. So the conversation drifted until Dan was forced to bring it to a close because of a phone call from a client.

Once more, after the video call, Hannah wrote in her Evernote journal.

His hacking mentor kissed Dan and Dan would like a repeat performance. His hunch about him flirting, or her flirting, turned out to be accurate. I warned him about the danger of falling in love too early, of loving the idea of love. At his age you'd think he'd know all this, but he's not had a girlfriend before and that makes him vulnerable.

If he and his mentor do get it on more seriously, where does that leave Dan and me? Will he need to keep our friendship up if he's getting his emotional needs met elsewhere? Will he gain a love interest and at the same time I lose a friend? He's been good for me, helping distract me from my sadness. Will I have to go back to relying on the fickle nature of social media for emotional comfort?

73

Dan crossed the threshold with ease. All of the training with D@@Mladen on her training server, and the growing experience he was building of hacking into companies for real was paying off. Businesses were getting easier to break into, finding and taking their accounts and payroll details was simpler than ever.

Dan felt a growing sense of achievement. He took pride in his work and the rewards of his intellectual efforts were accumulating, building up his self-esteem and letting him feel like he could 'do something' really well.

Dan paused outside the locked door of this particular head office's accounts department, gathered his breath, and applied his tools, one at a time, to picking the cyber lock.

At the same time, an operative from a Chinese syndicate did exactly the same thing. With only a modicum less care, because this was the seventh business the Chinese hacker had attacked on their shift today and they were tired. Hacking might look easy to an outsider, but hackers know how draining the business can be.

Dan breached the door and entered the room, taking care to look for false clues and fake files. Nothing looked out of place. He wanted to enter and exit quietly, not letting the business know there was anything to worry about until it was all too late and their bank rang them to say their account was empty.

The Chinese syndicate hacker also entered the room. Each was oblivious to the other. The Chinese hacker saw the payroll and accounts files and went to crack them there and then, rather than what Dan was doing, which was copying the files for later cracking and perusal. The Chinese hacker made a fatal mistake—they attempted to open a file that was not what it said on its filename. Both Dan and the syndicate hacker's computer screens lit up and webcams started snapping away.

Luckily for Dan, he'd ensured his laptop's webcam was covered with tissue paper. The Chinese hacker had covered up his webcam too, but in the excitement and the movement of the hacker's laptop it slipped from its place and exposed the hacker. Which angered them when they realised what had happened.

Dan's ego did, however, get the better of him and so he

left a calling card, in the shape of a text file, in the room where all the excitement was going off. He felt invincible and wanted to have a little brag about how good he was. D@@Mladen would have been furious, if he ever told her.

Dan thought rapidly about the wisdom of leaving a calling card when alarms were going off, and deleted it from the server, but not before the Chinese hacker had seen and opened it.

'THESE FILES HAVE BEEN ACCESSED BY VEXTANT. SOUTH AUSTRALIAN BORN AND BRED.'

The Chinese hacker believed that it was Dan that set the alarms off, because that text file wasn't there when they first entered the room. The file only briefly appeared before the alarms went off. The name 'Vextant' and place 'South Australia' bore into the hacker's brain as both the hacker and Dan made their way quickly out of the business' server and shut down their own laptop to kill any traceable connections.

Once the adrenalin had worn off, the hacker gathered their thoughts and pointed their browser to the dark web. Who was this 'Vextant', they wondered, and what punishment can be inflicted upon them?

The hacker left a message in a forum for Dan:

'VEXTANT. YOUR STUPIDITY ON A SERVER HAS CAUSED US PAIN. WE WILL FIND YOU AND EXTRACT PAIN IN RETURN. THE PHANTOM SYNDICATE.'

74

The workload was insane. More cases of cyber-hacking than anyone could keep up with. It was as though the hacker world had decided that South Australia, and South Australian companies, were the *fruit du jour*.

Stephanie McBride had been in touch with an Adelaide-based colleague in the Australian Federal Police, Detective Tony Gregson, and the situation there was just as rough. And, according to Tony, it was replicated in all the States. Australia was, for some reason, a popular destination for hackers at that moment. Everyone in law and enforcement was stretched to breaking point. ACORN was taking record numbers of reports from the general public.

The Australian Cybercrime Online Reporting Network (ACORN) was a national policing initiative of the Commonwealth, State and Territory governments. It was a national online system that allowed the public to report instances of cyber-crime; it also provided advice to help people recognise and avoid common types of cyber-crime. Reports came in, then it was up to the individual police forces in each State and Territory to chase and follow-up the information. The AFP took the big cases involving the larger multinationals, and the smaller corporate clients were handled by the States and Territories where those companies were headquartered.

When you added in the workload created by mums and dads who feared their bank details and credit cards had been hacked, you had a tsunami of cases to be attended to.

Each new day brought Stephanie a new batch of cases to be processed—the trivial and the not-so-trivial, the anxious grandparents, the equally concerned mortgage-struggling parents, and the twenty-somethings still living at home.

And so it was that Stephanie came to work, just like any Thursday, a little after eight-thirty in the morning. She had no idea that her world would be rocked.

Rocco slid into his chair just after nine, then slid out again as he did the usual Thursday coffee and bun run to Vili's bakery. Every alternative Thursday was payday for Stephanie and her colleagues in the police force, and to celebrate the milestone Stephanie organised a coffee and bun run each and every Thursday. Before Rocco had arrived as her 'project' she would collate the orders and email them down to the café. Rocco took that role on, at first begrudgingly, but as the discomfort of the office chairs and small monitors became more apparent, with growing approval and anticipation. It was always a nice walk in the sun to the café, and the café staff made sure everything was labelled and marked so that no-one's orders were mixed up when he got back.

This particular Thursday Rocco was down at the café picking up his order when one of the staff started staring at the tv set on the wall. It was a terrorist incident going down live in Melbourne.

Rocco watched for a couple of minutes while nothing happened, a stand-off between police and the terrorist, or terrorists, no-one could say, at a breakfast-serving restaurant when all of a sudden a mighty explosion shook the reporter's camera with its force, and smoke and debris shot out of the front of the building. The tactical police then swarmed the building, poured inside and shots could be heard.

Rocco put down his order and dialled Stephanie's number.

'Boss, it's me. There's a terrorist incident in Melbourne, it's on tv. Channel 7.'

Stephanie called up Channel 7 in a browser window and plugged in her headphones, catching the live feed.

'Hey, everybody! There's a terrorist incident in Melbourne. Channel 7 has a live feed on their website!'

The website interspersed their coverage of the incident with highlights of the explosion so that no-one would miss out on the excitement.

After the explosion, there was a calm, then paramedics rushed in. Several tactical police officers walked slowly out of the restaurant, faces still covered with goggles and heads-up displays. Stretchers made their way in, and after many minutes they made their way back out, each occupant supposedly still alive, because there was no sheet covering them, but no indication of how light or serious their injuries were. And there was no walking wounded, at least not yet. More and more stretchers went in, and more and more injured bodies came out. Ambulances were lining up down Swanston Street.

The television station news talking head was reporting that the police had said there were no deaths at this stage and that all the terrorists had been disarmed and were 'helping police with their enquiries' at the scene. However, the police did say that several restaurant patrons had probably sustained critical injuries because of their proximity to the explosive device when it was triggered. The reason for the terrorist attack was at this stage unclear.

Stephanie removed her headphones and turned to look at her colleagues. Another terrorist incident, again in Melbourne. Always Sydney and Melbourne, she wondered aloud. Why not somewhere else?

She received no reply to her rhetorical question. Instead, an office full of shocked, blank faces, men and women who were committed to righting the wrongs of crime and who currently had no answers to their own questions.

Oh well, she thought. Time will provide answers. Right now, I need to focus on what I can do, which is bringing criminals like D@@Mladen, *Crackerjack* and two score more to heel.

Rocco returned with lukewarm coffees and started handing them out.

'Rocco, let's go for a drive and track down *Crackerjack*. They've been at it again, this time with a clothing company.'

'I'm with you, boss.'

'Is that laptop in good condition?'

'They gave me a brand new one, boss, how's that?'

'Outstanding, Rocco! You must have done something right with the gods who look after computer requisitions.'

'Ha ha. The girl behind the counter couldn't resist me, boss.'

'That would be it, Rocco. There are days when I have to hold myself back.'

'Ha ha. You crack me up, boss.'

'I try, Rocco, I try.'

75

In the carpark, Stephanie McBride's white police-issued SUV awaited her. She was walking from the back door of the office building to her car, with a young Italian man to her side. Rocco was dressed in a smart Jack London narrow-trousered pale grey summer suit, thin tie, crisp white shirt that his mamma had ironed with love. Stephanie was dressed in a navy-coloured scalloped broderie dress with grey ankle boots. They made a dashing mother-and-son-ish couple.

Stephanie beeped the car open, and Rocco took his place, keeping the laptop open. He plugged the computer's power cable into the power inverter. The Bluetooth tracker that the car rental company had put into their Lexus revealed their target vehicle to still be in Blackwood. Stephanie put the car in Drive and headed out onto South Road.

'Boss, don't you come from Melbourne?'

'Yes, I do. Why's that?'

'Oh, I was just wondering about that terrorist bombing. If you were still in Melbourne could youse have been caught up in it?'

'No, Rocco, I lived out at Geelong and worked in Spencer Street. I was nowhere near that restaurant.'

'That's good. I mean, I feel sad for all the people who've been injured today, but I'm glad that you couldn't have been one of them.'

'Oh, Rocco, that's very sweet of you, thank you. But no, I would have been safe.'

'The Lexus is on the move, boss. Heading out east.'

'Keep watching and let me know if you get any definite idea where the car is going.'

'Upper Sturt Road, heading towards... Crafers.'

'We'll double back and take Anzac Highway to the freeway. That will get us there quicker.'

'Why don't you put the flashing lights on, and sirens and stuff?'

'Because the car doesn't have any, Rocco, and I'm not licensed to drive a car over the speed limit. Just because I'm a cop doesn't mean I get to play with all the fun stuff.'

'Well, that sucks big time, boss.'

. . .

'They're into Crafers, boss. No wait, they've turned off and are heading into Stirling.'

'We'll be there shortly, Rocco. Good work.'

'Okay, they're in Stirling. Now they're heading south down Longwood Road. Any ideas where they could be heading?'

'No, I have no clue. They could be driving the hills to find a secure spot to meet up, or they could be visiting a mate. I hope we find out soon enough.'

'Stock Road, boss. Heading south-east into Mylor. Do you know it?'

'Only of it, Rocco. Apparently it's very pretty. Has a pretty oval and a good café. That's all I know.'

'Okay, they've slowed down. They've turned right into Lot 870. I'll Streetview it. Okay, it's a green two-storey house. The satellite says there's one other car there. '

'Well done, Rocco. We'll be there in five minutes.'

'Should we call for backup, seeing as how there's another car there?'

'Let's drive past first and see. No point calling up the fire brigade for a little fire we can stamp out ourselves, is there?'

'You're the boss. I just would hate to ruin this suit, that's all.'

'Well, Rocco, you've got to stay in the car anyway while I make my arrest. You can't be actively involved in it, otherwise the defence lawyer will tear our case to shreds.'

Stephanie slowed down when she approached Lot 870, but not so slow as to cause concern for anybody watching. But she ducked into the next driveway she came across, got out of the car, and headed up a fire track back towards the house where *Crackerjack* might be.

The house sat on a slight hill, next to a nature reserve, and blended in with its surroundings. In the driveway sat two cars, and one hidden from satellites under the carport. Two of the cars were cheap old bombs, the sorts of first cars teenagers buy to learn the ropes and smack into things. The third car was a crisp white Lexus LX, with the numberplate surround showing the rental company's name and phone number.

Stephanie turned around and made her way back to Rocco.

'Well, that's the car. The registration plate is the one the rental company gave us. Let's call for backup now, Rocco, and see if we can't nip this in the bud. If we do, I'll shout you lunch in Stirling.'

'Bloody brilliant, boss. I'll be up for that.'

Stephanie rang the Stirling station and explained her situation. A car, with two uniformed officers inside, was duly dispatched. They didn't waste any time.

Ten minutes later, they pulled up alongside Stephanie and Rocco in the driveway and planned their approach. 'Quietly, quietly' was the recommended tactic, and Stephanie and the two police officers, one male, one female, strolled casually up the fire track. The female officer stayed with Stephanie, while the male officer snuck around the back of the house.

Stephanie knocked on the front door. She heard movement, someone coming downstairs, but the door didn't open.

'Police!' yelled someone from inside and Stephanie heard them running through the house, probably to the back door.

Stephanie's female officer took a step back and landed a mighty kick on the door by the lock. The wood splintered, and the lock gave way, allowing both she and Stephanie to rush in, Stephanie taking the stairs to the immediate right of the door, and the uniformed officer to the interior of the downstairs area.

Upstairs Stephanie found a large rectangular common area, with sofas and chairs and a large tv. There were expensive prints on the plain cream walls and several pot plants. At either end of the rectangle were more doors, probably bedrooms. To go left or right, she thought. Which door do I go through first? Left, she decided and barged her way through the door into what appeared to be a teenage girl's bedroom. Neat, tidy, and no one there.

Back to the other room at the other end of the rectangle. If someone's in there, they would have had plenty of time to shut down their computer. Well, there was someone in the room, a teenage boy, and they did have a computer. A laptop. Which, by the time Stephanie had crossed the room to snatch it, was closed. Powered down. No matter, the computer's history would show what websites it had been looking at, what programs and documents had been recently accessed.

Sounds of struggle emanated from downstairs. Things being broken. Time to get this particular teenage boy downstairs and into some handcuffs.

The teenage boy in question didn't feel like doing that, and so a scuffle ensued. But Stephanie's training and superior position (standing up versus his sitting cross-legged on the bed) meant that his acquiescence was inevitable. With his arm twisted behind his back, Stephanie marched the boy down the stairs and eventually into a now-quiet kitchen. At another chair in the kitchen one other boy sat, and another boy stood, both watched over by the male police officer. The female officer called out from another room; she had a young man in custody. She also had a laptop, open and powered up.

The female officer brought the young man in and it struck Stephanie that this could well be *Crackerjack*. He was about Rocco's age; old enough to rent a car but young enough to still be in contact with teenagers who were 'enjoying' their school holidays. His laptop was still in the other room, and Stephanie retrieved it before the screen-saver locked her out.

The male uniformed officer called in to Mount Barker station, informing them they had the suspects in custody and would return shortly. The boys were rounded up and tied together so they couldn't escape. Once that was completed, the female officer and Stephanie headed back down the fire track to the waiting cars and Rocco. He'd heard the door being kicked in, but little else. That's because it was all over quickly; unfit teenage boys, no matter how many tough-guy movies they've watched, are never a match for fit, trained officers.

The two cars pulled into Lot 870's driveway, and this time Rocco was allowed to come into the house and see the suspects. He just chose not to. He claimed he had a headache and just wanted to sit quietly for a while. His real reason for not getting out was that he and *Crackerjack* knew each other, and he didn't want word of his work for SAPOL to filter down into hacker conversations. But that connection was nothing that Stephanie McBride need know about, he told himself.

The two officers adjusted the restraints and eased the three males into the back seat of their SUV. Stephanie closed the rear door and tapped the car on the roof. The male officer drove away, the female officer stayed to look after the house until the owners could arrive home to inspect the damage.

'Well, Rocco, sorry to see you're not well. You've gone a bit pale. Lunch another day, perhaps. Right now we have to sort out the evidence here, then get back to Keswick and plan the interview with a man I can only hope is *Crackerjack*, but who is most certainly the renter of a new Lexus SUV. That's at least according to the photo the rental company sent me of him.'

76

Having secured the evidence, Stephanie made her way into Stirling, to Ruby's Café in the main street. There, with a coffee in hand, she and Rocco sat at one of the outdoor tables and Stephanie made her next call. To a Mr Dan Robinson. But she hit voicemail. Stephanie left a message: would it be okay to meet Dan at his place of residence at ten-thirty in the morning on the following Tuesday? If so, could he call back on her mobile number?

It was a conversation she was looking forward to, if not the long drive down and back.

But an hour after Stephanie had successfully apprehended the younger man she hoped would be *Crackerjack,* she received a phone call on her private mobile.

'Mrs McBride, this is First Constable Rhonda Delaney from Melbourne. Do you have a son named Joshua?'

'Yes, I do, why?'

'I'm afraid I have bad news. Joshua was injured in a terrorist attack this morning. He is currently at The Alfred, where I understand he is in a stable condition. However, you are best advised to liaise directly with the hospital for the latest on his condition. I have a special number you can call.'

Minutes later, Stephanie had been in touch with the hospital and discovered that Joshua had multiple cuts and grazing, a perforated eardrum, concussion, burns and bruising to the groin, and a broken right tibia and fibula. His condition was stable, but he was resting and could not take a call. Additionally, he was unlikely to stay in the Emergency Department but would be moved to a ward shortly. Did he have private health insurance, Stephanie was asked. Indeed, he did. Then would Stephanie approve of moving him to a private bed at, say, The Royal Melbourne, at some stage? Indeed, she would. Good. When could he have visitors? Not for a little while yet. 'Give us a few hours'.

Stephanie rang her husband.

'James, Joshua was involved in the terrorist incident in Melbourne today. He's at The Alfred. He's okay, but he's not well enough to see anybody yet, so I can't send your parents or Matthew in to check up on him. He's got a broken leg and a perforated eardrum, plus some cuts and grazing. I'm coming home now. Can you pack my suitcase for me, please, and book me a flight? Thanks. No, I don't know how long I'll be back in Melbourne; as long as it takes for my boy to heal.'

<hr />

77

They met up as before, Dan waiting in his car in a carpark in some unlit back street, D@@Mladen keeping him guessing as to what she'd arrive in. To his dismay, it was the black BMW motorbike from before. And she was clad in skin-tight leather, as before. Only now there was a kiss between them. He hadn't imagined that kiss, and he couldn't just forget it either.

'Hop on,' D@@Mladen shouted above the engine.

But what if she's changed her mind? It had been a week since that kiss and no contact other than a message to be in a certain carpark at seven thirty at night. Earlier than he was expecting, it meant he hadn't had dinner yet. Perhaps this was a night of further instruction, where dinner was considered unnecessary. He hoped not; he enjoyed his food.

D@@Mladen weaved her way around the traffic of Adelaide, eventually heading out on Payneham Road to the north-eastern suburbs. Marden, Felixstowe, Glynde... the kilometres slid by.

Eventually, after twenty minutes, they pulled up outside a pizza bar in Athelstone, *Da Marios*, and strolled inside. Unpretentious décor, fluro lighting, tiled floor, big screen tv playing the highlights of some Premier League game.

'You're probably wondering what you're doing here in a pizza bar, Dan.'

'I figured you'd tell me when it was the right time to know.'

'Well, that right time is now. I asked you to meet me earlier than before because I figured you wouldn't have eaten. And I'm guessing eating is something you like to do.'

'I've been known to eat, it's true.'

'Good. Well, I got up earlier than usual today and I'm hungry too, so I figured we could come here and have a good pizza together. And they serve good pizzas.'

'Excellent. I rarely get pizza, there's no pizza shop in

Meningie, so I have to stay up in Adelaide after seeing a client. I usually get a takeaway and eat it on the drive home.'

'Great. So we both like pizza. That is a good sign. Here's the menu—what do you fancy?'

'Okay. Well, I'll have The Lot, with anchovies.'

'Good choice. I'll go and order.'

'No, I'll get it.'

'It's okay, Dan, you don't need to be chivalrous. Let the person with the bigger wallet pay this time. You can get the next one, okay?'

'Okay, if you insist.'

D@@Mladen returned with two glasses and a bottle of water.

'So, Dan, the reason I asked you to meet with me is... is...' she hesitated. 'I want to know how your hacking has been going.'

'Good, I think. I've been much more cautious and not randomly clicking on things because they look interesting. So far, as far as I'm aware, I haven't set off any alarms. I've not noticed anyone hacking me back, either.'

'That's good. Have you been able to put to good use the information you've found in your expeditions?'

'No, I haven't. I'm clueless how to make money out of my hacks. But I'm not sure what I want to achieve with my hacking. I don't have a big goal, like blackmail or accounts fiddling or anything. I did have a big goal once, and that was hacking the farm to make them pay for sacking my mate Davo. But now, I'm just enjoying the intellectual thrill of it all. I'm not looking to make any money.'

'Well, you don't have to make money. I have hacked into corporations and planted HR files and packages. That's what gives me a cool bike to ride and an X7 M SPORT to drive. Someone in Sydney will be mighty pissed off when that little hack comes to light. But I'll know about it before the cops find out and will take appropriate measures so that nothing comes back to bite me. You could upgrade your Corolla, Dan.'

'Nah, it would only trigger suspicion with mum. She'd wonder where I was getting enough money to buy a new car. My business is tidy and ticks over a small amount, but it would never turn over enough to see me in a new car.'

'Then stay as you are, there's nothing wrong with hacking for the sheer enjoyment of it. Test out the security systems of small businesses and then contact them to offer advice on how to beef up their security. You know enough now to go out as a security specialist.'

'That's a good idea, I like that. It's legitimate and fun at the same time. I get to hack into companies then tell them where they screwed up, for a fee.'

'You could make a tidy income from that, Dan. And, as you say, you could do it all legally. Enter into an agreement with the company first, hack their systems, then report back on what you found and advise them on how to stop others from breaking in.'

'If I hacked into a company, noted what steps I'd taken, would you help me put a report together? So I can send that report to the company?'

'Sure, thrilled to. Now, the pizza's arriving. Do you have any other questions for me before I stuff my face full of food?'

'No. I'm starving. I likely won't be saying much after right about now.'

After they'd eaten their fill, they filled in time with some small talk about building security, or the lack of it. D@@Mladen boasted that the SAPOL headquarters was so insecure she could shut everything down, the lifts, the security cameras, the security gates, as easily as Dan found hacking into Derringerry. As she said, their cyber building security was so lax, 'what do you tell a building, or a battery when you expect or are in the middle of a cyberattack? The truth is, they can't tell the building anything.'

Dan let D@@Mladen know he'd received a call from a SAPOL detective, wanting to chat, and that the detective would come down to Meningie. Dan explained he wasn't worried; D@@Mladen advised him to keep his wits about him and admit to nothing. It was probably routine and nothing to worry about. They both had another glass of water, then headed back out to the bike.

Dan was getting used to leaning into corners by now, making riding and steering less of a fight for D@@Mladen. He was still a nervous passenger, especially when she wove her way through traffic, but he was enjoying more and more putting his arms around her waist.

Eventually, they returned to the carpark where the evening had started and Dan hopped off and removed his helmet. D@@Mladen turned the engine off, pulled the bike onto its centre stand and slipped her helmet off too.

An awkward silence.

'Dan, about our last meeting.'

'Yes?'

'I meant what I did, I hope I didn't scare you.'

'Not at all. I was definitely surprised, but I loved it. I'd like to do it again.'

'So would I,' she said.

So they did. A bit more tenderly this time. Longer. A cuddle while they both stood and kissed.

'Dan?' she said, after they came up for air.

'Yes?'

'My real name. It's Emily. You can call me Emily from now on.'

'Okay, Emily. Thank you. My real name is, well you know. Dan. Short for Daniel.'

'Tonight was nice, I enjoyed it. Thank you, Dan.'

'My pleasure. Now, is there a chance of another kiss?'

'Just this once, Daniel,' Emily smiled.

So they did.

Now he definitely had an erection.

78

A small and quiet carpark, Mile End. The carparks of the big chain stores too open, too exposed and too monitored to be suitable for another rendezvous. So this carpark was smaller, with no monitoring, even from adjacent buildings.

At nine-twenty-five at night, Dan was waiting in his Corolla for Emily. Emily D@@Mladen. Well, if he had a goal for tonight, it was to find out Emily's surname.

It had been a fortnight since he last saw her. She had to go away, she explained, otherwise it would have been much sooner they saw each other again, she'd said in their brief online chat. He would let her explain her absence in her own time, he thought, in her own way.

He saw the lights light up the carpark before he saw the car circle around him, then pull up beside him. A sleek black Beemer, an X7 M SPORT according to the tailgate.

Dan got out of his car. 'Hop in' came the disembodied voice from over the rumble of the engine. He did.

'Sorry I'm late,' Emily said and leaned across to kiss him

full on the lips. 'There, that's better. I've been hanging out for one of those. Now, have you eaten yet?'

'Yes, I had a pizza at *La Scala* on Unley Road.'

'You didn't go out to Athelstone? To where we went last time?'

'No, and for two reasons. One, I knew it was a bit of a way out and I wanted to be near the city in case you changed the time, and two, I only want to go there with you. That's our little spot.'

'Oh, Dan, you ARE a romantic! That's so sweet! Well, let's make *Da Mario*'s our little hideaway then. Now, for right now, do you fancy a drink?'

'I could always go a beer, yes. I'm not really up for scotches and brandies and stuff.'

'Well, let's find a beer for Mr Romantic. How about the *Historian*?'

'That's a pub, I presume. Sounds good.'

'Well, the old *Harris Scarfe* car park is just about opposite, so parking is easy. Let's go.'

In a short while, Emily pulled into the car park entrance.

'I thought you'd stay clear of well-lit car parks, what with their cameras and stuff,' Dan said, surprised.

'Oh, this car park is a friend of ours,' Emily replied. 'The system they use to monitor the car park is old. I'll just go in and edit the feed later on so we were never there. Simples. Sometimes hiding out in the open is the best defence, Dan. It's where you would least be expected.'

After a short walk to the hotel, Dan was sitting happily with a cold Pale Ale, and Emily had a chilled glass of Sauvignon Blanc.

'I'm sorry it's been so long since last time,' Emily said, 'only I had to nip out of the country for a few days. I thought about sending you a message, to let you know, but I was part of something big, and there wasn't any downtime.'

'Really? Wow, that sounds exciting! What were you up to?'

'Do you remember I mentioned the hacker Syrus and the S-Collectif? It was for her.'

'Wow. I did some research after you mentioned her. She is really big time, isn't she?'

'Oh, yes, she is. So when I got an urgent message to meet her in Milan I dropped everything and hopped on a plane. I had no idea how long I'd be gone. I just took carry-on. I planned to buy any clothes I needed over there. As it was, we were staying in a large hotel, and there was a laundry service, which was handy because I only had three days' worth of clothes. We worked flat out, working, sleeping, working, for ten days. All to help separate a Saudi billionaire from his money.'

'Why? What had he done?'

'Another Saudi billionaire wanted his money and property. And probably his wives, for all I know. You know how some of those Middle-Eastern women can be phenomenally beautiful. Anyway, all was achieved. As far as we know. If the first billionaire had insurance against hacking, it could all have been for nothing. But it was fun to be part of. We had people following him on foot, following his wives and children, spiking his food and drink, sewing listening and tracking devices into his clothes. It was all a lot of high-pressure fun.'

'Strewth! I would have loved to be a fly on the wall.'

'Ha ha. You and countless police and intelligence services, Dan. It was a huge operation, and at the end everyone just disappeared like nothing had ever happened.

Vapour trails. To all corners of the world. I was flattered to be part of it.'

'I bet. And well compensated, I would think.'

'Oh, yes! I walked away with a million US dollars. I can't complain about that!'

'So the drinks are on you tonight, then?'

'Ha ha ha! Yes, and the parking. But tell me, what have you been up to while I've been away?'

'Well, not much. Some low-level hacking, for the sheer pleasure of it. And my business has kept me busy during the days with lots of phone calls and training going on. The business is expanding quite nicely. It's not too rapid a growth for me to handle, but it's busy enough for me to fall asleep at night exhausted. The money is handy, too, but it's nothing like what you earn.'

'Well, with more practice and experience, you could earn my sort of money too, Dan. But there's always a huge risk involved. If the cops ever got hold of me, I doubt I'd see the outside again for a quarter of a century.'

'Yeah, I'm not sure I could live with that level of stress.'

'Which brings me neatly to something I want to discuss with you. But first, kiss me quickly. There you go, thank you. Well, I've been thinking about you and a possible security consultancy gig. There's someone I know of, DesCrackr, who has a side business as a security consultant. He hacks into companies, steals their stuff, then approaches them to help them keep others like him out. It's quite a good little business he has going on. He's based in Sydney, so there's no direct competition if you stay out of Sydney. I could ask him to give you a hand setting up if you like.'

'That would be really kind of you, thank you.'

'I don't know him personally, but it can't hurt to ask.'

Just then, the chap serving the drinks called out, 'Last drinks.'

'One more, Dan, or would you like to come back to my place and have a drink? No pressure, I just thought, you know, maybe if you wanted to.'

'Sure. That would be nice. But can we go and get my car and I follow you to your place, please? That way, we don't have to worry about driving after you've had a drink at your place.'

'Makes perfect sense. Let's drink up and go.'

———

79

'This is nice,' said Dan, after he'd got out of his car outside the front of Emily's house on Penfold Road, Stonyfell. He said it quietly so as not to wake the neighbours.

'Thank you. Let's get inside,' Emily whispered loudly as she worked the security alarm.

Once inside and the front door closed, Emily gave Dan the biggest kiss he'd ever had sober. For a while, he wasn't even sure if he was breathing. But soon enough, after the kiss, his equilibrium returned.

'So, what beers do you have, then?'

'Ha ha. You can take the man out of Meningie, but you can't take... Well, there's some Stella Artois in the fridge in the kitchen. Help yourself and pour me some Pinot Gris in the fridge door, too, please.'

'Glasses?'

'Hunt around, you'll find them. I'll just set some music up.'

Dan rummaged around in the kitchen, eventually finding a wine glass, and the Stella and wine in the fridge.

Something ambient washed the house with background music as Dan sat next to Emily on the white leather couch.

'This music you put on. It's... interesting. What is it?' he asked.

'It's called Ambient Drone. This particular track is by a duo called "Stars of the Lid". You like?'

'Not sure. It's not like anything I've ever come across before. I guess I could get used to it if I heard it often enough.'

'Oh, I love ambient drone music. I have it on all the time when I'm working. What do you listen to when you're working?'

'I don't really have any special music I play. Whatever I have handy on my phone at the time. Whether it's streamed or whether I have it on a playlist or in my music collection. But I suppose I am a bit partial to some classic "Gang of Youths", some "Stuck Out", and a bit of "Tame Impala".'

'Well, that's all a bit loud for me, except there are some nice quieter pieces that "Gang of Youths" have written over the years.'

'I think we have different tastes, ha ha.'

'No, your taste is wrong. Mine is correct,' she smiled, coyly.

'Let's fight it out. A kissing contest—first one to break the kiss loses.'

'Okay, that sounds perfectly reasonable. Let me get comfortable. Okay, do your worst, Dan.'

The kiss lasted several minutes, neither one wanting to lose the fight. But Emily had a chink in her armour—she was a heavy saliva producer. It didn't take long before she was feeling like she was drowning, hastily swallowing some of her own saliva and hoping that Dan didn't notice or at least wasn't worried.

Dan couldn't care less. He was luxuriating in the longest kiss he'd ever known, and just about sober, too; no party drugs or cheap booze to ruin the moment. He even had the foresight to not try to touch Emily in her girl parts. It was all about the kiss, and he was loving it.

Eventually, Emily's saliva production overcame her willingness to kiss Dan, and she chose to break it off, losing the fight. She didn't like losing; it wasn't in her nature. But it was either that or drown.

'Ha HA!' cried Dan. 'Victory is mine!'

'Yes, it is, my handsome beau. The music choice is yours, here's my phone.'

'I tell you what, how about you keep it on what you've got playing? It's your house and your drinks, after all.'

'That's very noble of you, brave Sir Dan, thank you. In which case, you shall be rewarded. Take your shoes off and lie down on the couch with me, and let's try this kissing thing again to see if we've got the hang of it.'

'I reckon I can do that, Miss Emily.'

And he did. And they did. And this time Dan let himself give in to temptation and touched her girl parts. And for Dan, who hadn't done this sort of thing in a very long time, it was good.

After a good half hour, Emily looked up into his eyes and asked him if he'd like to stay the night. He would. Very much. But he needed to quickly text his mum, who would be worried that he hadn't arrived home yet. So, he did. Then he followed Emily to her bedroom as more 'Stars of the Lid' played quietly in all the speakers around the house.

The next morning, they awoke at nine, Dan exhausted from a night's passion and feeling pleased with himself. Emily, too, was feeling pleased with how things had worked out. But now, the awkward 'morning after' conversation had to take place.

'Thank you for last night,' said Dan.

'You're welcome. I hope you enjoyed yourself, you seemed to be.'

'Oh, yes, I did. And you?'

'Oh, yes, thank you.'

'Shall we go and get breakfast somewhere?'

'Let's. There are some good cafes on The Parade.'

'Great.'

Silence.

'I'll just have a quick shower, then,' said Dan, breaking the silence.

'I'll get you a towel.'

'Thanks.'

Silence, as Emily slipped out of the bedroom and returned with a towel.

'Thanks.'

Dan hopped into the shower.

Emily, needing to shower as well, joined him.

They do say that showering with a friend saves water, and South Australia *is* the driest State in the driest continent on Earth. How very eco-friendly of her.

A week later, Mr Pendlebury did something unusual: he called Ros and told her to have the day off, as he wasn't opening the office that day. Instead, he told her, he was going to drive down to Kingston in the Mercedes and have a spot of lunch with a recently retired friend.

'I've decided I need to slow down a bit, as I'm not getting any younger,' he told her. Ros thought that if he slowed down any further he'd fall over, but she welcomed the chance to potter in the garden and sort out some washing. It was shaping up to be a beautiful day, and she might even indulge in a coffee at the bakery herself, once she had a load of washing on the line.

Mr Pendlebury eased his Mercedes onto Edward Street and headed off to McIntosh Way. The sun was warming, but not too so.

'A pleasant day awaits,' he told himself, and popped a cassette into the player. He sang along to Freddie Mercury singing about a man named Buddy who was kicking a can all over the place.

On a sunny day like today, the water of the Coorong was blue and the sand pale white. Tourists stopped and waved away the flies. Some tourists came armed with binoculars to check out the bird life. Mr Pendlebury noted the range of vehicles; mostly Japanese and Korean cars, the odd Holden or Ford, the lone luxury car.

The Coorong was no Disneyland or Movie World. Whether coming from Kingston or going there on route to Mount Gambier, the Coorong was one landscape that had children crying out, 'Are we there yet?' and wishing they were home with their toys and tv.

Past Salt Creek and the replica oil rig, cruising at a

comfortable 100-110 kilometres per hour. Plenty of time to listen to music and soak up the scenery and wonder how many bugs would be splattered on the front of the car. That was the only downside, Mr Pendlebury thought, to having his special car—the need to wash the front of the car carefully. Sure, there was an automatic car wash in Meningie, but older paintwork like the Mercedes required manual manipulation.

It was while Mr Pendlebury was singing along to ABBA and musing about money and how it must be funny in a rich man's world, musing also on his life and the things he was grateful for, that the front right-hand tyre blew.

This had a catastrophic effect on the car's steering. The car veered all over the road. Luckily for him traffic coming in the opposite direction had been light, and there was no one behind him.

But, in a moment of bad luck, there *was* a car coming in the opposite direction, and on a small hillock and bend Mr Pendlebury's much-loved red Mercedes sports car rammed into the rear passenger door of a white Hyundai i30 that was unsuccessful in avoiding him.

There was confusion at first, as Mr Pendlebury and the owner of the i30 recovered from the impact and sought safety at the side of the road. Mr Pendlebury rushed over to the Hyundai and apologised profusely to the driver, peering into the back of the car where his car had rammed.

There was a child, a ten-year-old girl he guessed, who was in a state of shock. The front passenger, the child's mother, was out of the car and rushing around to check on her daughter. The door couldn't be opened, but the window glass had shattered, covering the child. The mother was screaming, screaming in fear for her child and screaming at Mr Pendlebury. The i30's driver was also out of the car, checking on his daughter and yelling at Mr Pendlebury.

Mr Pendlebury stepped back from the car and pulled out his mobile phone. Calling ooo, he also requested a tow truck for each of the two cars. But this was country SA, only one truck would be available to take the cars away. An ambulance would be at least three-quarters of an hour away, whether it came from Meningie or Kingston. There was an ambulance response team in Salt Creek, but Mr Pendlebury didn't know whether it was manned on a weekday.

As it happened, the ambulance service at Salt Creek wasn't staffed during the week, so the ambulance came from Meningie, and it took forty-three minutes from the time Mr Pendlebury made the call to when the ambulance arrived.

By the time it arrived the child's mother had calmed down somewhat, and Mr Pendlebury had successfully apologised and explained about the shredded tyre. Looking at his own car, he could see bonnet, grill, bumper and side panel damage. What he couldn't see was that the chassis had bent, rendering the car irreparable.

Constable Andrew arrived with the ambulance, to make sure that the road was still accessible and to lay down safety signs to slow the traffic right down.

The Meningie CFS turned up and grappled the car door open, releasing the child into the arms of her mother and the waiting ambulance crew.

The tow truck came from Meningie too and took the i3o first. Constable Andrew put the family of three into his car and drove them back to Meningie, to the police station where they could make a statement. A police car came from Kingston to ferry Mr Pendlebury back to the Meningie police station. Once there, again he offered his sincere apologies. He also repeated his offer to put the family up at the Meningie Hotel while they organised a replacement car.

A day that had started out with such promise, he thought, had turned into such a calamity. And he'd nearly killed a girl. That would have been unforgivable. Still, the matter would be in the hands of the insurance companies, they could fight it out. But it was a pity about his car. He didn't yet know that it was irreparable, but a phone call the next day from Cliff Delman would bear the bad news.

His Mercedes was an expensive car to crash.

As it happens, Mr Pendlebury was not the only owner of an expensive car to have a crash.

82

The black BMW SUV sped effortlessly along the highway. Emily, not noticing her speed, was hitting 140 kilometres per hour in some spots. The relationship was turning out to be a winner for her. Here was a man, not a boy like she'd regularly dealt with, who had experienced some of what life had to offer. In Dan, she saw her hopes for 'normal' adult life within reach, a life of dinner parties and of picnics, of camping out and of staying in.

Sure, her cyber activities meant that she would never have to play the adult games of 'which bill can we afford to pay this fortnight' and 'we must turn the lights off in the room when we exit it'. She'd never have to worry about a mortgage, or a repair bill for the car. And even if she were caught and spent some time in jail, she had enough money invested in foreign bank accounts, shares, paintings and property that she could just pick up life as she left it.

She was feeling pleased with her life, with the choices that she'd made thus far.

Dan, for his part, was delighted how life had turned around for him. Previously in despair that he'd ever be worthy of getting a girlfriend, he now was getting regular sex from an attractive woman who guided him on his cyber enterprise to be more successful, and she was rich. Pretty much a royal flush. And here she was driving the two of them back down to Meningie to have the first dinner as a couple with his mum.

So pleased were they with how things had turned out for them, how effortlessly conversation, both deep and light, flowed, that they failed to notice the police car sitting in the centre strip on the highway until they had almost passed it.

'Shit,' they both said at the same time.

Feeling confident, Emily decided to wait and see if the patrol car gave chase.

Senior Constable Aaron Matthews would normally have not given chase, letting the highway safety cameras do their thing. But the safety cameras were offline for software upgrades. Aaron thought about the risks involved in a high-speed chase but ruled the most extreme ones out. The car was expensive and new, so it was doubtful that it was being driven by hoons from Mount Barker. It was more likely the driver, and he'd noted that the driver was female, was some upper-level executive who thought she'd show off to her mates. That would make it very likely that they would pull over when they saw the flashing lights. So, all in all, Aaron argued with himself, it was safe to engage the Commodore patrol car's powerful engine and run the driver down.

Spotting the flashing lights in her rear-view mirror, Emily made the executive decision to out-run them. Her right foot planted itself on the floor, and the X7 M SPORT roared to life with a sound of delight in its voice.

BMW M-series cars were never meant for an ordinary driving life, a life of suburban shopping centres and endless traffic lights. They were meant to be driven hard, to let the skilled and passionate driver within give vent to their surging life force. The M-series cars were, after all, drivers' cars. Deft handling, powerful acceleration, robust brakes. It was this pedigree that Emily channelled, as the flashing lights tried to catch her.

The Commodore police car, with its nine gears, was gaining, so Emily decided to show off to Dan and test the top speed of the BMW. One-eighty kilometres per hour; one-ninety; two hundred. Still the Commodore kept coming. The M-series SUV kept going, heading towards a top speed of 257 kilometres per hour.

There was an exit coming up, the turnoff to Callington, Dan said, that would give Emily the chance to disappear down some dirt roads.

But as they approached the exit, an 18-wheel truck was trundling along and was slowly being overtaken by a car. If Emily slowed down to let the truck pass the exit, the police car would be close enough to see and would follow. But the car overtaking the truck, obviously not looking in their rear-view mirror, had filled the remaining lane in the highway. Emily was going to tail end the car, and no doubt kill the driver and any passengers. All she could do was stand on the brakes and hope to pull up in time to not hit the other car.

Just at the exit there was a copse of trees in the middle of the highway, just before a gaggle of safety cameras. These loomed perilously close as Emily stood on the brakes.

The choice was before her: go into the trees and hope

for a softish landing, or plough into the back of the car in front of her.

She looked across at Dan, mouthed 'I'm sorry' and ploughed into the trees as she was rapidly decelerating from two hundred and two kilometres per hour to one-twenty, one-ten...

83

The police highway patrol Commodore pulled to a halt at the wreck. The BMW had ploughed through the trees and crashed through the barrier fence to the safety cameras, bringing the cameras down or else knocking them crazily out of alignment. Rolling several times, it rested upside down, all its windows smashed in and many body panels missing.

Aaron Matthews radioed for back-up to help manage the debris of car panels, and to have the Major Crash division notified. He rushed to the driver's door to see if the driver had survived. A woman, upside down, slumped sideways. He leant through the window and pulled her arm to free it, causing her to moan quietly above the ticking of the engine cooling down. Aaron looked over to the passenger side and felt goose bumps rise on his arms. The passenger was getting choked by the seatbelt and his lips were blue and the face utterly pale. Knowing the risk of a broken neck for the passenger, but more scared of the guy dying from strangulation, Aaron quickly cut the belt free and did his best to support the head of the unconscious passenger. He was stuck in this position when he noticed the driver starting to groan more consistently and move. Aaron yelled out for her to stay still but he was stuck in position as he noticed her starting to make more purposeful movements.

Aaron left Dan momentarily and scooted back to the Commodore to radio in for air ambulance support, and CFS support to have the passenger extricated from the wreckage. Ten minutes after his initial call, a CFS truck arrived and work began on freeing Dan from the wreckage. So too did a road ambulance and some more police arrived who co-ordinated the traffic around the scene. Half an hour after Aaron's distress call the air ambulance arrived, and they waited in the clearing just past the crash scene for the CFS to complete their magic.

By this time, Emily had somehow extricated herself from her upside-down prison and was staggering, confused, around the scene, to be attended to by the ambulance crews.

The CFS crew extricated Dan from his seat and let the air ambulance team intubate him and load him into the chopper. Emily would have to travel by the road ambulance that had arrived from Mount Barker. After Dan had been loaded into the chopper, and it had taken off, she passed out.

How both had survived the crash was down to good engineering in Germany and some lucky twists of fate from the gods.

The helicopter took off and settled back into its speedy return journey to the Flinders Medical Centre. Luckily for both Emily and Dan, Dr Ena O'Schady was the consultant on duty that evening in the Emergency Department at Flinders—she would ensure that both patients had the best chances of making the jump from crash victim to crash survivor.

Dr Ena O'Schady was Irish, a feisty character, short, short-tempered, and well skilled in the use of the words 'Jeysus Christ'. She was in Resus room 1 to greet Dan's inert body.

The room was large and contained all manner of machinery—everything that would be needed to treat everything from heart attacks to physical attacks to vehicle accidents, everything from the severely injured to the severely ill from any number of medical illnesses. The team of specialists and specialist nurses were waiting in preparation for Dan's arrival. Once he'd arrived, his clothes were cut off, and they examined him carefully, taking several X-rays and blood tests. An X-ray of his chest showed multiple broken ribs, but the endotracheal breathing tube was thankfully placed correctly. He showed multiple broken ribs from his seat belt, and lots of blood, which would later show no drugs or alcohol.

The doctors noted the seatbelt mark along the neck and combining this with the handover report from the paramedics showing Dan initially being pale and blue at the scene of the accident, they were quite concerned about the damage caused to his neck structures, not to speak of potential brain damage. Since the immediate examination revealed nothing but broken ribs, most likely from the seatbelt, and multiple lacerations from the splintered, shattered windscreen, the treating doctors decided to transfer Dan to the CT scanner.

The CT of his brain showed some concerning features of his injury, which could be due to both lack of oxygen and the pressure on the vessels of the neck. The CT of his neck, chest and abdomen revealed no other injuries besides the known rib fractures.

His condition deemed stable, he was wheeled around to the Intensive and Critical Care Unit, known in the hospital as ICCU. But there was no guarantee that there was no brain damage.

Emily eventually arrived at Flinders ED, and Ena O'Schady was still on duty to receive her. Emily was also wheeled into a 'Resus' resuscitation room, conscious but drowsy and very confused. Her clothes were cut off and placed in a paper bag under her bed. X-rays showed no structural damage to bones in the legs or pelvis, but there was a broken right forearm, and there would no doubt be heavy bruising from the impact of the accelerator and brake pedals slamming into her feet. She too had multiple bruised ribs and lacerations from the seatbelt and windows.

'Jeysus Christ!' exclaimed Ena, 'how did she get away with not having her femora broken and her pelvis shattered? The girl will be a walking miracle!' Her forearm was plastered, and her arm was put in a sling.

After a CT of her brain did not show any acute injury, her condition was deemed stable. After a few hours of observation in the time-critical Emergency Department, she was wheeled around to the Emergency Department's own Extended Emergency Care Unit, the EECU. She would have her own room, no door (allowing for quick access by medical staff should it be necessary) but with a curtain for privacy.

'Senior Constable Andrew Campbell, sorry to bother you this evening. I'm Sergeant Baz Smith of Adelaide Major Crash. There's been an accident on the Princes Highway, at Callington, and the passenger involved has a driver's licence with an address in Meningie. I wonder if you would be kind enough to notify the other resident at that address, Ms Rosalyn Robinson, that the passenger has been transferred to Flinders Medical Centre, where they are currently in the Intensive and Critical Care Unit.'

Andrew took down the details about the crash, as much as was known, and picked up his keys. He never liked being the bearer of bad news to good people. Even though he was off-duty now, he reached for his station keys.

Minutes later he was outside Ros' house, tapping on her front door.

'Oh, hello, Constable. I'm scared. My son and his girl-friend are late for dinner, he won't answer his phone, and now you show up. Please tell me there's nothing wrong.'

'Can I come in, Mrs Robinson?'

'Of course. Please forgive my manners.'

Ros led him to the kitchen where she fidgeted at the sink.

'Mrs Robinson, I'm afraid there's been an accident. Dan is alive, but he is currently in the Intensive and Critical Care Unit at Flinders Medical Centre. Dan was the passenger in a car that was speeding and crashed. Those are all the details that I know, I'm afraid. If you'd like to get your bag and a coat, I can drive you to the hospital, if you want. I don't think it's a good idea you drive yourself at the moment.'

In a trance, Ros got up and grabbed her handbag, coat and mobile phone from the living room. Andrew met her at the front door. He stayed with her while she locked the front door, then escorted her to the car where he chivalrously opened a back door for her and helped her get in.

Ros took a long time to get over the shock and asked Andrew several times to tell her all the details. He was happy to do so. After all, he'd want someone to show his mother the same courtesy should something similar happen to him.

After the third time he'd told her what he had been told, Ros slumped back in her seat, the air seemingly escaping her, deflating her like an old balloon, and she quietly sobbed to herself. Her only son, in hospital, and she many kilometres away. Too many. She wanted to be at his bedside right now, to take away all the damage and suffering he was going through.

Andrew made good time, occasionally going over the speed limit, and he pulled up in Flinders Medical Centre's police bay for the Emergency Department. He wasn't supposed to park there, because he wasn't there on official business. He had chosen to drive Ros to Dan out of the goodness of his heart; certainly, there was no requirement to drive her to the hospital in his operations manual. He would leave her in the care of the Intensive and Critical Care Unit team; he'd come and collect her if she wanted when she was ready.

He led Ros into the Emergency Department and elicited the directions to the Intensive and Critical Care Unit. A porter was called, and the porter walked them both round to ICCU, where Andrew explained to the duty nurse who Ros was and who her son was. He then left her alone and drove the two-plus hours back to Meningie. Ros would never find out that he had been her taxi service entirely off his own bat, and he would never tell anyone that, either.

87

'Davo, dear, it's Ros Robinson. I'm afraid I have some bad news for you. Dan has been involved in a car accident and is in the Intensive and Critical Care Unit at Flinders Medical Centre in Adelaide. Yes, he's alive, but no, he's not conscious, or up for receiving visitors at the moment. They don't really let visitors in at the hospital, it seems, but they have taken pity on me. Yes, I'm up here now. He's battered and bruised, and unconscious, and his heart is weak, from what they tell me. He's got some broken ribs and lacerations. From what the doctor said, it's a miracle he's alive. There is some concern that he might have suffered some brain damage, but nothing can be determined until he's conscious.

Yes, I'm okay for things at the moment, but if I need anything, I'll certainly ask. Of course, I'll keep you up to date on any news I get. Dan needs as many good wishes and prayers that he can get at the moment, so if you know anyone from the churches that can put in a good word, I'd be grateful. Yes, I'm also going to be calling Kelly and friends of mine about this. Naturally, I'll pass on your love to him when he wakes up. Thank you, Davo, and thanks too to Sarah, for both of your love for my son. I'm doing all a mother can do to help her son heal. He's in good hands with the staff here, they have been excellent looking after him and me. All right, Davo, love to you both and I'll be in touch as soon as I know anything. Bye.'

'Hello, Kelly dear, it's Ros Robinson here. I'm afraid I have some bad news for you. My Dan has been involved in a car accident on the highway and I'm currently in the Intensive and Critical Care Unit at the Flinders Medical Centre in Adelaide. Yes, he's alive, but only just. He's got some broken ribs, and he has cuts and bruising all over. He's currently unconscious, and the medical teams don't know how long he's likely to be that way. That's very kind of you, Kelly, but at the moment he can't have visitors apart from me. Only direct relatives can visit, it seems. Yes, I got a lift up with Constable Andrew Campbell, who was very kind and answered my endless questions. Well, I could probably do with a change of clothing at some stage. I have an overnight bag in my bedroom, if you could put a change of clothing in there for me, that would be good, if you are sure you don't mind. Okay, tomorrow early evening will be fine, Kelly. That is really very kind of you. I'm sure they have toiletries I can purchase here at the hospital, but a change of underwear and top will be really helpful. Oh, thank you, Kelly, you really are too kind. But I must stress that Dan can't have any visitors at the moment. I've already told Davo that he and Sarah can't visit. Well, you are too kind to think just of me. I really do appreciate it. Okay then, tomorrow early evening it is. Oh, I'd better tell you where the spare key is kept. Around the back of the house, near the garden tap, is a large cycad plant. Under the pot, you'll find the key to the front door. Oh, and if you could feed the goldfish in the living room, that would be lovely. Just a pinch of food, the tub is next to the tank.

Thank you so much, Kelly, dear, I really do appreciate all your kindness.'

'Ah, Mr Pendlebury. I'm ringing from the Flinders Medical Centre up in Adelaide. My Dan has been involved in a road accident, and I'm up here with him in Intensive and Critical Care. I'm sorry to have to ask, but is it okay if I have a few days off to sit with him? Oh, thank you. No, he's not conscious at the moment, and he has broken ribs, cuts and bruises, and there's some concern about possible brain trauma, but he's still alive and I'm viewing that as a positive. Well, that's very kind of you to think of me; someone is bringing me a change of clothes already, but if I need a second set, I'll certainly let you know. My car is back at home, Constable Andrew Campbell from the police drove me here in his police car, and he said to call him when I'm ready to come home. No, at the moment I'm being looked after really well by the Intensive Care team, and there's a shop here that I have bought a toothbrush and toothpaste from, and a restaurant where I can go for a meal and a break from sitting in an uncomfortable chair. All is as good as could be hoped for, considering the circumstances. Yes, it is challenging my views on life and my positivity. Thank you, Mr Pendlebury, you are very kind. Thanks for letting me have some time off and thanks for your kind offers to come and collect me. I'll let you know how things are going with Dan and me. Thanks again. Bye.'

EECU, the Extended Care Unit of the Emergency Department. A private room. A sleeping Emily King. The nursing staff in the Emergency Department resuscitation room had cut all of her clothes off, and the nurses in EECU had dressed her in a shapeless nightgown, in which she lay in her white hospital bed in crisp white sheets. The duty intern checked her e-clipboard, checked the machines to make sure they were behaving, then left her room.

Outside the room, a plainclothes detective stood, waiting.

'Excuse me, doctor, can I have a word, please?'

'Of course.'

'Is this the driver of the car involved in a crash on the highway at Callington?'

The intern nodded.

'Good. Is she able to answer some questions at the moment?'

'I'm afraid not. She's currently sleeping heavily. I'm afraid we don't know how long she'll be asleep for. We have given her a lot of strong pain medication which will contribute to that.'

'Okay. Here's my card, I'm Pauline Milosky from Major Crash. We want to ask the driver some questions. When she surfaces, can you or your colleagues ring us? We'll pop round.

'Sure, I'll put these details in her notes now.'

The Emergency Department clerical staff would have taken her details from her driver's licence and attempted to find a next of kin, but they would have had no luck. Emily had no next of kin registered on any public or private database anywhere. All they had to go on was the home address on her driver's licence, but they wouldn't have shared that with the police for reasons of patient confidentiality; the police wouldn't know where Emily lived. The police had a lot of questions they wanted to ask her, including why she was driving a car registered to a leasing company that reported it was leased to someone else entirely. A Mr David Mossman, whose address didn't exist.

***

The Minister for Home Affairs got up from his comfortable leather chair and padded across the thick carpet of his office to the laptop computer on his desk. He'd just taken a call from someone in one of the offices he controlled that told him that a Ms Emily King had been admitted into Flinders Medical Centre down in Adelaide and was in the Emergency Department.

He reclined in his comfy chair again, took a sip of his single malt, and searched his network for a name of someone at the hospital he could call.

Eventually, he got a result—a consultant for the Emergency Department and EECU, by good fortune. It was late, but the Minister rarely slept much anyway. He had several changes of clothes discreetly stored in his office, so tonight was Business As Usual. He put in the call to one of his apparatchiks.

'David, it's me. There's something I need you to do. There's someone in a hospital bed in Adelaide that needs to leave as soon as possible. Can you ring the following person and read them the Official Secrets Act? I want Ms Emily

King to have clearance to leave the hospital under her own cognisance as soon as possible.'

Dr Cat Thompson was the consultant of the Emergency Department that the Minister had identified. It was ten-thirty at night, and she took the call.

'Dr Thompson, I'm David Jacobson, Assistant to the Federal Minister for Home Affairs. I'm calling about a patient you currently have in the Emergency Department, a Ms Emily King. I'd like you to arrange for her release as soon as possible. If there are any police enquiries into her, please redirect them to me. This is a matter of national security and the utmost secrecy, do you understand? Good. This conversation never took place, and you will be charged under the Official Secrets Act if you tell anyone of the contents of this call or divulge the name of Ms King to anyone without my express permission. If you have questions, please call me on my personal number, the one I'm calling from now. Thank you very much for your co-operation, doctor.'

While his Assistant was calling the consultant, the Minister called a friend in Adelaide.

'Tony, thanks for taking my call at this late hour. I have a favour to ask...'

They say that sleep can be the best medicine. The body, not distracted by the surrounding environment, can heal itself. After twenty hours of sleeping, Emily came to painfully. She drifted slowly out of unconsciousness, but at the last moment of her gentle re-introduction to the world, she suddenly sat bolt upright, and air rushed into her lungs. Pain, lots of pain, all over.

She looked around her—a hospital room, smelling of sanitary wipes. A curtain pulled three quarters shut to give her some privacy, but no door in the room. No nurses to be seen. She looked at her arms. Scratches, bruises, cuts. A cast and sling on her right arm. The events that brought her to her room slowly filtered in.

Dan, where is Dan?

Emily tried to stand up, her legs buckling under her.

She collapsed to the floor. While lying there, she saw that the bottom of her bed contained a bag. Not being a bag she recognised, she slowly crawled over and retrieved it. A shopping bag from an upmarket designer shop. Inside were clothing in her size: a top, a skirt, some pumps, a bra and a pair of panties. And two envelopes. One envelope, DL sized, contained a letter from a consultant for the Emergency Department (which she guessed must be where she was) authorising her discharge. In the same envelope was a box of Endone, high-impact pain killers and a script for more. The other envelope, a bulging A5 size, contained what Emily counted to be two thousand dollars in one hundred- and fifty-dollar notes, along with her driver's licence, and credit cards. And her mobile phone, miraculously intact apart from scratches on the screen. The battery was flat.

With every ounce of energy she had, she pulled herself back on the bed and considered her options. She had to confirm where she was. She had to find out where Dan was, and if he survived the crash. She had to get to a secure location, with a secure computer, and find out who knew what about the crash.

Her first step, she concluded, was to get out of this room and out of the hospital. Get to safety, because she didn't know how much the information the police had about her and she wouldn't know until she could access their computers.

Emily had another attempt at standing up. This time her knees bent again, but she was able to pull herself upright if she held onto the bed. Progress.

The pain rocketing through her body was almost unbearable. Every sinew ached with a ferocity she had never experienced. If she could get to the water jug on the other side of the bed, she would knock back some painkillers.

If.

Taking the time to unhook herself from the various machines and bags she was connected to, she slowly, hesitantly shuffled her way around the room to the water jug, poured some water into a plastic cup, then swallowed four Endone. 'That's got to help,' she said to herself.

Now it was time to get dressed. Each piece of clothing was its own direct channel to pain hell, but after what seemed to her to be seconds, but was, in fact, forty minutes, Emily stood fully dressed and ready to meet the world. She gathered up the envelopes and boldly shuffled around the bed and to the edge of her room, hunched over in pain like an aged Mediterranean woman, expecting to meet some resistance from the nursing staff. She peered out from behind her curtain to see where the nurses and doctors were in the hallway. There were none. She turned left and hoped that an exit would open up shortly. She saw an internal fire door on her left, and she tried it gingerly to see if it would open. It did. No alarm. And off in the distance she could see hospital volunteer workers who would help her find the main entrance and a taxi.

At seven fifteen in the evening, one day after she'd been admitted, Emily King, otherwise known to a select few as the highly successful cybercriminal D@@Mladen, left the building.

91

Dan's reconnection with the living world was slow and hesitant, but eventually he opened his eyes and took in his surroundings.

He was in a hospital bed, which meant he wasn't dead, and his mum was asleep in the chair beside him. He was connected by various tubes and wires to various machines and sensors. He was in a small bit of pain, mainly around his chest, but apart from that felt a bit 'floaty' and comfortable. He figured that he must be on painkillers, and that would keep him from feeling the effects of the crash.

He tried his voice and found it didn't work; all that came out was a croak, not loud enough to wake his mum. So, he rested his head again on the pillow and was about to drift back to sleep when a nurse entered the cubicle.

'Hello, Mr Robinson,' nurse Rahima Al-Najjar said. 'I saw from your monitors that you were awake. How do you feel?'

'Dan re-opened his eyes and tried again to speak. 'I'm okay, I think,' he croaked.

'Here, let me give you some water to help that voice of yours.'

Duly refreshed, Dan tried again. 'I'm okay. I'm in a bit of pain, but not much. Am I on painkillers?'

'Yes, lots. Your seatbelt broke several ribs, and you are all cut up because of the windows and windscreen breaking. You were lucky to survive the crash, it seems.'

'The other person in the car with me, Emily, how is she?'

'I don't know, she's not in here with you. I've just started my shift; I'll make some enquiries.'

The sound of them chatting quietly was enough to wake Ros from her slumber, and she came to at the sound of her boy's voice.

'Daniel! Dan! Oh, how are you?'

'Okay, mum. Apparently, I've broken some ribs, so I'm on lots of painkillers. I don't feel too bad at the moment, but my chest hurts if I try to move in my bed.'

'I'm so glad you're alive, Daniel. Everybody's been asking about you. Davo and Sarah, and Kelly wanted to come up and visit you, but I told them that there were no visiting hours here. The staff here have been very kind and let me take over this chair.'

'Where am I?'

'The ICCU, the Intensive and Critical Care Unit at the Flinders Medical Centre,' Rahima answered. 'Strictly no visitors who are friends, but direct relatives can sometimes visit. Somehow your mother must have convinced the other nurses and doctors to let her stay.'

'I said I'd stay out of the way and just sit in this chair. They were very kind to let me fall asleep here.'

'How long have I been here?' Dan asked.

'Three days, Mr Robinson,' replied Rahima. 'Now, I must go and tell a doctor you're awake. I'm sure they have lots of questions for you, and probably some answers, too.

Excuse me.'

'Sure, thanks,' replied Dan. 'Have you been here three days, mum?'

'Yes, hovering over you in case you needed anything.'

'You're an angel, mum, thanks.'

'Well, when Constable Andrew came around, I stuffed my overnight bag with a few things and came as soon as I could. Kelly was adorable and brought me up a couple of changes of clothes as well, even though she couldn't pop in and see you. That girl is a gem, Daniel. She adores you.'

'Yes, mum.'

'Well, anyway, how did you get into this predicament?'

'I'm not really sure...' but just then a doctor swept into the cubicle and Dan directed his attention to this new presence in his life.

'Hello, Mr Robinson, I'm doctor Peter Swift. I'm responsible for looking after you this morning, and for making sure you have enough painkillers. How do you feel?'

'Well, from what I gather I've broken a few ribs, and there're cuts and bruising. I should be feeling a lot worse than I do. I just have a bit of pain in my chest when I try to move. And I feel a killer headache coming on.'

'Good, the painkillers are working. I'll organise some Panadol for the headache. Try not to move in your bed too much. Now that you are awake, the nurses will probably want to give you a wash, to clean away some residue blood, and to freshen you up a bit. You'd be amazed how that can pick you up.' Peter turned his attention to Ros. 'And how are you this morning? Those chairs aren't known for their comfort.'

Ros laughed. 'I'm okay, thank you, doctor. I feel like I've been in the spin dryer, and I've come out all knotted and twisted, but I'm just happy to talk to my son again.'

'Good.' His attention moved back to Dan, 'Mr Robinson, it's my duty to inform you that you suffered some head and neck trauma in the crash. Nothing in the CT scans showed a definite trauma, but the ambulance crews reported that a police officer cut you down from your upside-down position in the car because you were being strangled by the seat belt. You had changed skin colour, apparently, and that's never a good sign. So we are asking our friends at BIRS, the Brain Injury Rehabilitation Service, to come in and run some tests. Now that you're awake, someone should be in later today.'

'Strewth!'

'As I said, there's no definite proof that you have suffered a brain injury, it's merely a precaution. Once you leave here for home, you might return to normal within a few days as your body re-acclimatises with its familiar world. It's had a big shock, and there is a lot for it to cope with. Mood swings and other indicators of brain injury might be present for a few days until you have settled into a routine at home.'

'Is that all there is, mood swings, doctor?' asked Ros.

'That's the usual indicator. Either some outbursts of irrational anger or periods of melancholy and depression. They rarely last for long. There might also be some other signs of injury—difficulty walking, lack of insight, lack of gratitude. As I say, there may be nothing to worry about. But we have to make sure, hence why we are asking the BIRS team to come and visit.'

'Thank you, doctor,' Ros said.

'Well, I'll leave you now. I'll pop my head in from time to time, but for the main part of your stay, the nurses will look after you. And they are fabulous nurses. I'll arrange for

Rahima to come in and give you some Panadol for your headache. Goodbye.'

'Goodbye, and thank you, doctor,' replied Ros.

'Thanks, bloke,' replied Dan.

'Well, that was interesting, Daniel,' said Ros when they were alone.

'Brain injury, mum! That's scary.'

'I know. Well, let's wait and see what the brain injury team says. I'll just have to watch myself back at home when I'm looking after you.'

'Oh, mum. You don't have to look after me. I'm sure that I'll be okay to look after myself when they release me from here.'

'Nonsense. You are badly broken and cut up. Mr Pendlebury said I could take as much time as I need to nurse you back to health. So that's what I'll do.'

'I wonder how Emily is? Have you heard anything?'

'No, no one has told me anything. I asked at the enquiry desk out the front of the hospital, but no one would tell me anything because I'm not next of kin. All they said was that she wasn't in the hospital.'

'Strewth. She could be dead, then.'

Just then Rahima re-entered the cubicle with a couple of Panadol and a tray of wet and dry cloths. 'Hello again, Mr Robinson, Mrs Robinson. I'm here with something for the headache, and I'm also going to give you a bed bath, sir, and change your sheets.'

'Thanks. Did you find any news about Emily, the driver of the car I crashed in?'

'Oh, yes. Miss Emily was discharged from the hospital two days ago, after a twenty-four-hour stay in the Emergency and Extended Care Unit. It's a mini-ward in the Emergency Department. That's all that anyone knows, I'm afraid, without looking up her records, which is illegal. Sorry, but that's all the news I have.'

'Okay, thanks. Well, at least she's alive. Or was, two days ago. I really need to get in contact with her, mum. Can you arrange for someone to bring my laptop in for me?'

'I'm sorry, Mr Robinson, but there are no electronic devices permitted in here. The equipment here is very sensitive and could give false readings if interfered with. Besides, your body has suffered tremendous trauma, it needs time to heal.'

'Fuck. I need to talk to Emily, find out what is going on.'

'Dan, I'm not even allowed my mobile phone or iPad in here. And Rahima's right, you have suffered a huge trauma, and your body needs to rest and heal, not start bashing away at your keyboard again.'

'Fuck.'

'Daniel, that's not the language that's called for in here. Rahima's right, you need to rest. Now, I'm going to head down to the restaurant for some breakfast and a cup of tea. Rahima, would it be alright if I bring Dan back a takeaway coffee?'

'Sorry, Mrs Robinson, that's not allowed. Only food and fluids administered by us in this unit. We have to monitor them carefully.'

'Okay. I'll see you in a little while, Daniel. It's good to see you awake and alive again, my love.'

'Thanks, mum. Sorry for swearing in front of you.'

'And in front of Rahima, dear. Don't swear in front of your nurses.'

'No, mum.'

Rahima interrupted. 'Here's some Panadol. I'll go and get another nurse to help me lift you up and move you about so I can wash you and change the sheets.'

92

Stephanie kept up to date with what was happening in the office while she was in Melbourne. Emails to Rocco were usually timed around 3am, her access codes tracked her in the parts of the SAPOL system she was allowed to be in from 10pm through to 7am.

A routine internal email to all staff was circulated each day and mentioned the previous day's incidents. It mentioned Emily's crash and gave her name and the name of her passenger—Daniel Robinson. Amongst all the names in the daily email, Stephanie spotted his. She felt bad for him, but it was just another in a long line of cases she had; one less case to worry about for now. But to continue to work the case, she requested Dan's laptop from the Major Crash investigation team. It had miraculously survived the crash with only a splintered screen. Its login password protection was easily cracked, revealing the chat transcripts of the early conversations with Hannah.

Stephanie tracked down possible Hannahs through the various databases each State police force had, narrowing her search to five possibilities. She would reach out to each of these five when the moment was right.

93

A Rubanesque woman in her late 40s stuck her head around the curtain. 'Hello, Mr Robinson, my name's Ruby Matthews. I'm from the Brain Injury Rehabilitation

Service, and I'm here to administer some tests. Is now a good time?'

Now was as good a time as any for Dan, who had been lying in his bed wondering how long it would be before he could get to a computer and get in touch with Emily.

His mother Ros had finally taken his advice and gone back home, asking Mr Pendlebury for a lift, which Mr Pendlebury was delighted to provide. Now that her Daniel was safe and awake, there was no need for her to be constantly at his side. And she needed to change her clothes, they smelled of body heat.

'Sure, come on in.'

'Thank you. How are you feeling today?'

'Good enough considering, but you don't really care, do you? You're just asking to be polite.'

'Actually, I do care, Mr Robinson. I need to know what your emotions are before I run my tests.'

'Okay, well, I'm feeling in a slight amount of pain from my broken ribs and bruising, but the painkillers I'm on are doing a good job with that. I feel kind of "floaty" because of them. I'm bored and frustrated because I can have no access to any electrical devices, but I understand I might move to a ward if a bed can be found, so at least there I can access a laptop and my mobile phone. If the police ever return it to me—they found it at the crash site and have decided to keep it, apparently.'

'I see,' said Ruby, pulling a clipboard out of her pink canvas supermarket shopping bag. 'So can I take it you are recovering, are conscious, are feeling slightly above average because of the medication, but are bored?'

'Yep, that sounds about right. What tests do I have to take?'

'A series of simple language and comprehension tests,

some simple logic tests, and a slight bit of current affairs. All easy tests, no problems for a man like you.'

'Well, bring it on.'

'Okay. First off, can I have your full name, address and date of birth, please.'

Daniel duly obliged.

'Good. Okay, let's start with some simple language tests,' and Ruby spent the next forty-five minutes administering and coding various tests that Dan should have found easy. Except he didn't find them easy. Answers he would normally have tripped easily off his tongue were hard to find, causing him to dig deep.

More than once he swore, and more than once he swore deeply, offensively. His mother would not have approved and would have given him a cuff under the ear were he still a child.

At the end of the battery of tests, Dan felt spent. He had wracked his brain to answer simple questions, and he was mightily frustrated. At first, his frustration energised him, but at the end of the questioning he just felt exhausted. Even without asking Ruby how he went, he knew he had not done well.

His temper had flared, his language had guttered, his patience had worn thin. To top it off simple questions that he knew the answers to, like who was the current Prime Minister, and who was the most famous cricketer Australia had ever produced, he couldn't answer. He could tell Ruby what year it was, but not what month. He remembered he lived in Meningie, but not what road. He knew what type of car he drove, but couldn't remember the registration plate. He remembered Kelly's name, but not Davo's. To protect Emily, he said he couldn't remember anything about the crash, nor the events leading up to it. He said he had no recollection of who was driving, or why they were driving, or where they were going.

'Thank you, Mr Robinson,' Ruby said as their time together drew to a close. 'We'll have a report for you and your doctors within the next few days. I hope your rest and recuperation goes well.' She swept herself around the curtain and was gone.

'Fuck,' said Dan to himself as he lay back in his bed and felt stupid and miserable.

94

At the hospital entrance, Emily had grabbed a taxi and escaped to the city, having the taxi drop her off in the city at the East Terrace restaurant and bar *Africola*.

From there she taxied under a different name to *Paparazzi*, a cafe on Unley Road, went in, bought a coffee that she didn't drink, waited twenty minutes, then taxied under yet another name to a house three doors away from her home in Stonyfell. She had paid for everything in cash.

Her pain levels were screaming at her—nine out of ten. She imagined only childbirth could be any worse than what she was feeling right now.

She didn't have a key for the front door, it wasn't left for her at the hospital, so she retrieved the spare key from a pot plant of the house next door and entered her own house. Stopping only to enter the security code, she made a painful beeline for her laptop. The Endone had kicked in, but her pain levels had only dropped a couple of notches, and laptop in hand she woundedly made her way to the kitchen and clutched a fresh bottle of water from the fridge.

She felt like some English football hooligan had used her as a football, kicking her all over, between the thighs, in her groin, all over her chest, her sides, under her feet, her back, everywhere. No part of her body felt unbruised.

Her priority was to find out what had happened to Dan, to discover whether he was dead or alive, so she went online and quickly gained access to the patient records system of SA Health.

Emily let out a cry of relief when she saw that Dan was alive and recuperating in the ICCU. 'He's alive!' she said to herself over and over.

She read the various reports and status updates on Dan —broken ribs, lacerations, heavy bruising, concussion, possible brain injury. Emily added a note: a nurse had taken a call from a woman named Emily. 'Emily was fine and looking forward to seeing him when he got out of ICCU'. 'That should help, I hope,' she said to the laptop.

With Dan well, or as well as could be expected, Emily turned her attention to herself—what did the police know of her, had they identified her, was she to expect a patrol car to visit her soon?

SAPOL had an interesting security setup. On the one hand, it looked easy to hack into. On the other hand, Emily knew that the hacked were watching back with a 24/7 human monitoring system, so Emily had to pull some moves that pinpointed her as living on the island of South Georgia in the Atlantic Ocean. It was just about the opposite time zone in the world to Adelaide. Emily thought the half-a-world-away feint would be enough to let her into the SAPOL system without too many eyebrows being raised at first. Any watchers, she thought, would think it was a system anomaly and just discount it.

But she had to be quick, to not dawdle in the SAPOL

system for fear that ever-watching eyes would eventually figure out that all was not what it seemed.

She breached the outer walls, scooted over familiar territory to Major Crash Investigations, scrolled down the list of current cases and recognised her name and car.

Opening the file in a duplicate window to what SAPOL investigators would see, she saw that they had not yet realised she had escaped the hospital. They were still showing that she was a person of interest and located in the EECU at Flinders. They didn't have any address attached to her name, so that meant no detectives or patrol cars were likely to visit at uncomfortable hours of the day or night.

She recognised the name of the consultant who had signed her release—it was the same name as on the letter she had sitting on the counter top in her kitchen.

She read of her injuries—lacerations, bruising, a broken forearm.

The full report of the crash was still to be finalised, but initial investigations showed that she had been involved in a high-speed chase, had crashed into the middle strip of the freeway into trees, and had destroyed many of the safety cameras located at the scene. The wire fence surrounding the safety cameras had been torn down, and debris from the car, fencing and safety cameras was considerable.

The passenger of the vehicle was identified as a Mr Daniel Robinson of Meningie, and he was currently recuperating in ICCU. A Mrs Rosalyn Robinson, the passenger's mother, had been advised of the crash and currently staying with her son at the hospital.

That meant that her personal security rested on Dan not telling the police where she lived or who she was. This was asking a lot, she reasoned, of a man who probably thought she had tried to kill him.

Time to take stock of her situation.

She had escaped from the hospital with only minor injuries but a lot of pain, for which she had some pain killers. Her name and whereabouts were not known to the police, nor could they use the taxi or Uber services to track her down because she had used aliases all throughout her escape from the hospital.

She was now at home, in lots of pain, but with a box of painkillers at the ready, although a quick flick through Google would highlight that the painkillers didn't come without side-effects, including severe constipation, so she would need to go a chemist and get something for that.

Even though she had them, she daren't use her credit cards, all in Emily King's name, because that name was now tainted, so her gift of $2,000 cash would come in handy until she retrieved some cards in other names. She had some cards stored away, but she would have to wait until a bank opened and she could access a sealed envelope.

'The situation's not as bad as I thought it might be,' she thought.

She logged out of the SAPOL system, pushed the laptop away from her, and took a gentle swig of the water. She was tired, in pain, but home, amongst familiar things and understood geography. Time to catch up on the rest of her world, the world of D@@Mladen, the mysterious and successful Australian hacker.

Nervously fingering the material on her arm sling, she pulled the laptop back to her and entered into the world where she was most comfortable.

No messages from Dan, no messages from anyone. That was good; time to heal, she said to herself.

She would, of course, have to leave the house for a while, until the heat cooled off, and especially if Dan or his mother talked to the police. But for now, she winced her way to her bedroom and started the slow task of taking her new clothes off to have a shower.

This time there was no Dan to shower with; the room was disquietingly large without him.

95

Two mornings later, Dan had a visitor.

'Hello, Mr Robinson, I'm Detective Pauline Milosky from SAPOL Major Crash, do you have a spare minute?'

'I reckon I can just fit you into my busy schedule, detective.'

'Good to hear it. Now, do you have any recollection of the crash, or the events leading up to it?'

'Sadly, no. As I proved the other day with the BIRS team, my memory is shot.'

'Nothing at all about the crash?'

'Nothing, sorry. I've been lying here trying to figure out who might have been driving, but nothing comes to my mind. Sorry.' Dan was relieved that his mother had left him and gone back to Meningie, otherwise she would have butted in and told the detective all about who Emily King was.

'That's alright, Mr Robinson. Just do the best you can. If I said the name 'Emily King' to you, would that ring a bell?'

Luckily for Dan, he had been reaching for a cup of water as Emily's name was dropped into the conversation. His eyes flashed. This flash of recognition and understanding took microseconds to play out in his mind, and by the time he turned around to face Detective Milosky, his face had regained its blank composure.

'No, sorry. Who's she?'

'Okay, Mr Robinson, we thought you might remember her. She was the driver of the car that crashed, nearly killing you. Do you remember anything about the lead up to the crash, like why Ms King was driving, where she was taking you, where you had come from?'

'Sorry, nothing comes to mind. It's all a complete blank. Is that normal with crashes?'

'It can happen with some crashes, yes. The body is subjected to severe trauma and copes by shutting down parts of the body. In this instance, it's possibly shut down parts of your brain to do with memory. In my experience, that memory comes back eventually in eighty percent of cases.'

'Okay.'

'We'd like to talk with Ms King, but unfortunately she's been released from the hospital, and we have no address at which we can contact her. You don't happen to recall an address or phone number, do you? We would normally warrant that from the hospital, but we thought we'd ask you first.'

'Sure. No, sorry, I remember nothing.'

'Okay, well should your memory come back, even with just fragments of details, please call me on the number on my card. I'll leave it here on your table. Call me anytime; either I'll answer, or it will ring through to a special constable who will take down any details you can remember. Thank you for your time today, Mr Robinson.'

'Thank you, detective. I'll call if I remember anything.'

When the detective had left, Dan fell back into his pillow and breathed a silent sigh.

So, Emily was in hospital but was well enough to be released. The police don't know her address, but they probably will shortly when they get a warrant.

'Damn it! Why can't I have my phone back so I can ring her? Or was it broken in the crash? And mum is now the weak link; she might tell the police that it was Emily driving, and that we were coming down for dinner because Emily and I are romantically partnered.'

Detective Pauline Milosky stuck her head around the curtain for the second time.

'Sorry to disturb you again, Mr Robinson. I forgot to give you this. It's your phone. It's a bit scratched up and bent. And the battery is flat. Maybe they have a charger in here you can use.'

'Thanks, Detective. Unfortunately, I'm not allowed technology in here, so I doubt they'd have a charger. But thanks for returning it to me, much appreciated.'

'If you do get it charged, can you remember to check for an Emily King in your contacts, and let us know what you've found. Thanks.'

'Will do.'

Dan checked with the nurses, and Rahima had a charger at home. She took Dan's phone and charged it up overnight, bringing it back in the next day. Dan told her the passcode to get into the phone, and she took it out of the medical unit and powered it up.

Sadly, it was dead. It wouldn't power up, despite being on an overnight charge. She broke the news to Dan.

'Fuck!'

'But I have some news,' Rahima said. 'A woman named Emily called and said she was okay and looking forward to seeing you once you'd left here.'

'Fucking brilliant!' Dan involuntarily jumped in his

bed, but the pain shot him down ruthlessly.

96

Eventually, Dan was released into the care of his mother, and she drove up to collect him. There was still much healing to be done, and Dan's mood swings were worrying. But as the BIRS folk, and the ICCU nurses also said, being at home and surrounded by the familiar did wonders for stabilising a patient's moods.

When he got home, he hobbled ungracefully into the study, to order another laptop online from the desktop computer. He guessed that the one he had with him in Emily's car was broken beyond repair and he'd need a new one quickly. He fired up the office desktop, searched the Dell website for a cheap laptop with a numeric keypad, and hit the 'Pay' button. By the end of the week he'd have a new laptop to configure and play with, delivered to the Meningie Post Office.

New laptop purchased, his next task was to contact Emily. He left a virtual chalk mark on their wall and waited to see if he got any immediate response. He didn't.

Angry, he got up from his chair, pushed a pile of papers off the desk and onto the floor, and staggered out from behind the desk and out into the kitchen. Checking the fridge for beers and finding none Dan slammed the fridge door shut and stormed off to find his mother.

He found her in the living room, on her phone to a friend.

'Mum!' he interrupted, 'there's no beer in the fridge!'

'Excuse me, Phyllis. No, Dan, the doctors said you

weren't to have any alcohol yet because it interferes with your medicines. You'll have to drink water.'

'Oh, for fuck's sake!'

'Daniel, don't speak to me like that, please.'

'Sorry. Fuck.' Dan left the room and hobbled his way back to his bedroom, where he gingerly climbed onto his bed and lay down.

'Guilt. Now I have guilt,' he said to himself. 'I just lost my temper at mum, and now I feel awful. How could I have done that? Oh, God, I'm a shithead. When I get up, I'll go and apologise. Shit. How could I have been so awful to her?'

After a while there was a knock on the door.

'Daniel, dear, can I come in?'

'Come in, mum.'

'How are you feeling, my love? Is it nice to be back amongst your belongings?'

'Yeah, it is. Look, mum, I'm really sorry for swearing at you and behaving like a pork chop. You don't deserve that. I guess I was just so angry that everything came out. I'm really sorry.'

'That's alright, my love. Everybody said your moods would probably be volatile until you settled into a routine at home. We've just got to figure out a routine for you now. Did you order your laptop?'

'Yeah, it should arrive by Friday, which will be good. I'd much rather be running my business from my bed than the desk at the moment, but until I get a new phone sorted out with the phone company, I'm stuck. At least I have backed up all my contacts in the cloud, so I can just download and install them onto my new phone.'

'When did the phone company say they could get a new phone to you?'

'Thursday, all going well. Which is good, because I've

probably got a stack of calls from my clients, and they'd be wondering why I'm not getting back to them.'

'Have you heard from Emily?'

'No, I left her a message online, so hopefully she'll see that soon and get back in touch. I'm sure my insurance company will want to know who her insurance company is. But I don't really want it to go down that path, I'd much rather get my clients back up and running, my new laptop configured and running smoothly, and my healing getting on with itself. It would be lovely if she could get some new wheels and come down and see me. I'm sure she will if she can.'

'I hope so, my love. In the meantime, if I can help in any way, please let me know. Now, did you want me to ring Davo and Kelly? I'm sure they'd love to speak to you.'

'That would be magic, mum, thanks.'

'I'll go and get my phone.

97

The next day was Dan and Hannah's scheduled catch-up. He'd missed one while he was in hospital, and without his phone he couldn't be sure that she'd be online and ready to chat. He'd already hopped into the Misfits group on Facebook, looking for her, but not seeing her presence, he had left a message in Messenger and hoped she'd see it in time to catch up.

He needn't have worried.

'Oh, Dan! I was so worried. You were out of touch for ages, I thought the police had arrested you.'

'Nah, all good. I just had a massive car accident.' Dan

brought Hannah up to speed on the crash, the hospital and how Emily, apart from one second-hand message, had just disappeared with no trace—he couldn't find her anywhere, but he didn't have his phone and wouldn't have a new one until tomorrow.

'That's awful,' Hannah said. 'So, you're okay apart from the broken ribs and all the bruising?'

'Yeah, plus I get big mood swings. One minute I'm okay, then the next minute I'm the Incredible Hulk. After that, I calm down and become Mr Sorry for Himself.'

'That's funny and sad at the same time. Oh, Dan. What a mess!'

'I know. According to the doctors at the hospital, I'm lucky to be alive. Even luckier to not have broken arms and legs and neck and stuff.'

'That's amazing. Hey, I heard a good joke the other day, I reckon this might help cheer you up: 'If we are what we eat, I'm fast, cheap and easy'.'

'That's very good, Hannah. Ha ha ha.'

'It was posted in the Misfits group the other day and I know you would have commented on it, so when you didn't I got more concerned.'

'Well, you don't need to worry about me being caught. I had a police detective leave a message on my phone saying she wanted to meet with me, then she rang back a day later saying that she couldn't now make the meeting and she would ring me back at some future date. Sounds harmless to me.'

'Harmless? Are you crazy? You have the police inter-ested in you. That means your name is in their database as a person of interest. That tag never leaves you, you remain in the system for life. I'd be worried if I were you.'

'Nah, 's all good. I have Australia's best hacker giving

me instructions on how to stay out of harm's way. I trust her implicitly. She's never been caught, so why should I be if I'm following her exact steps?'

'I respect your confidence, Dan, I really do, but I reckon you're wrong on this.'

'Well, I won't know anything until they decide to chat with me again, if they ever do. No point stressing about that now, is there?'

'Well, just as long as you stay out of harm's way. I would lie low for a while, not hack into anybody's computers for a while, just to be on the safe side.'

'There's the thing. One of the first things I do when I get my new laptop is I'm going to reload all of my hacking software and go hacking some sites. To make sure I've still got it, and I don't have any brain injury.'

'Oh, Dan. Don't do that. At least rest and heal first. Give yourself the greatest chance of hacking with ease by being fully rested and restored. At the moment, it sounds like your brain is all muddled. Let it settle down and let sanity restore itself. Please.'

'I'll think about it.'

'Out of curiosity, who would you hack?'

'I'd probably have another wander through Derringerry, for old time's sake. Or Anthol Logistics; I never did get the chance to use the backdoor I planted on their system. Or I might just pick a random business, like a temp staffing agency or something, and see what I can do in there.'

Dan, please don't go hacking straight away. Let your mind and body settle. Let them heal. Those companies will still be there when you get better, but if you are a person of interest already someone somewhere will be keeping a watch on you, and if you make one error, they will have you. Trust me, that's what my dad taught me.'

'Okay, Hannah, I'll wait until I'm feeling better. But I hope I don't succumb to boredom.'

'Hopefully when you get your new phone, you can catch up on all of your client calls and that will keep you busy. At least you don't have to worry about driving up to see them for a little while.'

'That's true. But I enjoyed the journey—I listened to music, I answered emails, I sent texts, all via Siri from my car. It was very productive.'

'Well, I hope that level of productivity is manageable when you get your new phone and laptop. Don't forget, you've had a major trauma, your body needs to heal, even if your mind is still active.'

'Yes, nurse. And as an example of how the trauma is affecting me, I'm actually feeling tired just from our conversation. So maybe I'm not as fit as I think I am. Would you mind if we ended the call and I take a little nap?'

'No, not at all. I totally understand. End the call and rest up. Just remember, there's a lot of people who love you who would hate to see you in prison because you made a silly error out of tiredness. Don't go back to hacking straight away, Dan, okay?'

'Okay. Message received and understood. I'll leave off my hacking pleasures for a little while longer.'

'Good. Glad to hear it. Take care and see you next week, my friend.'

DAN WASN'T ARRESTED, HE WAS IN HOSPITAL! OMG I AM SO RELIEVED. I HAD VISIONS OF HIM IN A REMAND CENTRE, BEING PUSHED AROUND BY THE PRISON GUARDS AND OTHER INMATES. HE'S NOT HARD ENOUGH TO

SURVIVE IN THAT SORT OF ENVIRONMENT. EVEN THOUGH I'M SORRY TO HEAR HE'S BEEN IN A SERIOUS ACCIDENT, AND HIS GIRLFRIEND IS MISSING IN ACTION, I'M SO GLAD TO KNOW HE HASN'T BEEN CAUGHT.

THE RELIEF COMPLETELY TOOK MY EMOTIONS BY SURPRISE. I'M FLUSHED WITH EMOTION, WITH HAPPINESS. I'M ELATED. I KNOW THERE WILL BE A PUNISHMENT FOR THIS, FOR THIS HAPPINESS. I KNOW THAT MY BRAIN WILL TRIGGER A CORRESPONDING SWING TO THE DARK SIDE TO COMPENSATE. BUT FOR NOW, I AM REALLY REALLY HAPPY THAT DAN IS SAFE, IF NOT WELL.

98

Being an insomniac has its benefits. For one, you need never miss out on what is happening at work even if you are a State away, you just call up the work computers at three in the morning and see what is going on.

For another, you have the quiet of the night in which to think, when the busyness of the day, with its incessant emails and phone calls and meetings and discussions, blocks out any reflective thinking.

Three am is the hour of writers, painters, poets, musicians, silence seekers, over-thinkers, and other creatives. Walk around a city at that hour and you can see them. They have their lights on.

Three am is the hour that Stephanie McBride sat down with a glass of Auchentoshan scotch and reflected on the work she was still heavily involved in, even while she was back in Melbourne, tending to her son Joshua and his injuries from the terrorist incident.

Only two other people in Stephanie's work world knew of her insomnia: the HR officer that entered the details into her file, and her boss, both of whom were sworn to secrecy. Everyone else she worked with thought she was some kind of Wonder Woman. Which, in a way, she was. She didn't carry a whip or a shield, but she tracked down criminals and brought them to justice at a rate that outpaced her colleagues.

At this point, she had fifty seven cases on the go. That is the workload that she and her colleagues were under. Those fifty seven cases could be organised criminals, or they could be teenagers out for kicks or out to create a name for themselves. Or they could be overseas players out for a fun night in, or to stretch their crime tentacles.

She thought about the Derringerry and Anthol Logistics hacker. Sure, the hacker followed traditional paths in their method. But they were organised enough to clean up after themselves. If it hadn't been for the artificial intelligence engine at work none of the break-ins of this hacker, whoever they were, would have been discovered. That, to Stephanie, was a sign that they were more than just a bored teenager out for some kicks. Either they had received instruction, or they were naturally talented at the game.

It was the former that Stephanie was betting on. And not just instruction from anyone—instruction from D@@Mladen.

Stephanie had no clues other than the neatness and regularity of the hacks to make her think that her nemesis had anything to do with this particular hacker. Indeed, the regularity of the hacking, initiated about two or three minutes after seven pm, was a weakness, a chink in the armour. A slip-up that an experienced hacker would never make.

There were no obvious, direct ties from this hacker to D@@Mladen, but Stephanie's intuition told her that there was a connection. She'd pursued hackers with far less surety and still come up smiling before. Look at Rocco—he'd been picked up using a signature move of D@@Mladen's, and he didn't deny it. Only he said he'd never actually met him and so didn't know what he looked like. Every contact, Rocco had said, was made online, all the training was via video conferencing, hands-off and remote. D@@Mladen could be anywhere in the world, Rocco had said. D@@Mladen left no calling card, no secret boast of what they'd done and why. Like when you take your finger out of a glass of water and look at the hole left behind, sometimes there was no trace of a hack. But knowledgeable minds looked at the bigger picture of hacking in Australia and saw that this very absence of a calling card was itself a calling card.

So, while other high-end hackers boasted of their successes in forums, and were tracked by an ever-watching police presence, D@@Mladen was noticeably quiet about his activities. All the police felt they had to go on was that he probably had several trainees he was looking after, how many was unknown, even those of his trainees who had been caught, like Rocco, had never heard of or knew of anyone else.

It was this interest in finding D@@Mladen that drove Stephanie. She would love to be the one to track him down, to bring him to justice. And the case of the neat and tidy hacker with the predictable timetable who had hacked into a farm and then the farm's parent company, was her current only lead.

She took another sip of scotch and composed an email for Rocco.

Rocco, I need you to focus your attention on the Derringerry and Anthol Logistics hacker, please. Liaise with Senior Constable Andrew Campbell in Meningie and see if you can see any activity in Meningie at seven pm tonight. I have a hunch that the hacker we are looking for is local to Derringerry and is possibly hacking other sites as well. Can you scour the dark web for any clues to the hacker's identity, please, they might have boasted about their hacks in some forums.

Let me know how you get on. Use your car to drive to Meningie and back and take a note of your odometer readings when you start out and when you get home, I'll sort out reimbursement.

Thanks, Stephanie

99

'*Fanculo questo!*'

Rocco pushed his chair away from his desk and looked around the room, hoping that someone would have noticed him. No one looked back.

'I was going to go to my cousin's house this evening,' he announced to no-one in particular, 'but now I have to drive down to Meningie. Shit. I'm going to get a coffee.'

Not even the prospect of coffee was enough to garner a response. Without Stephanie, his audience had shrunk to none.

He got up and sulked his way up to Vili's café, knowing full well that he'd have to go back to the office to collect his car keys and also spend some time digging around the dark web for word of the Derringerry and Anthol hacks. If the hacker were being trained by D@@Mladen, he thought, there would be no word. D@@Mladen's trainees are told very early on that their exploits are to remain secret. 'Loose lips sink ships' they are told, emphatically, and examples reeled off of showboating ex-hackers who had been caught because they had been mouthing off in the various hacker forums. Being mouthy was a sure way of being dropped from the team, and no-one wanted the reputation of being a one-trick show pony.

He sipped his coffee, and took a bite from his bun, and made his angry way back to the office.

A search for word of the hacks turned up nothing, as he expected. But a search for D@@Mladen turned up something interesting. Someone was using an alias known to the police as belonging to the uber-hacker. There was the alias name, Robin, and a single word, 'caring'. Rocco made a mental note to monitor that post, to see if anyone responded. It was doubtful that they would, though, he told himself. All that would happen would be whoever was supposed to see the message would meet up somewhere secure. A pre-determined time, place and channel. Still, a clue is a clue, and worth following up even if nothing eventuates.

Rocco fired off an email to Stephanie, letting her know of his discovery.

He then rang Andrew Campbell in Meningie and arranged to meet him at the police station at five in the evening.

Those tasks out of the way, Rocco picked up his car keys

and laptop and headed out to fill up his tank. He would go home and enjoy a nice lunch at home, then crank up the car stereo and enjoy a leisurely trip down to Meningie. He had all the time in the world, and, except for a court case that would come around eventually, very few cares.

———

A pleasant lunch at home was enjoyed, and Rocco took a brief nap before leaving at two-thirty in the afternoon for Meningie.

A two-hour journey of loud doof-doof music found him feeling peckish by the time he landed in the town. Remembering that there was a Vietnamese takeaway that Stephanie had enjoyed the last time he was in town, he navigated Google Maps for directions and pulled up out the front of Phuoc and Han's shop.

'G'day, what would you recommend to someone new to Vietnamese cooking?' he asked Phuoc.

'Well, the cold rice paper rolls are always popular. You can have either a vegetarian filling or pork and prawn. Buy three rolls and you have a snack, buy six for twelve dollars and you have a meal.'

'That sounds great, I'll have six of the meat filling,' Rocco replied, aware that he had a long drive home ahead of him.

He thought of hacking and wondered if the owner of the shop had any ideas who it might be.

'Say, did you know one of the local farms had been hacked into recently?'

'Oh sure, everyone around here knows about it. 'Không

có bí mật trong một thị trấn nhỏ—there are no secrets in a small town',' Phuoc replied. Han's eyes were focused on the meals she was preparing, but her sharp ears listened intently to her husband and the stranger.

'Do you have any opinion on who it might be? Is it someone local, do you think?'

'Well, it depends on who is asking. Who are you?'

'I'm another hacker, and I'm interested in talking with the person who hacked into the farm.'

'Well, in that case, there's a man known as Davo, some people down here wouldn't be surprised if it was him; after all, he was the one who was sacked by the farm. But I don't think he's smart enough to do it,' said Phuoc. 'Tội nhân rõ ràng nhất đôi khi không phải là thủ phạm thực sự—the most obvious sinner is sometimes not the real culprit'.'

'Who do you think is smart enough to do it?'

'That I don't know, Mr Hacker. You are going to have to do some digging yourself to find the culprit, even though they might not be from around here.'

'Okay. Well, thanks for the rolls.'

Phuoc turned to his wife once Rocco had left the shop. 'That was no hacker,' he said.

'I agree, that was the police. Aren't they young these days? Constable Andrew is so old by comparison. Who do you think is the hacker?'

'I reckon it's Mr Dan. He's a computer geek, he has fixed our computer when it was playing up, I reckon he did it for Davo's sake. I have no proof, it's just my hunch. But I'm certainly not going to tell the police that. They can do their own dirty work.'

'I disagree with you. I don't think Mr Dan did it, he's too nice and friendly.' And with that, Han went back to her food preparation.

Rocco pulled up at the station just after five and strolled inside to meet Andrew. Introductions made, Andrew made some space at another desk for Rocco and his laptop.

'What I'd like to do,' explained Rocco, 'is drive around Meningie with you from around six-thirty to seven-thirty. The hacker who broke into the farm usually goes online around seven pm, and I have a black box here that can hack into modems and routers and let me see where people are going when they're online. I'm hoping to match up the address details we know of with the person visiting them.'

'You want me to drive?'

'Yeah, that way I can concentrate on doing this black box magic. Sounds do-able?'

'Totally. We've got a bit of time to kill, want a coffee?'

'Sure. I'll check my emails an' stuff.'

'Fill your boots.'

When Andrew returned with the instant coffee, Rocco had a near seizure, but he did his best not to let on. 'I'll just let it cool down.'

'No worries.'

'Say, I was talking to the guy who runs the Vietnamese takeaway. He reckons someone called 'Davo' might be the hacker, although he did say that Davo wasn't that bright.'

'Yeah, Davo is a nice enough bloke, but the roos are out of the top paddock. He's not a suspect. I'll tell you who is, at least in my books. It's his best mate, Dan Robinson. Dan is the local IT guru, fixes everyone's computers when they play up. Has a business looking after the IT of some

Adelaide companies. Makes the journey up to Adelaide a couple of times a month to see his clients. Now he has the smarts to hack into other people's computers, I reckon. I've been round to see him about some other matters, but he's always stayed clean.'

'How about we focus our attention on him this evening? Is that possible to do without making it look obvious and stopping him from carrying out a hack?'

'Possibly. We could park just down the road, maybe a hundred metres away. Would your black box work from that distance?'

'Doubtful. But what if we used my car instead of yours? He wouldn't recognise my car, and we could get closer, perhaps.'

'We could. The trouble is that the house is just near an intersection and is the only house in that vicinity. There are no other houses to screen us.'

'Fuck. Well, let's give it a go anyway. It will be worth trying. I can leave a payload in his modem and router that will enable us to track him in the future.'

'Well, that's got to be a good thing, if I knew what you were talking about. But let's do that. Now, I'll let you get on with your emails. Did you sort out some dinner?'

'Sure did. I got some cold rolls. That should last me until I get home.'

At six thirty, Andrew and Rocco left the police station in Rocco's car, Andrew driving. They made their way up McIntosh Way to East Terrace, then on to Cemetery Road. There were only two houses on Cemetery Road, the Macklethwaite's down near the cemetery itself, and Ros Robinson's petite three-bed brick veneer home.

'I tell you what,' Andrew said as they slowly approached the house, 'I can park in the Trees of Tribute monument opposite.' That should be close enough for you to get a reading but still give us a bit of cover.'

'Okay, sounds good, go for it.'

Rocco pulled out his black box, connected it to his laptop, and started scanning. First, he had to identify the modem and router, then he had to crack its password. That was easy enough with the tools he had at his disposal. He then jiggered and poked with his laptop to place a quiet monitoring program on the router. Mission accomplished, Rocco retraced his steps, wiping his digital fingerprints. Just as his mentor had taught him. All up it took ten minutes.

Six forty-five on a beautiful evening. The sun was low in the sky, casting amber rays across the walls and roofs of Meningie. Time to wait and monitor the web traffic coming from Ros Robinson's house.

There was constant activity, showing an open connection to Facebook and Gmail. There was a connection, too, to HackerNews. That's not your typical domestic traffic, Rocco mentioned to Andrew. But that was also nothing that could get a guy in trouble.

They kept watching, Rocco his laptop, Andrew the house.

At six fifty-five, Andrew saw movement. 'Dan Robinson is getting into his mother's car with his laptop and pulling out of the driveway. Do I follow him?'

Dan had just had a rare—but increasingly frequent of late—fight with his mother. He was itching to get back into hacking, to prove to himself that he still had the skills. His sense of self, of manhood, was wrapped up in his ability to hack into a company's computers, even if he did nothing when he was there. It was all about the successful act of penetration.

Dan told his mother that he needed to get out and that he was going for a drive in her car. He would have taken his, but it was still parked outside Emily's house.

'Dan, what are you thinking? Your ribs are broken, you're on painkillers, you can't drive. Don't be silly, put down those keys and let me make you a cup of tea,' Ros had said.

'No, mum, you don't understand. I'm going stir crazy. I need to get out.'

'Dan, my love, you can't possibly drive with your body wrapped so tight in pain and painkillers.'

'But I can, mum. I can twist enough to be able to look around and see that the road is clear.'

'Oh, Daniel! You're silly. Put the keys down and come and sit down with me.'

'No, mum, I'm going for a drive!'

'Daniel! You're on painkillers and shouldn't be driving. The insurance company won't cover you. Now come back here and sit down. Please.'

'Fuck off, old lady! I'm going for a drive and that's that!'

And with that Dan stormed off and got in Ros' Polo. Luckily for him, he lived on a quiet road and didn't have to twist and look behind him to reverse out of the driveway.

Ros didn't pursue him because she was not a chaser.

She hated conflict of any sort and sat shell-shocked by the exchange she had just had with her son. As the front door slammed shut, she sighed and tears escaped her eyes.

Dan was in his mother's car, driving away from the house, and Andrew had asked Rocco whether he should follow him. Rocco thought about it, then decided. 'No, he'll probably recognise our car. Did he look like he was carrying a mobile phone?'

'Too hard to tell. Why?'

'Because he might be using that mobile phone to tether his laptop and access the web that way. Or he might not, he might be on his way to a friend to fix their computer for them. I've heard he does that a lot. Either way, our work here is done. We've planted an eavesdropping program in his house, and I can monitor that from anywhere. Let's head back to the station, and I'll write up my report and head off.'

'Okay, heading back.'

Back at the station, Rocco wrote a long—for him—email to Stephanie telling her what he'd done, the conversations he'd had and the progress they had made. They now had a suspect that they could track, although if he used his laptop and mobile phone to perform hacks they were still blind. Stephanie would later reply that she was coming back the next day, to visit Meningie and capture Dan. Good work, Rocco, she would say.

All in all, Rocco thought, a good day's work. It started badly, but he'd had a nice lunch and a nap, a thumping drive down to this country town, a track, a hack and he had a nice meal waiting in the fridge for him to heat up when he got home. All in all, a good day's work.

———————

Six fifty-five pm. 'You ready?' Stephanie asked Andrew.

'Ready as I'll ever be.'

Stephanie was back in South Australia, just to wrap this case up. She checked her phone again, waiting to see if Dan had once again entered Anthol or Derringerry's computer system. No, it was still quiet. So they continued to wait, parked on North Terrace out of eyeshot of the Robinson residence.

A text on her phone. Rocco, confirming that he saw no activity. The previous hacks had all occurred on or just after 7pm.

Just then, Ros's car drove past them on East Terrace, probably heading out to Bowman Street and the Princes Highway.

To give chase or to let him go. Andrew said to follow, he could be going somewhere and hack in using his laptop and mobile phone connection. Stephanie said to wait. 'There are no other cars on the road at this time of evening, so a police car will stand out'. Stephanie was the ranking officer, so her view was the one that mattered. An example of 'The Hippo', Andrew thought—the highest paid person's opinion.

'Let's call it a night and try again tomorrow,' Stephanie decided. 'Tonight, after it's dark, can you attach this gadget to the underside of Ros's car, please? Use wire or gaffer tape to make sure it stays in place.'

'Sure.'

'Thanks. Now, take me back to my car, and I'll come down tomorrow afternoon.'

106

Stephanie looked at her iPad and saw that the Bluetooth tracker Andrew had planted under Ros's car had come to a stop at the corner of Hacket Crescent and McCallum Street.

Dan was parked at the side of Our Lady Help of Catholic church, using his second, burner, phone for network access. Once again he entered Derringerry's server, sort of like an old lover to go to in times of stress, this time looking for other files to adjust, and ego to fuel.

He remembered Emily's words: 'get in, get it done, get out, quickly'. But this time would be different, he thought. This time he was on safe ground because he'd enter via the backdoor he planted. There was less of a risk of being caught.

He deliberately slowed down, looking around his cyber surroundings and noting what files and folders are here. He felt more like a seasoned pro hacker now. He knew that being aware of one's surroundings was key to advanced hacking, Emily had told him that. He looked for rogue programs owned by SAPOL or Derringerry. His additional training with Emily prepared him for their presence and if he found any he was confident that he could calmly dismember them.

Stephanie saw *Evie's* message on her phone and received a confirmation text from Rocco seconds later. Time to act. According to *Evie*, the intruder was the same as the intruder of Anthol Logistics of not so long ago. A deep level geo search would take a little longer, but already *Evie* was reasonably confident the hack was originating from the south east of South Australia.

Dan was transferred by *Evie* to the dummy virtual site, complete with empty files with the correct filenames, but this time with a couple of extra 'real' files donated by Stephanie. One of which was the payroll spreadsheet, this time carrying a payload that would bounce back and start infecting the hacker's computer. Dan was wandering around, comfortable and confident that he'd find something worth looking for. He didn't bother putting tissue paper over his webcam.

Stephanie turned his webcam on and took screenshots of both him and the screen he was looking at.

Dan's meandering through Derringerry's folders saw him finally uncover a folder that contained the MD's personal files. Or, at least, was supposed to. The filenames were innocuous enough: 'February', 'Project Rain', 'Rental assistance'.

Dan paused for a moment, cracked his knuckles. 'Which file to read first?' He decided on 'Project Rain'. But the Word doc wouldn't open.

Stephanie watched as Dan's mouse hovered over a dummy file, kept clicking on it, hovered again, clicked again a few more times, then hovered once more. She watched as Dan tried another file, then another.

Dan's confusion and frustration escalated quickly. He was swearing. Stephanie could hear him through his laptop microphone.

She dropped a real text file into the folder.

Readme: Dan Robinson, you have been caught illegally entering into the computers of Derringerry Farm. Please present yourself to the Meningie Police Station immediately. Stephanie McBride.

'Time to go, Andrew.'

'Where to?'

She told him.

'The Catholic church. I hope he's praying for salvation,' Andrew responded.

'He will be shortly. He's certainly got plenty of guilt for the Catholics to feast upon.'

Stephanie eased into the passenger seat, and Andrew eased the patrol car south. From what Stephanie had told him, there was no need to hurry, Dan would be there for a good fifteen minutes.

Frustrated with the un-openable files in the MD's folder, Dan moved out of there—without seeing Stephanie's note—and navigated the folder structure until he found the salary file again. He was revisiting his old conquests, and his attention was focused on opening it.

Stephanie and Andrew pulled up, blocking his exit. They got out of the patrol car quietly, didn't close the doors, and softly softly tip-toed their way up the grass to Dan's car. He never heard or saw them coming.

It was all over in a disappointing few seconds. No shouting, no hysterics, none of the 'you'll never take me alive, copper!' antics you see on tv—Andrew tapped on the driver's window, Dan looked up, saw the uniform and knew it was all over. Stephanie opened the passenger door, leant in, took Dan's laptop and took a cellphone picture of the laptop screen.

While Andrew got Dan out of the car and put the hand-cuffs on, Stephanie made a call.

'Rocco, we've got him. Tidy things up, please.'

It was all very calm, polite and matter-of-fact. An anti-climax, as these things so often were.

He was caught. No alibi. God, his mum would be angry, he thought. And disappointed in him. This would be his last hack of Derringerry. Emily had taught him to do the least possible damage and get out before anyone could know he was in there. Well, she'd obviously not taught him well enough. He was performing one last penetration to prove to himself that he was still good. He wasn't supposed to get caught.

The drive back to the police station was sedate, as was his entrance into the station building. Andrew took him down to the cells, to let him feel the weight of his crime before Stephanie started asking him questions. He sat on the single bed and pondered—how did he feel? Did he have any regrets? Andrew had asked him if there was someone he wanted to contact, a lawyer or something?

The only lawyer he knew was Mr Pendlebury, Davo's uncle, and he guessed that he was as good as anybody in a situation like this. No point in trying to deny what he'd done. Best to plead 'guilty' and hope the magistrate takes pity on country men.

Mr Pendlebury was informed of what Dan was about to be charged with, as well as the circumstances leading up to the arrest. He was led into the interviewing room, where Dan was already waiting.

PART FOUR

107

It didn't take long. It never usually does. Once Dan admitted to the hacking, and Stephanie had probed him about D@@Mladen, Andrew took over and asked him about the thefts from Derringerry.

He was at first silent about his best mate. But it only took a little persuasion—along the lines of, 'we only want the truth', and 'possibly no charges will be laid if we can recover the equipment in working order'—for Dan's resolve to waver.

Stephanie reminded him that his co-operation would serve him well with the magistrate, 'should it come to that'.

'Okay, it was Davo that helped me with the robberies. He drove the ute, but it was all my idea and prompting.'

As with the admission of guilt with the hacking, Dan felt a tremendous sense of relief in his confession, as if he trusted that the police would look after him and Davo. He guessed that the sense of relief was the same as Catholics must experience when they confess to a priest. A lightening of the load, a trust in a higher power to look after them and make things right. Mummy and Daddy would fix things.

Of course, the police were going to press charges against Davo. It was their job. But something in Dan convinced him otherwise, that the police would stand by their word and drop their investigation once they'd recovered the equipment.

Andrew: 'Where did you leave the equipment you stole from the farm, Dan?'

'South on the highway, down about eight point five clicks from town. Just after the entrance to Yungip Farm, there's a 100km speed sign. Next to it, on the right, there's a dirt track hidden behind the swamp paperbark bushes on the side of the road. Runs along the eastern edge of old man Johnson's farm. You'll find the generator and the welder there, under some camouflage netting.'

'Thank you,' said Andrew. That made his job considerably easier. This was a big brown area to search, and it had been taking up a lot of his time.

'Dan, I will type up a statement that I will ask you to read and then sign. I will be gone for about twenty minutes. No doubt Ms McBride will take a break, too, so I'll leave you with Mr Pendlebury here to fill in the time and prepare you for the next stage in your adventure. Okay?'

'Okay.'

Left with Mr Pendlebury for company, Dan had time to process all that had happened.

He was fine at first. Just a little curious about how things would play out here at the station.

But slowly the enormity of what he'd done crept up on him. He'd committed cyber-crime. That was a serious felony. And more importantly to him, he'd let his mother down. Let alone Davo, Sarah, Kelly and his new friend Hannah, who had been warning him all along.

Dan broke down and cried. It was the first cry he'd cried in twenty years, the first since his mother had taken him from the family home and transplanted him in rural Meningie. At the time she had said, 'Hush, don't cry. Big boys don't cry', and he'd believed her. His sobs now were not just for the present, but for all the pasts he had endured.

'I am one of life's incompetents. Someone who means well but doesn't have the competency to make a go of anything. After six years in the RAAF, I have not been able to find a job, so have tried to set myself up in business. But it's such slow going, and it takes so much energy. I am a professional failure. I am useless and hopeless, a smiling and laughing dead weight and an intellectual lightweight. I am a ne'er-do-well, not from any criminality, but just from malignant incompetence. Someone that mothers warn their daughters about and advise them not to marry.'

But after the streams of his tears, there was calm. For a brief moment he had been someone. He had been someone powerful. He had walked without stooping for once, and had spoken confidently. He had a girlfriend and a semi-successful business. He was to never forget that.

And he remembered one more thing. A saying he'd come across on the internet that forced a chuckle from him: 'My entire life can be summed up in one sentence: It didn't go as planned'.

Mr Pendlebury received the call from Andrew in the middle of his favourite tv show. He'd just returned from handling the affairs of Dan Robinson.

'Be prepared, Mr Pendlebury. We will bring your nephew Dave Wilkins in for questioning, with charges of unlawful trespass and multiple counts of theft. I strongly ask you to not contact your nephew before we bring him in for questioning, I've only called you now as a professional courtesy.'

'Understood Constable and thank you. I will prepare to represent my nephew accordingly.'

He waited until Constable Campbell ended the call.

'What's he done now?' he thought to himself. 'Ever since his parents died in that awful car crash he's been a boat without a rudder. I thought Sarah could keep him on an even keel, but it seems not.'

He picked up his briefcase and checked that he had his favourite fountain pen, a LAMY Studio, and a black Leuchtturm1917 notebook, still with him after the Dan Robinson session. He felt that serious matters were always best considered with serious writing materials. He checked that the ink reservoir in the pen was full and noticing that it wasn't he padded to the kitchen and pulled on some disposable gloves. He emptied the ink in the pen out down the kitchen sink, flushed the reservoir full of clean water ten times, then carefully filled the pen with Noodler's 'Borealis Black' ink. He then dried the nib and barrel with tissue paper and put the pen into the correct spot in his briefcase.

Now he was ready to represent his nephew.

There was a knock at the front door.

'I'll get it, hon,' called Sarah, who was near the door anyway.

She turned on the outside light and opened the door, surprised to see Constable Andrew Campbell standing there.

'Hello,' she said, 'How are you? Come in.'

Andrew took his hat off and entered the living room.

'Mrs Wilkins, I've come to see your husband. Is he in?'

'Sure. DAVO!' she called out.

'Coming! Who is it?' Davo called back from the kitchen where he was making Sarah's lunch for the next day. He turned the corner and stopped in his tracks.

'Oh,' he involuntarily let out.

'What 'oh'?' asked Sarah of him.

'Nothing. Constable Andrew, what brings you to us at,' he checked his phone, 'nine thirty at night?'

'I'm afraid I have to ask you to come with me to the station, Mr Wilkins. We'd like your help with a small enquiry.'

'What enquiry?' asked Sarah. 'Davo, what is this?'

Constable Andrew replied on Davo's behalf: 'I'm afraid we can't discuss it here, Mrs Wilkins. But your husband is able to help us with a police matter, and I would be very grateful if he would come with me to the station now to clear some details up.'

'Can't this wait until the morning? Why the urgency?' asked a slightly emotional Sarah.

'Now is the best time, I'm afraid,' Andrew replied calmly.

'Davo, what's going on?'

'It's okay, hon,' lied Davo, 'this won't take long. I'll fill you in on all the details when I get back. Let's go.'

Before his wife could ask any more probing questions, questions he didn't want to lie to but equally didn't want to answer right now, Davo grabbed a jumper and led Andrew out to his car. He guessed that this could be a long night.

'Thanks for coming,' Andrew uttered, started the Commodore up and reversed out of the driveway. It was only a short trip from Baker Street to the station. Neither man said anything more on the journey.

***

'**Would you like to come in here** and wait for a moment, please?' Andrew asked, pointing to the interview room. Davo complied and sat in one of the plastic chairs facing the door, next to the table.

'Would you like a cup of tea or coffee?' Andrew again asked.

'Tea, please. Black, no sugar.'

'Certainly. I'll be back in a minute.'

Left on his own, Davo was confronted by his choices. He'd let his emotions get the better of him again and went along with Dan's suggestion of enacting revenge on Derringerry by stealing equipment. Dan had said they wouldn't get caught.

'Bugger!' he said to himself. He'd been caught. It was not going to end well. Sarah would give him a huge telling off. At least his parents weren't around to see this, he reasoned. They'd be mighty pissed off at him, and really disappointed.

Andrew reappeared with a mug of tea for Davo and an offer of help.

'Your uncle, Mr Pendlebury, is here helping us with another matter. If you like, I can ask him to come in here and represent you.'

Davo thought about it. A friendly face was welcome right about now.

'That would be good, thanks.'

Minutes later, Andrew opened the door and ushered Mr Pendlebury in.

'David.'

'Uncle John.'

'Gentlemen, let me start the proceedings,' announced Andrew. 'Mr Wilkins is here to assist us with our enquiries into missing farming equipment. I'm going to record our conversation and give you, Mr Wilkins, a copy of the conversation when it is finished. Is that okay with you both?'

Both men nodded their consent.

Andrew typed in some metadata into a recording machine and loaded a couple of coloured dvds and a cd. He hit the record button and the interview proper started.

'Mr Wilkins, some equipment used by the Derringerry Farm recently went missing. Do you know anything about it?'

Davo was faced with a dilemma—did he pretend he didn't steal anything or did he come clean? If he pretended he knew nothing about it, how long could he get away with the lie? Could he reasonably expect to keep the police clueless as to the thieves' identities? And why was Uncle John here? Was he going to be charged? If so, Uncle John's presence was not a good sign. What will Sarah say if he is charged? Will he be able to go back home to her to await a court case, or will they take him to a remand centre and he won't see the outside world again? What if Sarah leaves him?

Davo was silent for a good few minutes while he fidgeted and weighed up his options. Andrew was sensible enough to let Davo be the next person to speak.

In the end, Davo chose what he believed was the best option—tell the truth. Sarah would forgive him eventually, and even if she didn't, and she left him, it was what he deserved.

With his heart plain for all to see, with his head down, Davo sighed and confessed.

'Yes, it was me that stole the equipment. Me alone.'

111

Alone at last with her thoughts, Ros leant back in her armchair. Where had she gone wrong? Was she too strict with Dan? Was she not strict enough? Was she too selfish when she left his father and took him with her? Was she too picky to not give him a good adult male role model to grow up with? Had her staying single been the wrong thing for her son?

'He's been such a good boy,' she mused to herself.

All the thrashings of her mind were for nothing. So too, were all the positive affirmations and sayings she'd been sticking on her fridge. In this time of need nothing came, no cheery saying spoke to her.

On her fridge at this moment:

'WHEN THINGS GO WRONG AS THEY SOMETIMES WILL,

When the road you're trudging seems all
uphill,
    When funds are low and debts are high,
    You want to smile, but you have to sigh,
    When care is pressing you down a bit,
    Rest if you must, but don't you quit.
    Life is strange with its twists and turns
    As every one of us sometimes learns,
    And many a failure comes about
    When he might have won had he stuck it out;
    Don't give up though the pace seems slow—
    You may succeed with another blow.
    Success is failure turned inside out—
    The silver tint of the clouds of doubt,
    And you never can tell just how close
you are,
    It may be near when it seems so far;
    So stick to the fight when you're hardest hit—
    It's when things seem worst that you must
not quit.'

She felt a failure. Her usual cheeriness had failed her, and she spiralled down into melancholia. Not a place she frequented much.

When she had the chance, she would apologise to him, she decided.

Ros had sunk to a world of self-loathing, of endless sorrow, of punishment for sins known and unknown.

There were tears now, and wet mumbled admissions of supposed guilt. Ros was flailing against the tide. Her sadness kept washing over her like an endless series of waves, each with the sole purpose of battering her into submission. She suddenly found herself blind with grief.

Her son was emotionally not himself and now a criminal. That's a hard burden to bear.

Until the judgement of the court case, there would be no peace for Ros Robinson. To Ros, she had let her son down, somehow, in some way, and a mother's guilt knows no bounds.

112

For Hannah, her conversations with Dan now became one-way on Messenger, stretched out over the days.

'DAN, I'D LIKE YOU TO CALL ME.'

'DAN, I WANT YOU TO CALL ME.'

'DAN, I NEED YOU TO CALL ME.'

'DAN, CALL ME, IT'S URGENT.'

'DAN?'

By Sunday night Hannah still hadn't heard back. This was unlike Dan. 'What if he's been caught?' she thought. 'No doubt they'll trace his computer conversations back to me. Oh well, it was coming. It was only a matter of time. I've been waiting for this, I'm prepared.'

Monday: There was a message for Hannah on her phone's Messenger app.

'HELLO, HANNAH. THIS IS STEPHANIE MCBRIDE FROM THE SOUTH AUSTRALIAN POLICE. CAN YOU CALL ME BACK AT YOUR CONVENIENCE? THANK YOU. HERE'S MY NUMBER.'

While the girls were having their naps on Monday,

Hannah picked up her mobile and dialled Stephanie's number.

'Thank you for calling me, Hannah. Tell me, do you know a Dan Robinson?'

'Yes, we're online friends.'

'Do you know him well?'

'A little, I guess. We chat about things going on in our lives. Is he okay?'

'Dan is currently helping us with some matters.'

'I see. Am I able to speak to him?'

'I'm afraid that isn't possible at the moment. Perhaps soon. In a few days.'

'Ok. Well, can you pass on a message to him for me?'

'I can do that. What would you like me to say?'

'That I miss him. I miss his jokes. I hope that the enquiries he's helping with work out okay.'

'I'll certainly pass that on, Hannah. Now Hannah, how often did you chat with Dan?'

'We met up online once a week, for about 20 minutes. On a Wednesday.'

'Were the meetings recorded?'

'Not by us. I don't know if they are stored by the hosting service or not.'

'Okay, thank you. Did Dan ever talk to you about stealing things, either physical things or electronic things?'

Hannah paused. Did she tell the truth, or did she lie? A policeman's daughter knows that liars never prosper when it comes to conversations with the police, that the police have long memories and big ears. 'Yes, he did. He told me he had stolen some farm equipment and also hacked into the farm's computers.'

'Did you tell anyone else about these crimes? Like, say, your father?'

'So, she knows about my father,' Hannah thought. 'Then she would know that I'm an accessory to several crimes for not reporting them to him. Bugger.' 'No, I kept them to myself. I tried talking to Dan and getting him to stop his criminal activities. Maybe I didn't do a very good job.'

'Perhaps Dan is a headstrong man who doesn't listen to good advice. Thank you for your time today, Hannah. I'm sure I'll need to speak to you again; is there a number I can easily reach you on?'

'Sure, this number is best.'

'Thank you. That probably wraps up my call for the moment. Is there anything else you'd like to say?'

'No, I can't think of anything.'

'Well, thanks again, Hannah, and I'll be in touch.'

Brilliant. Dan has been caught and therefore I will probably be charged with being an accessory to his crimes. I will need a lawyer. I don't know whether I need a South Australian one or a NSW one, or even a Federal lawyer, because this might fall under the remit of the federal police.

I probably should go and see Dad and tell him what's happened. And I need to tell Carlo, too. Both of them will be furious with me for being so stupid. It's probably best if I tell both at the same time. I'll ask Carlo to meet me at Mum and Dad's, or else get them to come over here and ask Carlo to get home on time.

Oh, my depression was low before this, now I

FEAR IT WILL HIT ROCK BOTTOM. I CAN ALREADY FEEL THE SELF-LOATHING RISING UP WITHIN ME. MAYBE I SHOULD SEE MY GP AND GET SOME TABLETS AFTER ALL.

I THOUGHT ABOUT DELETING THESE EVERNOTE ENTRIES BECAUSE SOME MENTION DAN, BUT THESE JOURNAL ENTRIES ARE NOT JUST ABOUT HIM. THEY ARE ABOUT ME, ABOUT WHAT'S GOING ON IN MY LIFE. SO NO, I WON'T BE DELETING THEM. IF THE POLICE WANT TO ACCESS THEM, THEY CAN HAVE THEM. I'VE GOT NOTHING TO HIDE. EXCEPT FOR MY GUILT ABOUT NOT TELLING DAD OR ANYONE ABOUT WHAT DAN WAS UP TO. OH SHIT, WHAT HAVE I DONE? I HATE MYSELF FOR BEING SO STUPID.

TEARS ARE FLOODING OUT OF ME AS I TYPE THIS. I AM IN AGONY. WHAT HAVE I DONE TO MY FAMILY?

113

Kelly heard about it from the farm hands on Lochiel Farm. According to one of the guys, who'd heard it on the radio, some computer jockey in Meningie had been caught hacking into a farm, Derringerry. The police were going to make an example of him, they said.

'The bloody idiot,' she said to no one in particular, from the safety of her driver's seat. 'What's he gone and done now?'

She had to wait until she got into Tintinara and had cellphone signal. She rang Dan's number, but it rang out and went to voicemail. She wanted to ring Ros Robinson at her work but figured she would have her hands full and probably wouldn't be at work anyway.

Kelly thought of Dan's business and his clients. Someone should contact them and let them know what has happened. She'd volunteer to take that on. Dan is going to need all the help he can get, she thought.

'Oh, Dan. What have you done? And why? Your business was growing, you were growing yourself into your role. Why did you throw it all away?'

Kelly pulled into the Shell Roadhouse and searched Google on her phone for news of a hacker in Meningie. It didn't take long for a result.

'Meningie man arrested for hacking farm's computers. Police officers have arrested a 28-year-old man in conjunction with a series of computer break-ins at Derringerry Farm. Dan Robinson from nearby Meningie was allegedly caught while conducting a break-in. Officers from the Australian Federal Police are assisting with the investigation, and the accused man has been moved from Meningie to police holding cells in Adelaide.'

She decided to call Davo, to see if he knew anything. But as with the call to Dan, the phone rang out and went to voicemail. She left a brief message, asking him to call her back. She didn't have Sarah's number, otherwise she'd ring it. There was nothing to do except carry on with her day and call into Ros Robinson's in the evening.

When she got to the Robinson house, she parked as close as she could. Approached by a few reporters who, in the evening light of summer, could still get good footage of her with their smartphones and cameras, she ignored them all, brushed aside their intrusive micro-phones and went up to the front door. Mr Pendlebury opened it up, alerted to Kelly's arrival by the hub-bub noise outside.

'Thanks, I'm Kelly, a friend of Dan's,' she announced quietly. 'I've come to see if I can be of any help.'

'Sure, come on in,' Mr Pendlebury replied and ushered her into the living room.

Inside there was Ros and a couple of her friends who were holding her hand and nodding sagely. Kelly could hear a mumbled, *sotto voce* conversation taking place in the kitchen.

'Hello, Mrs Robinson. I've come to offer my help if it's needed,' Kelly said at a volume just above the murmuring.

'Thank you, dear. I'm not sure what you can do, but a friendly face is always welcome at times like these.' Even in times of tragedy, Ros still managed to sound like a positivity guru.

'I tried ringing Davo Wilkins to find out what was going on, to not bother you, but I only got voicemail,' Kelly explained.

'Oh, dear, you haven't heard? Davo has been caught stealing from Derringerry. He's down at the police station, as far as I know.'

'Goodness!' Kelly exclaimed. 'No wonder I couldn't get hold of him. Now, Mrs Robinson, what should we do about Dan's clients. I think they have a right to know that their contracts will have to be terminated.'

'That's a good idea, dear. But I don't know how we are going to find out who the clients are. Dan's computers and all of his paperwork got taken by the police late last night. Police officers came down from Adelaide to package every-thing up. They took it all with them. They were here until three in the morning. I had a very nice policewoman sit with me while they went about their business.'

'I remember the name of one of the companies, but I don't know the others. All I know is that Dan had four clients, all in Adelaide.'

'Never mind Kelly, dear. I guess the police will have all of those details and will either let us know or else call the companies themselves as part of their investigation.'

'I think you're right, Mrs Robinson. There's nothing we can do for now. So tell me about Davo, what happened there?'

'Oh, I feel sorry for poor Sarah. This all happened behind her back. I bet she's livid, I would be. Well, apparently Davo and Dan were responsible for the break-ins on the farm. This all happened after Davo was fired from there, you know.'

'I'd heard. I'd heard it was because Davo had stuffed up a few big contracts and clients.'

'Yes, well, I don't know about that. What I do know, now, from Sarah, is that the two of them hatched up a scheme to get revenge on Davo's sacking. 'Sticking it to the man' as we called it in the 70s and 80s. Anyway, the police questioned Davo, he told the truth, and apparently told them everything about the break-ins, including where they'd hidden the equipment they'd stolen. He's in custody at the moment, awaiting a charge to be laid by Adelaide detectives. They're coming down tomorrow, apparently.'

'Oh, poor Sarah!' Kelly sympathised. 'What a horrible shock to both of you.'

'I knew Dan and Davo were as thick as thieves, but I never expected them to live up to it. And they are, aren't they? Thick.'

'I would have expected more from your son, Mrs Robinson. His business was slowly taking off, and he was making progress with his people skills. To throw it all away for silly revenge is just plain, well, stupid, yes. Yes, they are thick. The pair of them. To think they could get away with it. To even start down that path. Madness.'

'If only Dan had a good girlfriend to keep him occupied, none of this would have happened.'

'Well, Davo has a good wife, but that didn't stop him, did it? No, I fear a collective madness overcame them both, and they both did some incredibly stupid things because of it. Do you know what the procedure is with Dan? Will they put him in the remand centre with the druggies and rapists?'

'I don't know. Possibly,' said Ros.

'I hope not. They both need more positive role models in their lives at the moment. Do you want me to do anything for you, cook you a meal, or something else to help?'

'No, thank you, dear. You're very kind to offer, but I'm not hungry at the moment, and there's nothing that needs doing. Cheryl and Bridget here have offered me the same, and I told them the same thing: I'll eat again when Dan comes home.'

'Okay. Well, I won't stay and clutter up the place. If you need me, please don't hesitate to call me on my mobile. Take care, Mrs Robinson, and don't forget to call me if there's ever anything I can do.'

With that, she left. It would be a little while before she again would be visiting the Robinson house.

115

Andrew felt no sympathy for Dan or Davo. He felt nothing at all. It was just another case. More blokes who'd thought they could outsmart the system. They couldn't. The only time Andrew had seen someone 'get away with it' was a domestic violence case back in Mount Gambier. The prosecutor was going to make a good case, but the victim was so scared of her husband she recanted her story just before going into court. The magistrate and prosecutor guessed what was going on but were powerless to do anything. So he's probably still thumping her about.

That thought made Andrew sad, so he sat down at his computer and started filling in his paperwork to chase the thought out of his mind.

'Bloody paperwork. Always the bloody paperwork,' he said to no one there.

116

To: Gregson.Tony@afp.gov.au

From: McBride.S@police.sa.gov.au

Hi Tony, I've just arrested the man responsible for some cyber activity on a country farm. Daniel Robinson. He is currently being transferred from Meningie PS to Adelaide Central. When do you think you'll be able to pop over to chat with him?

Regards,

Stephanie McBride

Senior Civilian Officer

117

Phuoc turned to his wife, Han.

'It ended as I predicted. Badly.'

'You were right. I didn't think Dan and Davo were the types to do what they did. They've thrown away their lives,' Han replied.

'Two fewer customers, too. And they were good customers. Sometimes I think we made a mistake coming here. We haven't been successful.'

'It's true we haven't made any money yet,' Han agreed, 'but the children love the school and their friends. And we've made more friends here than we did in Adelaide. Back in Adelaide, you were just working crazy hours, and we never saw you. Down here, we are a family.'

'You're right, Han. I didn't think of it that way. I get to see my children grow, and I get to spend more time with you, which is also great.'

'Exactly. Let's focus on that. Now, help me move some boxes out the back, the customers will start coming in soon for lunch.'

118

And that was it. Mission Accomplished for Rocco Santofanti.

A short phone call from Stephanie to say it was over, and an instruction to tidy up.

That meant asking Wei to reinstate the uncorrupted, unaltered files back on Derringerry's server, the ones with the extra bits of code in them that enabled Rocco and Stephanie to track any future hacker's movements and leave a breadcrumb trail.

It also meant writing up a brief document that explained what he saw, what he did, and what he was told to do.

Rocco felt no pity for Dan Robinson. Dan was a hacker who got caught, just like he had. Dan was probably bored with his life, like Rocco was, and saw hacking as a way of spicing things up. And Dan would probably help Stephanie McBride out, just like he had, for a promise of a reduced sentence. All in all, she wasn't a bad boss. Could be worse.

What a couple of days it had been, Mr Pendlebury thought to himself as he settled into his favourite armchair and reached for his scotch.

His nephew had confessed to stealing from his former employer, his nephew's best friend had confessed to hacking into the former employer's computers and causing malicious damage. This sort of thing doesn't happen in a small town. At least, not HIS small town.

He felt bad for his nephew most of all. A promising career and a loving marriage, thrown away by a crazy sense of revenge. He didn't know if Dave's wife Sarah would stand by him, but if she did, it would be a rocky marriage full of mistrust for quite a while yet.

He'd got closer to Ros Robinson, comforting her as best he could when she found out her son was in hospital and then when she found out her son was a criminal. He'd liked getting closer to her, feeling the bonds of affection draw him in.

But stop it, he sternly told himself. She's an employee. Those sorts of thoughts will never do. Best put thoughts like that on a back burner, for when she retires from the practice.

He let his train of thought stop and instead thought about what he'd seen on the evening news, the destruction, the politicians who had lied and been caught out, or else played wildly with the truth, the stories of human betrayal and human endeavour. He still had hope for humankind, but it would be a rocky path to safety for some.

120

Another day, another hacker. It was a good thing she enjoyed the intellectual challenge of bringing them to justice because there seemed to be a never-ending stream of bored teenagers trying to either make a name for themselves or make a million.

Except for this case, she reflected. This case was different. Dan Robinson was an old man in hacking terms, someone who should not be mingling with the young and the wired up. Stephanie felt genuinely sorry for him. The others were either street-savvy enough to bounce back from their crime, and vow not to get caught next time, or else they were misguided boys and girls who'd fallen in with the wrong crowd.

Rocco was a misguided boy. Once he'd done his time he'd be back at home, with mamma to look after him, do his washing for him, cook his meals and remind him about right and wrong. Rocco would be looked after. But Dan. Dan would have his mum, yes, but would she look after him like an Italian mamma would? Would she clip him around the ear and lecture him on right and wrong? Dan was older, not a boy anymore. A grown man, who had his own business. Had. That was now history. There's no way he'd be allowed to have any technology again for a long time.

Except for D@@Mladen.

D@@Mladen might be Dan's meal ticket, just as D@@Mladen was for Rocco. If Dan had information on D@@Mladen that he'd be willing to share, maybe his life might get a tiny bit easier. Because make no mistake, Stephanie said to herself, that hacker is the main game in town.

Time to go have another word with Mr Robinson, she thought, as she clinked her coffee cup with an imaginary colleague.

Emily heard from Dan one more time.

Well, from his account, anyway.

A message was left at the online dead letter drop.

WE HAVE VEXTANT. YOU MIGHT AS WELL GIVE IN AND MAKE IT EASIER ON YRSELF. MSGE ME BACK TO ARRANGE A PLACE TO MEET TO DISCUSS. MCBRIDE.

'Damn!' she thought. Her mind was torn, worrying not only about Dan and his fate in the police's hands but also for her own security. What if Dan confessed to the police her name, her address, her identity? It was good that she was now living in her safe house, a two-bed maisonette in Erindale. But what if he didn't tell the police but instead made friends with a roommate in prison and told that new roommate about her? There's nothing to stop that roommate grassing on Dan for an easier time or extra privileges.

There was nothing for it. She had to jettison the Emily King identity and leave Stonyfell behind. She still had her BMW motorbike, but she needed to organise a new set of car wheels. Who would she be from now on? A Ruby, a Cindy, a Jerry, a Sarah? The credit cards she was now using were in the name of Rachel Havens. 'That will do for now. Time for Rachel Havens to buy a new car,' she thought. She liked the X7 M SPORT, liked the way it drove and handled; it was better, she felt, than the Porsche Cayenne S. Still, the BMW had bad memories for her, so she walked to her local shopping centre and Ubered over to Glen Osmond Road in Rachel Haven's name to the Porsche dealership. She found a second-hand white Cayenne S in good condition that she could drive away. She ran one of her credit cards through the machine and signed some papers, and within an hour of arriving at the dealership Emily King, now known as Rachel Havens, was driving away in a smart set of wheels.

As it turns out, Dan was only kept in the Remand Centre for a week, then released on bail back into his mother's care. So Emily, now Rachel, was able to visit him and plan what they were going to do and how they were going to handle the future, depending on whether the magistrate determined that jail time or a hefty fine was the punishment fit for the crime.

But back to the present. D@@Mladen put down her phone after checking the dead letter drop message, turned her attention back to her car, indicated and turned her white Porsche Cayenne S into the steady stream of traffic on South Road. She was headed down south, to another rendezvous point with Rocco, to meet another wannabe hacker. Separate cars. Always in separate cars.

The end.

Lee Hopkins

Lee is a London-born, Adelaide-raised gentleman. Like all good authors, he has had an interesting and varied career, including spending time as a call centre operative, marketer, social media guru, artificial intelligence evangeliser, conference speaker, entrepreneur, counsellor, emergency room clerk, husband, stepfather and grumpa.

He lives in Adelaide, where he delights in the beauty of the Adelaide Hills and wishes his summers away, aching for a cooler time of year. Autumn and Spring are particularly pleasant in Adelaide, he notes.

You can find him online at the following places:

Twitter: @leehopkins
Facebook: LeeHopkinsAuthor
Website : LeeHopkins.com
Email: lee@leehopkins.com

Finally, you can sign up to his free monthly-or-there-abouts newsletter at https://leehopkins.com/newsletter/, where you can read work-in-progress and see what Lee is currently reading himself.

Cold

Excerpt from the next novel featuring Stephanie McBride, 'Cold'.

The roads from Sydney to Adelaide are reasonably well populated by cars and trucks, even at night. It's only after 10.30pm that things quieten down a bit and roadhouses prepare for a long quiet night with few distractions. The cleaning, the preparation of food for the day shift, the re-stocking of the shelves.

At that time of night, a man or woman can think. The busyness of the day is behind them, and the slumber of the night is not that far off.

The A20 from Wagga Wagga in New South Wales keeps a curved line until it meets the M1 at Tailem Bend in South Australia, some eleven hours' comfortable driving away. Dale Stevens and Enrico Tarales had been taking turns driving, stopping for coffee and food *en route*, taking it easy. They had plenty of time on their hands to make their meeting in Adelaide at 3am and hand over a Transit van full of ice.

They'd taken in turns the music playlist, too. Whoever

drove got to have their playlist on the van stereo. House, technobrega, dubstep, shibuya-kei, happy hardcore... all had received a fair airplay.

At 10.57 on a cold winter's Sunday night, Dale and Enrico pulled into the BP roadhouse for some fuel and a snack.

Dale was 23 and a couple of years older than Enrico, or Rico as he preferred to be called. Dale was lightly built, springy, and had a lightweight boxer's energy about him. He kept fit at a training gym and he was due to have a spar with lightweight runner-up Tommy Fulmoa in a couple of months' time. He was looking forward to it. His blonde hair was cut short, just a bit longer than a crew cut, and he surprisingly had no tattoos marking his skin.

Rico Tarales was hot-headed to Dale's calm. Rico had lots of tattoos, mostly sleeves showing loyalty to his Sydney gang and his family. He was impulsive, dark-skinned and handsome in an edgy, street-wise way. His sister, María de Jesús, was a newbie hacker, stealing dollars and cents from online bank accounts and generally making a small-time name for herself in the gang, when she wasn't running classes in her day job as a freelance fitness instructor. His brother, José Luís, was at university, studying to be a pharmacist.

But Rico never inherited scholastic genes like his brother, nor entrepreneurial genes like his sister. He instead inherited the 'follower' genes—he loyally followed his leader, whoever that was at the time, into mischief and mayhem. Rico was a loyal foot soldier, a spear carrier in the world's affairs, but a loyal one who could be relied upon to carry out his mission.

Dale was driving, and he pulled up at the pump, but in need of a visit to the bathroom first. Rico got out of the passenger side, the same need uppermost in his mind. Locking the dark blue van behind him, Dale followed Rico to the toilets at the side of the roadhouse. So they wouldn't have seen the white BMW pull up and park just out of the range of the pump security cameras.

A man and a woman got out of the BMW and followed Dale and Rico, the woman walking side by side with her partner into the male toilets. Both of them carried a SIG Sauer P226 with silencer, a great pistol known for its concealed carry options, and both took ten seconds from entering the toilets to exiting.

Dale and Rico were shot standing up, in the back of the head, thump thump, their skulls splintering and splattering the wall in front of them. The male shooter fished around in Dale's pockets for the keys, found them, then walked calmly out of the toilet. His partner walked back to the BMW while he walked to the van, unlocked it and got in. The van still had a quarter of a tank of fuel left in it, enough to get to the sparkling lights of Adelaide and the petrol station at the bottom of the freeway. Both van and car started their engines and made their way out of the roadhouse and back onto the freeway.

The time was 11.04 on a cold winter's Sunday night.

Made in the USA
Middletown, DE
22 July 2020

12680621R00177